REMODELING EVE

Helen Kantor

TREELINE PRESS
USA

REMODELING EVE
Helen Kantor

Copyeditor: Kate Guiney
Book Design: Ooty Moorehead Graphic Design Group

This is a work of fiction. The author has made up names, characters, places, and incidents, all of which are used fictitiously. Any resemblance to actual persons, living or dead, business establishments, events, or locales is entirely coincidental, a circumstance of the way creativity happens in the universe.

Published in the United States by Treeline Press
ISBN: 978-0-9907898-0-2

Text set in Bembo

For Uncle Dave Wightman who told me to write it down.

Eve 1

The table was perfect. Set for tea with delicate china and polished silver, it only needed guests. But no one arrived for the party. Eve sat down. This had been her daughter's idea, which was a surprising request not because Audrey was turning seventeen, but because she hadn't wanted a party for the last five years. But Audrey had helped plan it, shopped for a new dress, and handed out the invitations to girls Eve had never met. New friends, Audrey told her. Audrey sat down next to her, that mane of brassy hair falling forward and hiding her fair face.

"Where is everyone?" Eve asked.

Audrey tossed her hair back and exhaled a rush of air through her lips. She started to reach for a sugar cube.

"No more," Eve said. "You've already had five. Have a finger sandwich."

Audrey picked up a book of matches and then brightened.

"I can make flowers bloom orange," she said.

She held the book and match too close to her face.

"No, wait. Let me," Eve said.

Eve struck the match and touched it to the wicks of each small candle.

"Was something else going on this afternoon?" Eve asked. "Something at the school? Was someone else having a party?"

Audrey pressed her eyes into the V of her elbow and rested her head on the table. She wasn't like other girls her age. She never had been. She was very imaginative. That was all. She was highly sensitive. Some wanted to label her; autistic, Asperger's. But she didn't really fit the profile. It wasn't clinical, it wasn't all the time. Audrey could get dressed, go to school, and pass her classes. She just didn't socialize, except with Eve. A few times a year, when Audrey was particularly difficult, Carl would insist Eve schedule an appointment with a therapist, a specialist, a hypnotist. At first, Eve agreed. She interviewed two counselors and three doctors but none of them were right for Audrey. They'd frighten her with their beards or glasses or cold questions. Each time Carl brought it up again, Eve would agree and then forget, or she'd agree and things with Audrey would get better all by themselves. Most of the time, she was fine. Things could be worse. Teenagers could be far more difficult than this. She didn't smoke or drink or cut herself. She didn't hang out with a bad crowd. She just didn't hang out with any crowd.

Audrey scooted her chair closer to Eve as if the bond between them had pulled her over. Their bodies were almost the same size, Audrey's having somehow become adult despite her childlike demeanor. She rested her head on Eve's shoulder. That warmth, that desire to be near dissolved Eve's frustration. When Audrey reached her arms around Eve's neck and kissed her, Eve wanted nothing else except to put her arms around her daughter, too. There was no other bond like this. With anyone.

"Audrey, it doesn't matter about the party," Eve said, embracing her little girl, her teenager.

She was beautiful, breathtaking. But she was fragile. Eve's fiercest impulses would never let anything destroy Audrey's vulnerability.

The tiered tray of finger sandwiches remained untouched. The white sugar cubes remained in a perfect pyramid. Audrey let go of Eve to pluck a sugar cube from the silver bowl in the center of the table.

"Sweetheart, please don't."

"It's not for me."

"Don't take sugar cubes up to your room."

Eve hated to reprimand her, but the sugar cubes brought ants.

"I'll tell you what, beautiful," Eve said. "Why don't you and I have our own tea party?"

She motioned for Audrey to pass the tray of finger sandwiches, but they were out of reach. Audrey rose from the chair and walked around the table in her pink party dress. The more sophisticated silk sheath Eve urged her to purchase had been refused. When Audrey first pleaded to have a tea party, Eve was surprised, but then seduced. An afternoon affair for elegant young women had a certain charm. It didn't have to be something from second grade. Brushing against the silver ribbons of a dozen purple and pink balloons, Audrey incited a riot of thudding latex. Her eyes widened and she flinched at the jungle drumming. Reversing course, she trotted back, and snagged her dress on the corner of the table. Shrieking, she changed direction to free the fabric. As she reached for the dress, her arm knocked over the tiered trays.

But Eve was already up, already close enough to catch the trays and avert disaster.

Audrey wailed over the ruined fabric of her delicate dress.

"I can fix that, let me see. Let go. I can fix that Audrey. It's okay. Sit down," Eve said, patting a chair. "It's nothing. See?"

The tea candles steadied themselves and Audrey calmed down, too.

"Feed me," Audrey demanded, and she placed a tiny watercress sandwich in Eve's palm. Eve steadied the flat of her hand as Audrey nibbled with her lips, the way a horse might. The tickling and nuzzling made Eve soften. Her daughter's pale cheeks and invisible eyelashes made her innocent and vulnerable. She had no interest in make-up, had never even experimented with Eve's. When the sandwich was gone, Audrey turned two china cups over and made them trot around the place setting as if they were hooves at the ends of her hands.

The whole idea of a party did not seem like something her daughter would want, but Audrey had insisted. She'd even handed out the invitations herself.

"Where's your backpack?" Eve asked, suddenly understanding why all the RSVPs had come at once, why all the chairs were empty.

Audrey blinked and glanced at the staircase. Eve jumped up and ran in the direction of Audrey's room. By the time she got to the stairs, Audrey caught up to her and grabbed at her ankle but couldn't restrain Eve, who twisted out of her daughter's weak grip.

"Mommy, no."

Eve pushed open the bedroom door, unzipped the pink backpack on the chair and rifled through it. Deep in the bottom, she felt a handful of envelopes, and slowly removed them. The porcelain collection of unicorns stared from the shelf. Audrey stepped timidly into the room.

"Why, Audrey?"

"No one would have come."

"You didn't have—I thought you wanted—We could have just—"

Audrey went to the shelf, trying to hide the watercress sandwich she offered the unicorns. But Eve could see all of this. She tapped the stack of invitations against her forehead, waiting for her heart rate to slow. The envelopes were thick with marbled Italian paper from Florence, and Audrey had insisted in writing out all the names in calligraphy.

Audrey bent her head, quickly ate the bread so that she was at once the unicorn and the girl feeding the mythical creature.

"Audrey, stop feeding them!"

"They're hungry."

"They're not real."

Audrey collapsed to the carpet, holding her arms over her head as if the sky were falling. A murder of dark birds circled this vulnerable, pulsing heap of her child. Eve knew her own frustration would only undo Audrey, but she slipped sometimes and an angry tone invaded when she needed to go gently.

"Why did you ask for a party, sweetheart?"

"I thought it would make you happy," Audrey whispered.

"Your party should make you happy, not me."

"Unicorns don't like parties."

"Audrey, you're seventeen. You're a beautiful young woman. But you're not a—"

"Don't say it!"

Audrey yanked away as if avoiding a bridle and bit, pushing Eve away, fending off her embrace. Eve blocked the bedroom door, lunged at Audrey and held onto her. Audrey's strength was no match for hers. She hated herself for upsetting her beautiful girl, so she waited for Audrey's tears and hugged her tightly. The sobs, the raspy choking gave Eve a single focus. Comfort.

She moved them both to the bed and held Audrey's head and shoulders in her lap. Audrey buried her face against Eve, kept her arms wrapped tightly around Eve's waist. There was nowhere else Eve would rather be except here, keeping her daughter company, holding her until rapid breathing diminished to an occasional huff. She tucked Audrey's hair behind her ear, and gently stroked the curve of it. Audrey's pink cheek felt warm against the backside of her hand, and she blinked wet eyelashes as she stared blankly at the walls of airbrushed unicorn posters. Audrey had surrounded herself with an idyllic garden of creatures that watched over her with round eyes and strange beauty.

She would do anything for Audrey, especially if she could help her find a way to let go of her childish obsession and step toward being a young woman.

Audrey 1

When we were alone, I offered the sugar cube to my unicorns. I had slipped it in my pocket when Mommy had not seen. She didn't like when I fed them so I had to be tricky sometimes. Some were made of glass, some of china. The oldest one was white with blue flowers in her mane. Sapphire Jones.

"You," Sapphire Jones had whispered when my grandmother first brought her to me. "If you are my keeper, I will share my world."

No one else could hear her speak except me.

The magic of that moment changed everything, even the color of daylight, which I could still see when I remembered how we first met. A hush fell across the rooftops outside, and across my heart. She lifted her porcelain head and blinked at me. But my grandmother did not see. Only I did.

"Let's go outside," Sapphire Jones said to me. So I took her.

She had been the first. Her mane was as white as my grandmother Daphne's hair. Others will seek you out, Daphne told me, and they did. In gift shops, and bookshops, and street fairs, unicorns raised their heads, calling to me to tell me they belonged in the herd. When I got them home, I introduced them to the others, and there was always a celebration. There are more of us, they sang. They gathered before me on the shelf, included me as one of their kind.

I admired their delicate grace, the way they balanced on slender legs, each one unique, all of them beautiful. They communicated to me with their graceful heads and dark, round eyes. I brought them sugar cubes and small pieces of apple, even though Mommy said don't, because ants came. The unicorns accepted me as one of them, even though I didn't look graceful and strong.

Twenty-three of them stood on the shelf, munching softly on that single cube. And it was enough for all. Their smooth muzzles tickled my palm when they nibbled. I tasted what they tasted until the crystal sweetness was gone. Long manes of white and silver draped from their necks, some in waves and some straight. Their heads could fit in my hand, and I could cradle them with one arm if they wanted to be carried. They all stood on four legs except for a mother that lay next to her beautiful colt. They were perfect. Not one was chipped because I protected their grace and beauty.

After I fed them the sugar, they stood in silent thanks. I changed out of the pink dress, fingering the place where it had torn. I wanted to wear the t-shirt with flowers on it and my soft jeans. This party dress was not me. It was for a popular girl at school, someone who knew how to talk to boys and wear make-up. I didn't need to know those things. I had beautiful creatures that cared about me.

My unicorns wore noble expressions. They knew more than they could tell me, their eyes full of secrets. Sapphire Jones stood in a circle of lavender flowers, always beautiful and calm. I cradled her thin porcelain body along the length of my forearm, holding her close. I tried to tell her about all the lovely dishes downstairs that had been let out of their dark cupboards and put on the table where they could sparkle and shine. She wanted to see. All of them wanted to see.

I would have to be fast, so I brought three of them downstairs and put them on the table. It was all so much more beautiful with them on the table, too. They made the party magical. Plus, I would not have to do homework because the table was covered with everything. The candles flickered and the unicorns glowed. I ran up to get five more and placed them around the table, too. They shared cups and stood next to plates, but they had to wait for the rest before they would each get their own sugar cube. Before I went to get more, I galloped around the dining table in a circle because I love how circles bring me back to where I start.

Mommy talked to me from the kitchen, but she didn't come out. "Audrey, you remember that the kitchen is going to go away? Well, not go away, but become different. New. Better. You remember the contractor? His name is Nick. He'll be here a lot until the kitchen is done. But that's okay. He's making it better."

"I remember," I said.

When there were eleven unicorns, they asked for fresh grass, so I went quietly to the backyard and felt the top of the grass with my palm to find the softest tips, the youngest blades.

"Audrey, no grass upstairs," Mommy said when I came back in. "What's in your hand?"

She came out of the kitchen. I hid my hand behind my back, but she made me uncurl my fingers. Then she saw the table with all the unicorns. Mommy hung her head, turned away. Then she sobbed. And she tried to stop breathing and a sob shook her insides.

"I'm sorry. I'll take the grass back outside."

Mommy shook her head, waved me away. But I went out, let the grass fall from my hand and watched the wind scatter it across the wooden deck. When I came back in, I put my arms around her. She sank into a dining room chair and covered her face.

"The unicorns and I came to help you pack."

"That's very sweet," she said, and started to kiss me on my forehead.

"Not there," I wailed.

"I want to bring the others down. They are my guests."

"No. We need to pack everything."

"But they're all thirsty."

She looked at Sapphire Jones. I started to race upstairs to get more of them.

"I said no!"

She grabbed my arm to stop me and I knocked a teacup off the table. It fell to the floor and shattered into sharp pieces. It had been right next to Sapphire Jones.

"Shit fuck," Mommy said, then covered her mouth.

The sight of jagged pieces that used to be a lovely cup made Sapphire Jones afraid, made them all afraid. This could have been her. It could have been all of them. I picked her up, shrieked, and raced away. Mommy grabbed me and put her arms around me while I held onto Sapphire Jones.

"It's okay. Don't cry. It's just a cup. I have others," she said, and showed me a box filled with cups. But one was missing.

Mommy held me tight so I couldn't disappear, and I wept for the cup because it would never be what it once was. It was destroyed.

"Shh, sweetheart. It's okay. There are other cups out there in the world."

I stopped struggling.

"Hey, let's get out of here," she said, the sun coming out in her face.

"And go see Daphne?" I asked, sitting up straight.

"I was thinking we could go to the mall and try on make-up."

"I want to see Daphne."

"Go up and put some shoes on so you don't cut yourself," she told me. "I need to pack the kitchen into boxes."

I looked through the doorway at a slice of blue kitchen, but didn't see how it could fit. Mommy and Daddy told me over and over that the kitchen was going to go away. But every day when I looked, it was still there with its blue wallpaper and blue floor and blue counter. I brought the unicorns back to my room. The others wanted to know about the crashing sound. But I didn't tell them about the cup. I couldn't tell them. It was too awful, even though keeping secrets from them was bad, too. When I went back downstairs, the shards had been swept away. The tea party had become stacks of cups and saucers like tall buildings downtown. Brown cardboard boxes waited for all of them, and a tape dispenser lay on its side, ready to seal them up.

Eve 2

Eve drove east, away from her quiet coastal neighborhood, toward the assisted-living facility that was halfway to downtown Los Angeles. Her heart and lungs became trapped in the cage of her ribs. Breathe, she reminded herself. Pay attention to traffic. In some ways, the request to see Daphne was very mature on Audrey's part. Eve was proud of her for that, for the bond she shared with Daphne. Sitting in the passenger seat, gazing out the window, Audrey looked like a young woman, looked capable of behaving like an emerging adult. Her translucent skin exaggerated her dark, round eyes. Long, silky hair framed her expressive face. She has no idea how stunning she is, Eve thought. Seventeen could be the year Audrey turned a corner and grew up a little.

"I want to remind you about tomorrow. The kitchen contractor is coming."

"Nick," Audrey said.

"That's right. He's going to take out the old kitchen and build a new one."

Sometime in the 1960s that kitchen had been astonishing, with its circular windows on the double oven. The aqua stovetop, hood, and linoleum must have been daring, not antiquated. Eve had collected pictures, searched the Internet, watched cable programs, studied showrooms, and spied on other people's kitchens. Dreaming became a blueprint with a budget. A wider window would frame a bigger view of the ocean. An island and new appliances would transform the outdated. Everything except how to finish the walls had been figured out. The possibilities of newer and better had infected Carl, and they interviewed a dozen contractors until they finally found the right one. But maybe it was too soon. Maybe Audrey wasn't ready for this kind of disruption. She might go into full panic because of the changes, the noise, the dust.

Eve glanced at Audrey again, silent in a flowery pink t-shirt that belonged on a twelve-year-old.

"Hey, beautiful. What are you thinking?"

"Why don't unicorns live in cities?" Audrey asked.

Eve exhaled, gripped the wheel tighter.

"Unicorns don't live in the city because—"

"Because they don't like it," Audrey shouted, cutting her off.

Arguing was pointless. Audrey was smart, highly functioning but reclusive.

Imaginative. Her teachers never complained and she got almost all A's. There was a delay. About womanhood. Eve had given her a beautiful childhood and she didn't want to leave. She'd given her exactly what Daphne had failed to give Eve.

They passed under the 405 freeway. Signs on shops and billboards changed languages and alphabets. They could be in Korea, but in a few more blocks they could be in Guatemala. The patchwork of flavors and colors that made up Los Angeles offered mysterious neighborhoods she'd never found time to explore. Mid-Wilshire came and went. Apartment buildings cropped up between strip malls. Eve slowed as they approached the care facility, navigated around the potholes in the parking lot, pulled in to a spot, and turned off the engine. Audrey got out of the car, ran in circles and jumped over puddles; a teenager who could become a lively delight at any moment. Eve stood and watched, enthralled and alarmed. The teenage slouch, the hip jutting out in defiance, expressions of boredom; at least none of this infected Audrey. Carl had found a place her mother's money could afford. It was hard to say how long she'd be able to afford even this. And he knew better than to suggest Daphne move in with them.

"Look," Audrey said, pointing to the puddles. "Clouds have fallen down."

Eve looked into the puddles of rain that reflected white puffy clouds. Suddenly the sun emerged and the world was dazzling. Audrey jumped across a puddle like she was eight, raised her arms upward, then skipped over and wrapped her arms around Eve.

"I just hugged you with an armful of sky," she whispered.

Brightness stung Eve's eyes and she put her arms around her precious daughter. The impulse to protect and enfold was automatic. No one ever prepared her for how that would happen, certainly not her own mother.

"Let go, Mommy," Audrey said, escaping her embrace, pulling her hand, leading her toward Daphne's care facility.

Its pink stucco was supposed to be cheerful, but Eve's mood did not lift to match Audrey's. They had moved Daphne here after Carl discovered her sitting in her studio in a corner, confused, unable to speak. Her dementia had grown steadily worse over the last two years and there had been little choice. Carl had handled the entire mess, done all the research, found the place and convinced Daphne to give him power of attorney. He'd been quick to step in, take control, make it all better, because he knew Eve couldn't deal with it. He knew how to charm Daphne, and she'd signed off on everything. Only a few more pieces of darkroom equipment needed removal before they could put Daphne's studio on the market to pay for the care facility.

Three white-haired women and a man sat on benches outside the entrance like ancient sentries. Their heads turned to follow as Audrey skipped past, consuming her youth and energy with their eyes. When she got to the glass door, Audrey waited for Eve to push it open. It was Saturday. There should be families surrounding these people, but Eve and Audrey were the only visitors in the lobby. Audrey rushed in but slowed as she sniffed the air. The place smelled of floral perfume and disinfectant, infrequent bathing and incontinence. Several more geriatric people sat with their walkers and canes staring into what little was left of the future.

Eve signed in at the front desk, led Audrey down the hall and knocked on her mother's door.

"Daphne," she called softly.

Her mother had insisted on a first-name basis since Eve was a child. Her long white hair spread out around her thin shoulders. Her face slumbered. Somewhere in her skull, her mind had turned to dust, forgetting the cruel past Eve remembered.

Let's leave, Eve started to say, but Audrey raced to the bed.

"Audrey, wait. Let her sleep."

"I'm awake," Daphne answered, voice soft and gentle, eyes closed.

"I miss you," Audrey said, and leaned over to kiss Daphne's papery cheek.

"I miss you too," Daphne said, opening her blue eyes. "But who are you?"

Audrey laughed. Eve stopped in the doorway, anxious.

"I'm a unicorn," Audrey whispered.

"Unicorns are rare," Daphne said.

Eve clenched her jaw, remained in the doorway, fingered a button on her coral-pink sweater, and looked around the room. The walls had been empty last time, but Carl had framed and hung some of the iconic photographs Daphne had produced through her brilliant career. Eve scanned the images that had made Daphne a well-known artist. A wooden fence pointlessly bisected a grassy slope. A chain-link fence rose into the sky as if it could divide the clouds. An ancient rock wall suggested the timeless attempt at ownership. A barbed wire fence threaded itself between refugees and soldiers. The gray scale, the resolution, the quality of the light transformed the viewer's experience from the practicality and purpose of these man-made boundaries into the extraordinary, into a statement about what people can and cannot separate. Eve knew the location and date of every image. Carl admired Daphne's work endlessly, and must have hung these because he thought it would please her to look at them. Maybe it did. But now, in their own way, they fenced her in.

"You're a beautiful unicorn," Daphne said to Audrey. "It's nice to meet you."

I have never met a unicorn."

Audrey tossed her head. "Yes, you have," she snorted. "Last time I was here. You keep sugar cubes in that bowl for me."

"Do I? Let's see. Would you like one?" the frail woman asked, reaching for a bowl next to her bed.

The impulse to prevent her daughter from eating white sugar pulsed through Eve, but she did not intervene. She needed to let this moment of sweetness happen between her mother and her daughter so that she could believe in it. Audrey bent her head to the woman's wrinkly hand and took the cube with her lips. Eve remained in the doorway.

"Do you have other unicorns to play with?" Daphne asked, and shifted her gaze to Eve. "It can be hard to be alone. Very, very hard."

Eve's heart hushed itself and listened to see if her mother might be speaking of the past in some coded way. She stepped toward the bed, toward the softness she heard in Daphne's voice that must surely understand loneliness. Let this be tenderness she could trust from the mother she wanted Daphne to be.

"Who is this?" Daphne asked Audrey.

"That's Mommy," Audrey said, rolling her eyes and tossing her hair as if Daphne still joked.

"Hello, Daphne. You look good."

Daphne smiled but in a way that didn't offer recognition.

"Do I? Hand me that mirror and brush," Daphne said, and Eve stepped into the room to do as her mother asked.

Warmth passed between them, a quick flicker of gratitude as Eve handed her the mirror and brush. Daphne struggled to brush her hair, her arm and shoulder too stiff. Then she let Eve take the brush and brush her hair. Eve's fear for this visit had been misplaced, and she looked at Daphne in the mirror she held. Daphne looked back, their eyes meeting briefly in a tender gaze.

"I see an old woman," Daphne said, lowering the mirror. She shrugged Eve away.

"Oh, Daphne. Don't say that. You look great."

"Don't you have anything better to do than visit an old woman?" she asked.

"Audrey wanted to come. It's her birthday. I think it's very sweet." A long silence followed. Daphne looked tired. Perhaps the visit should be brief. "We can't stay long. I need to get home to pack up the kitchen. We're getting ready to remodel and I have to clear everything out."

Eve put the mirror and brush back on the counter. Daphne stared at her. "Do we know each other?" she asked.

Maybe the word 'pack' had triggered her departure, Eve thought. It was hard to follow Daphne's mind. "I'm your daughter. Mother, it's me. Eve."

"Mother? You're telling me I'm the mother of some housewife who's redoing her kitchen?"

Eve stepped back. Some housewife? The challenges of surrounding her daughter with love and care, teaching her to tie her shoes, to decide what to wear by herself or to form her own opinions about English essays meant so much more than being 'some housewife.'

Please let the tenderness come back. Let Daphne not go on the attack. Let her anger not well up on Audrey's birthday.

"Good heavens. Look at you. Wearing a sweater set, talking about a kitchen. My daughter?" Daphne laughed. "One would remember her own daughter."

"If one had been around," Eve said, immediately regretting having let such a hard reply slip out in front of Audrey. "You left me. So you could take pictures," she added, trying to explain a lousy childhood to her daughter in a handful of words.

Daphne turned toward the wall. "Tourists take pictures. I take photographs. There's a difference."

"You mean you used to."

Another sharp remark meant to remind Daphne her career was over. Eve hated being resentful of Daphne, but sometimes she was powerless in her mother's presence to do anything but deflect attack and protect herself. Too many visits served regret to both of them. No wonder families didn't fill this place on the weekends.

"Audrey, could you go down the hall and get Daphne a box of tissues from the front desk? Hers is empty."

Audrey nodded and loped out the door and into the hallway.

"Daphne, it's her birthday. I brought a card for you to sign."

Eve pulled the card from her purse and held it out.

"I don't take pictures. I take photographs." Daphne folded her arms and turned away from Eve.

"Carl did a nice job framing these. When did he hang them?"

"Last week," Daphne said, able to recall anything that had to do with Carl. "He's a thoughtful man, that Carl. I'm surprised no one has snagged him for a husband."

Eve exhaled, picked a hair off her sweater.

"I went everywhere. I went places no one else wanted to go, saw towns and villages that had been destroyed by men and their wars. Places that had been forgotten and left behind. And you? Are you the person you wanted to be?"

Daphne waited for Eve to answer, but Eve had no response.

"I want out," Daphne said, examining her fingers. "Why am I here? I want my Nikon and a plane ticket."

Her Nikon sat helplessly on the dresser with its single, staring eye. There was nothing here to see, nothing worth photographing inside these four walls. Daphne closed her eyes and sank into her pillow.

Audrey raced back in holding a tissue box in front of her. Daphne took the box and Eve slid the unsigned birthday card back into her purse. Without warning, Daphne launched the box of tissues at the camera but missed and hit a photograph, making it hang crooked. Audrey jumped in alarm.

"I wasn't meant for this. I was never meant to be trapped," Daphne shouted.

"Grandma, why are you yelling?" Audrey asked, her voice shaking.

"Don't call me that. I'm Daphne Delfin."

"Mommy?" Audrey said, looking for some way to make sense of this outburst.

"Look at you," Daphne continued to Eve. "Who are you? What happened to you?" Daphne began to rise and lowered her white-blue legs to the floor.

"Daphne, don't get up. Let me get someone."

Osteoporosis had weakened Daphne. The staff had put Eve and Carl on alert for the danger of falling. Eve placed her hands on Daphne's bony shoulders to keep her from standing and Daphne screamed. Audrey snorted, tossed her head and fluttered her lips.

"Audrey, it's okay," Eve said, and turned away from Daphne to embrace her daughter, to calm her. But it was too late. Audrey pawed at the air. Her whinny rose to a scream as Daphne stood. In full panic, Audrey swiped at the collection of prescription containers on the dresser and tore around the room.

"What's wrong with her?" Daphne shrieked. "Don't you have any control over her?"

Audrey leapt onto the armchair and off and on again, then ran at the wall and crashed against it, backed up and crashed again.

"Audrey, stop," Eve shouted, trying to prevent her mother from standing and her daughter from crashing.

"You need help. She needs help. But I do not need help," Daphne said.

Daphne took a step toward her bathrobe on the chair, but lost her balance and fell, knocking her head against the nightstand. Audrey continued to stampede. Eve knelt beside Daphne and yanked the emergency cord by her mother's bed. Her mother did not move. Audrey froze. Seconds gathered like bystanders until finally Daphne opened her eyes.

"Don't get up. Someone's coming," Eve said.

"What do you want from me? Who are you?"

Eve moved away as a male nurse stepped into the room. He took a quick look at Daphne and radioed for assistance. Daphne groaned, opened her eyes. Stared at Eve.

"She tried to get out of bed and fell," Eve explained.

"Get her out! She's trying to steal from me. My camera, my photographs. She's trying to take my life's work," Daphne yelled.

"Ma'am," the aide said, indicating the door. "If you could give us a few minutes."

Eve extracted Audrey from where she crouched in the corner of the room and walked her to the hall. She gave Audrey sanctuary in her arms as they waited for three staff people to evaluate Daphne and return her to her bed.

"Did she lose consciousness at any point?" the nurse asked, stepping back into the hall. He made some notes on a clipboard when Eve answered that she had not.

"Probably nothing broken," he told her, "But she'll feel some bruises tomorrow. She's resting now. We gave her something to help her sleep. But you can say goodbye."

"No," Eve said. "I don't want to upset her."

"She has to have a kiss goodbye," Audrey insisted.

Audrey turned and stared at the woman already asleep in the bed. Then, with courage that surprised Eve, Audrey tiptoed back into the room and leaned over to kiss Daphne's forehead. Tears welled into Eve's eyes. Damn middle age. Tears for what? For the emptiness where love should live? For the tenderness that Audrey offered Daphne that Daphne could not find for Eve?

Where did she go? her mother had asked. *Was she the person she wanted to be?*

Those questions didn't seem to rise out of dementia.

Just some housewife.

Eve retreated to the hall, blotting tears with the sleeve of her sweater before her beautiful daughter returned from the triumph of giving Daphne a good-bye kiss. Then Audrey locked arms with Eve.

"Mommy, I want to go to the mall with you," she said. "Please can we? I want to try on make-up and look older."

This was a sacrifice, an offering of love. Eve started to press her lips to Audrey's forehead but remembered not to kiss her where that imaginary horn grew. Lips pressed against Audrey's temple, Eve closed her eyes for a moment to inhale. Soap and sweetness. The scent of her daughter's well being. The only thing that really mattered.

Audrey 2

A face stared back at me from the rectangle of mirror, blinked if I blinked, turned if I turned. It was plain and blank and clumsy with a round head and stubby neck, not a face that had friends who came over for parties. My hand left a five-fingered print on the warm glass of the cosmetics display, soiling the clear surface that protected pretty presents and small boxes inside.

"A blank canvas," Mommy said to the woman at the counter whose blue eyelids wrinkled when she smiled.

The make-up lady's red lips made her look like a fish, which made a shiver race down my back. Her overpowering smell poisoned me with sticky sharpness as she made me sit in a tall chair and stood too close. I pressed my hands to my nose to protect myself and breathed rapidly through my fingers. Mommy said my name, brought me back to the fence rail of knowing, of calm. I closed my eyes. The department store, with its white plastic figures and racks of fabrics, disappeared behind the darkness of my eyelids. Here, in the underside of seeing, I could escape. But the perfume cloud moved closer. The warmth of the fish-woman's powdered skin radiated toward me. My lungs fought against the inhale that would pollute me. But I had to breathe. When I exhaled, the rush of air from my mouth fluttered past my lips. Laughter from the frozen mannequin-women wearing nighties in the lingerie area bounced and stabbed across the make-up counters, making me flinch. There had been no laughter at my party, I had not pleased Mommy, and I could not explain to her why I had pretended other girls were coming. She was happy picking out candles and little cakes with tiny flowers on them. But I should not have made her do all that. Maybe if I tried on make-up like the girls at school it would make her happy again.

The fish-woman turned on a light and pointed it at my face, chattering about pore sizes and the pale color of my skin. She leaned in with a sharp pencil to poke my eye. I flinched. I flared a warning breath out of my nostrils. From the horizon that defined sky and earth inside me, a stampede of hooves beat forward as a whinny formed and escaped my throat and jaws. The majestic creature that lived in me was ready to protect or to run.

"Audrey don't," Mommy said.

The herd circled and slowed and waited. The fish-woman offered me a cautious smile, then retreated.

"Just close your eyes, sweetheart," the woman said, and stepped too close again.

"Close your eyes, Audrey."

"You don't need to squeeze your lids. Just relax."

I made my eyelids two smooth moons but my stomach wiggled and squirmed.

"I don't feel good," I whispered.

"You're becoming a lovely young woman," Mommy said.

"Do you go to high school?" the woman asked.

Again, shrill laughter rang out from the plastic women in nighties who pretended they were frozen. The laughing pecked at my blindness. I jolted away so I could open my eyes and see who really laughed. The pencil jabbed me. White pain attacked. A tangle of hoof and muscle made me bolt from the chair, my arms and legs flashing and pawing in front of me.

The woman said sorry sorry sorry and waved a white tissue, which Mommy grabbed. Mommy made me sit. I bent over and covered my face and would not uncoil until the ribbons of Mommy's arms wrapped around me. Then I was safe, even if I was blind in one eye.

"I am ruined," I moaned.

Holding both wrists, Mommy moved my hands away and made me look in the mirror. A jagged line ran up my eyelid toward my eyebrow, a scar of eyeliner that made me ugly. This didn't belong. This was not like a graceful creature whose rareness made everyone hold their breath.

"I don't want to do this," I said. "I feel sick."

Mommy poured some white lotion into the tissue and stepped in front of the fish-eye woman. "I can fix it," she said.

The woman apologized again and moved out of the way while my mother gently stroked my face smooth and clean.

"Let's give it one more try, Audrey. We came all the way here."

At home, there were invitations in my backpack, chairs around the table, and an empty blue kitchen. At Daphne's, there had been throwing and yelling. Hollowness filled me and made me heavy at the same time. I slumped into the chair. My mother went back to her chair.

Two mannequins laughed just as two girls stepped out from behind them. Mitzi Schultz and Madison Moncrief, girls from school who always wore make-up and who would never want to be friends with me. I closed my eyes again, but when the fish woman moved away, I peeked. Those girls wore low-cut jeans and tops and had decorated themselves with jewelry to make themselves look older than they were. The woman raised the pencil in her hand so I would know what she was going to do, but I moved her arm away so I could see Madison reach for the plastic mannequin's private area and rub. Mitzi shoved Madison and they both blurted cruel laughter. I did not understand what they did to the plastic figure or the word they both said at the same time.

Frigid.

I closed my eyes for the fish-woman.

"What is frigid?" I asked.

"Where did you hear that?"

Mommy followed my gaze to the mannequins. Mitzi and Madison were gone.

"It means…" my mother said.

"It means cold," the make-up woman said.

I had to shut my eyes again and when I could finally look, I saw a stranger in the mirror staring back at me. She had purple-brown eyelids drawn with exaggerated lashes and lines. She was not me, she didn't smile. But Mommy and the fish-woman did.

"I really don't feel good," I said.

Mommy leaned in closely. "Is it your period?"

No, it was not that awful wound between my legs! I wanted to jump the rail and run because of thinking about it.

"Look how beautiful," Mommy said, tilting the mirror.

I let go of the chrome hand rests, confused by the girl-woman in the mirror.

"Let's see what a little foundation and blush will do for you. Then we'll go get hot chocolate," Mommy said.

The blue-lidded woman rubbed and smoothed color into my cheek so that one half of my face was coated, the other pale and clean. Mommy moved a strand of hair back behind her ear, then folded her arms tightly around her chest. She was beautiful, tall.

"Audrey, what about just having lunch with some girls at school?" Mommy asked. "Think about how you'd feel if they asked you."

"Like they were desperate," I said.

Mommy laughed, but I hadn't told a joke. Again, my stomach rose toward my throat.

"You look stunning," the fish-woman said, and reached over to reposition the mirror. I looked at the diamond in the corner of my eye as it slid down the flawless powder on my cheek.

My mother put her hand on my shoulder just as I burped. Then bits of watercress and white bread came up out of my mouth and spread across the glass protecting the expensive boxes underneath. Mommy pulled tissues rapidly from a box and wiped my mouth and chin and pink flowered blouse. I wanted everything to stop moving. I wanted everything to not be ruined and it kept getting ruined.

"Excuse us," Mommy said to the make-up woman as she hurried me to the glass doors that released us from the building's insides.

When we got home, Daddy walked in too. He put his keys and phone on the kitchen counter.

"You're not going to believe my day," he said. "I was cleaning out Daphne's studio and I found three prints I've never seen before. Prints I think no one has ever seen before. Eve, I brought them home and I want you to take a look. This could be huge. This could be the centerpiece of a solo exhibit. The attention it creates could generate a revival of her work. Who knows?"

Mommy folded her arms. "It's your daughter's birthday," she said.

Then Daddy wrapped his arms around me and squeezed so hard my breath stopped for a moment.

"Hey, beautiful," he said. "Happy birthday."

"She's not feeling well. She threw up at the mall."

Daddy let go, held me away from him and looked me over. "The mall? What about the tea party? Is that make-up? Your mom might be able to show you how to put it on a little better. But honey, you're beautiful."

"No one came to the tea party because Audrey didn't actually invite anyone."

"After all the fuss about invitations last week?" he asked.

"I was just pretending. But we went to see Daphne," I said, bouncing toward the teacups on the table.

"How is she? Did you see the photographs I hung for her?"

Mommy didn't speak.

"Daphne didn't know Mommy," I finally said. "And she fell down getting out of bed."

He looked to Mommy. "She okay? They didn't call me. They're supposed to call."

"Carl, we were there," Mommy said. "She's fine. Probably some bruising. They checked everything out."

"That's awful," he said, sitting down next to the stacks of china. "I should go see her."

"It's Sunday night. You can't. Plus Audrey has homework. You were going to help her. Or help me pack up the rest of kitchen."

My heart dropped off a cliff. I wished the kitchen were gone. I wished there were a hole in the house already and that blue kitchen had been taken away.

"But the table is covered," I pointed out. "And I was sick."

"Come on, sweetheart. Let's get this over with."

Daddy made me sit with him at the blue counter in the kitchen to help me with algebra. I could see the dining table from there, with its skyline of china that didn't want to be put in boxes. Nothing Daddy said made sense. He had come from another planet and spoke a strange language to the book and paper while we sat in the ugly kitchen and I nodded so that the alien monster would not eat me.

"It's so dark in here," Mommy said, scowling at the tiny window. "This whole wall is going to let in light. And all this," she said, speaking to the blue floor and the old oven. "All this is going to disappear."

Squiggles and letters on the pages of my book made my stomach small and rocky. The ink on the paper was impossible to understand, no matter how many times Daddy said the same thing over and over. Plus, I didn't want to understand. Ever.

"I don't get it," I said, when he asked me if I saw.

I would rather read about Pandora and the jar. I wanted to know what terrible things would come out and what would happen to her. I wanted to understand Medusa and how something beautiful like a horse with wings could come out of someone so ugly. Maybe there was a horse with wings inside some people. And while the part about her head being cut off made me feel dark and afraid, I loved when Pegasus arrived. He had been trapped inside her, and I felt better that he finally got out. Maybe that was the point. That beauty could come from ugly.

"You're not even listening to me. Come on, Aud, you have to focus."

"Carl, don't call her Aud. How many times have I asked you not to?"

I touched my forehead with my fingertips to feel where my horn was. Daddy exhaled and his breath lifted up my notebook paper. I wished it would fly away and take the squiggles with it.

"I give up," he said. "This isn't working."

He walked out of the kitchen, then walked back in.

"Hire someone, Evie. She needs a tutor, someone who can walk her through this, help her understand. Just hire someone."

"Carl, we've tried that."

"Try someone else."

They argued like I wasn't there, so I pretended I could drift out the small kitchen window and float up to the stars that hung over our house in the night sky. From there, I could see the ocean's white waves rushing to the sand even though the moon pulled them back again and again.

Eve 3

After Audrey had gone to bed, Carl emerged from his office and sat next to Eve at the dining table. If she waited long enough, he would speak first. And it would be about Daphne, again. She felt for the invisible edge of the packing tape, which had adhered to the roll.

"How is Daphne? I mean honestly?" he finally asked.

"When she remembers me, she's vicious, like I'm a stranger who intends harm."

"But she was able to remember that I'd been there. That's something."

"That is something."

They'd discussed this already.

"I'll tell you what's something. Those three photos. I put them in my office. Will you come look?"

"I need to finish all this."

"Do you want my help?"

"I want to do it. I know what to keep and what to put in the giveaway boxes."

Carl shrugged. As he headed upstairs, Eve studied the swing of his arms, the tilt of his head, the way he carried his shoulders. His contours contained the man who once took her breath away, who turned her world upside down with love. She had done what Daphne was incapable of; she'd build a home with her husband and mothered their child.

She turned to a stack of unassembled cardboard boxes that leaned against the kitchen wall waiting for her to make them three-dimensional. It was hard to visualize the new kitchen, hard to imagine the demolition that would wreck and rebuild. She worried that the intrusion would provoke Audrey, but perhaps it would be good. The chaos might just unsettle the world of her imagination enough to help her let go a little.

She finished packing up the rest of the china. It was liberating to clean out what she didn't want. Getting rid of the duplicate blender, the deep-dish pizza pan they never used, the worn wooden salad bowls, this would be an unburdening. She put them into a separate box, turned away from the kitchen and went into the dining room. A ghost of herself looked back at her from the sliding glass door that held the night outside.

Beyond the window, the Pacific Ocean remained hidden in the dark. Behind her, the lights of Los Angeles spread east, disappearing into desert. This house, built in the mid-60s, clung to the edge of the coast above the Pacific Ocean, where cool air rushed across the Santa Monica shore during the day, held its breath at sunset, then reversed itself each evening.

Upstairs she undressed and let her coral sweater set and pants collapse on the floor by her feet. Wrinkles would set in, and she'd make more work for herself later if she didn't hang them up now.

Housewife.

She carried her clothes to the closet, body heat still clinging to the fabric. An array of expensive blazers and dresses hung before her. Her mother's words lurched and clawed again. Carl slept, undisturbed by any of this. Eve dropped to the floor with her clothes, crawled further into the closet, and grabbed blindly until her hand felt a cardboard box, which she pulled out. Sitting there in her bra and underwear, she ran her hand across the Gilbey's gin box.

The flaps unfolded easily. They were powdery with age, and the box released a musty smell. She hadn't opened this box in a long time.

"Here you are," she said.

The box was filled with all the t-shirts she had collected from the countless concerts of her teens and twenties. More than a decade of her life fit into this hidden box. With care, she lifted a t-shirt from the top and let it unfold. Aerosmith, Rocks. Cheap Trick in concert with Kiss. And then with Kansas. I Want You to Want Me. Surrender. Dream Police. And behold, Van Halen. Arena rock exploded out of the box. She exhumed The Pretenders, The Clash, and beneath them she found Led Zeppelin, the Stones. Somewhere near the bottom of the box she found Quadrophenia, but she'd been too young, hadn't followed them until after Keith Moon died. Oh, yes. She'd lifted the shirt from a roadie who was wearing it before they made out in his truck.

Beneath all of them, tucked at the bottom, was a shoebox. It had been some time since she had opened it or added to it. She couldn't remember how much cash was in there. When she was twelve, her mother told her she was old enough to be on her own, and she'd leave money on the counter for Eve during those long absences. So she started saving. Even when she was older and working for the concert promoter, she kept adding to it. Habit. Always evading the 'what ifs' that followed her around. There were even sporadic additions when she became mother and wife. The cash had accumulated into a substantial sum that she counted out on the carpet: just over four thousand dollars.

Her safety net. Her means of survival if she were ever abandoned or needed to get out. It was still here. Proof she did not need it. She lifted an armful of shirts whose graphics celebrated rock music. These were far from Audrey's childish t-shirts with rainbows and flowers. Eve inhaled. The bouquet of cotton released an ancient scent; time laced with a hint of herself. Memories of arena concerts flooded her.

Each concert had been an adventure. She would work her way through the fans and find sanctuary at the foot of the stage in the crush of other concert-goers. The bigger the band, the bigger crowd. Then loneliness left her alone. The shove and jostle confirmed that she existed, that she took up space. The music, the light show, the nearness to seemingly immortal performers; all of this offered confirmation that she was where she should be, something she could not find in her mother's apartment. Later, she might work her way to the loading dock, meet a sound technician or a stagehand and make the magic continue.

Van Halen.

He'd been her first.

But not in an arena.

In the Starwood on the corner of Sunset and Crescent Heights. Yes, she'd sneaked into it.

Someone handed her a flyer at school, and she went by herself. Fearless.

That moment changed her when the club, packed with so many other kids, responded to the music, to the rebellion and volume and how Eddie had his way with them. Everyone knew they were part of history, as they stood packed together in awe of talent that was destined to become huge. It happened again in Santa Barbara when Tom Petty gave it up to a college crowd in a university gym. Then Caljam. At fifteen, she learned to make herself look eighteen and live the independent life of a twenty-three year old. She learned sex was not love.

On the floor of the closet, Eve extracted The Chili Peppers, Quiet Riot, Journey, REO Speedwagon. This was not disco. This was not her mother's migraine jazz. The next t-shirt she lifted, she pressed to her face. Heart. Tour for the self-titled album. *"Never," "Nothin'," "What About Love?"* That night, an all-access pass caught Eve's eye as it dangled and danced on the lanyard around a young man's neck. He took her to the after-party, and she took him home.

Carl.

He should have been just another affair, but here they were after so many years. That night she first brought him home, he followed her into her mother's apartment and remarked on the photos that hung on the walls.

"Who collects Daphne Delfin? These are from *Divide*," Carl said, naming the exhibit that hung at a local gallery.

"You know who she is?" Eve started to pull away. No one she'd ever brought home knew who her mother was.

"I would have studied photography except my father insisted on law. My office isn't far from the Zane Gallery. I've seen the show."

"She isn't here. She never is."

"This is… You're her…" Carl struggled for words. "She's not who I'm interested in," he said.

He had taken her shoulders between his hands, would not let her pull away. The heat and softness of his palms spread through her entire body. She pulled him to her, reached for the button on his jeans, desperate to get as close as she could.

"This is moving a little fast," he said.

"Make love to me," she told him. "Hold me."

Afterwards, in the circle of his arms, she told him everything he wanted to know about being the artist's child, about coming home after school and being so afraid, about looking into the abyss of the freezer for meals or keeping her mother's bedroom door closed so the photography equipment could not remind her of Daphne's absence. He asked questions about her loneliness, let her describe all of it, and didn't make excuses to leave. They talked until dawn colored the sky an optimistic pink.

At the diner over eggs and toast, the sizzle between them grew.

"Eve, you are her masterpiece, whether she sees it or not."

Carl confused her, confused the answer to Heart's question about love. The second time they saw each other, Carl picked her up, took her out, paid for dinner, and left the motor running when he dropped her off.

"Please come in," she begged.

"How about a movie next Thursday?" he said, as if they had never experienced every inch of each other.

His approach intrigued her. Slowly, she stepped away from the backstage life she'd fashioned and perfected. She chose marriage, then motherhood. Everything Daphne had been afraid of. All that had that led her to this closet floor, where she sat with a box full of t-shirts and getaway money she would never need.

Sometime before sunrise, the crush of Carl's arm pressed down on her ribcage and she woke from a vague dream in which she could not breathe. She tried to turn, but Carl's arm pinned her. With more effort, she freed herself. The house was still, but something had woken her.

A gasp or a cry came from the dark direction of Audrey's room. She stood up and left her slippers behind. The floor's cool surface against her bare feet made her more alert. She navigated the graphite shadows of the hallway, trying to hurry but straining to sense distance and wall.

Standing in Audrey's doorway, she waited until she could make out her daughter's thin body in the bed. The vulnerability of that shape made her heart seize. Some kind of nightmare had visited. The shelf of unicorns stood watch, posters of them crowding the walls. Lot of good they did. A gasp in the darkness drew Eve to her daughter. Audrey struggled to suppress a sob.

"Audrey? What is it?"

Don't, her daughter mumbled, but her small frame did not move in the bed. *Leave me.* She brushed Audrey's cheek, wet with tears. *Alone.*

"Hey sweetness, I'm here."

The phrase escaped Audrey's lips, the same phrase Eve had heard on other nights. *Don't,* Audrey said again. But she seemed to sleep though she spoke, unaware Eve was near. *Leave me alone,* she pleaded against antagonistic forces Eve could not see. *Don't.* She uttered a plea of protest against someone. Or was it a plea for companionship?

Don't leave me alone.

"I'm here," Eve said, bending to kiss Audrey's forehead.

But she stopped herself. She'd been admonished so many times for trying to kiss Audrey's forehead, never knowing when the silver horn protruded or when it was absent.

Her heart froze, paralyzing her with her daughter's loneliness. This force had no unit of measure. Finally, Audrey calmed, turned her head, and after a minute her breathing relaxed and deepened. Eve's own breathing did the same. She straightened the folds in Audrey's bedspread, sat a few minutes longer to be sure the nightmare had passed. This bedroom, her daughter's sanctuary that surrounded her with unicorns, felt like stepping back in time to Audrey's five-year-old world. Audrey's interests had never moved forward. She had no use for electronics or hairstyles or the clothing her age group reached for. Socializing on the Internet defaulted to looking for unicorn images.

If Audrey were aware of her mother's presence, she didn't indicate it except to sleep in peace under Eve's sentinel. The darkness outside shifted to gray by almost imperceptible degrees. She turned from the window and took a last look at Audrey before heading back to her room. *Don't leave me alone.* Audrey's words echoed in her mind. A call for companionship, a plea against the isolation of being trapped by the mythical creature she had created out of herself. Morning would finally arrive once she hit deep sleep and the agony of waking would start the day. Chaos waited on the other side of sunrise. Her daughter might not be well enough to go to school, but would find little rest at home when the contractor laid siege to the house. The crew would thump around and commence destruction.

Eve climbed back in bed, her side cold with absence.

"She okay?" The back of Carl's head cratered the pillow with its weight.

"Crying in her sleep."

"Nightmare again?" Carl asked, turning toward her, reaching an arm across her. "We should have had her evaluated long ago. We still could."

"Audrey's a normal teenager," Eve said. "How many times have we had this conversation? We agreed not to label her with something awful, something that doesn't give her any room."

"I still wonder if there's something we could be doing and aren't because we don't know."

"She gets the best grade in her English class. She taught herself calligraphy. She's creative," Eve said.

"She *is* pretty creative. Remember when she was eight, she drew an entire chalk landscape in our driveway?"

"That unicorn habitat," Eve said. "It covered the entire thing. We had to park on the street until it finally rained."

Carl had been complicit in championing their daughter's creativity and imagination. But Audrey's bad dream was a small reminder of the delicate balance between the real world and the fantasy world her daughter worked hard to maintain.

"Carl, maybe we should wait on the remodel."

"No, Evie. We've waited. We can't keep dancing around, trying to make the world accommodate her preferences. She has to learn to deal with reality, with change. And I think you need a project to get involved with."

"Because I have nothing to do all day?"

"A project other than Audrey."

Eve folded her arms as she lay in bed.

"Carl, she didn't hand out the invitations because she's shy. Teens are moody. Don't you remember?"

"Get some sleep," Carl said, his exhale the last sound before silence resumed between them.

Audrey 3

Strands of dream evaporated when I woke, but I could still see some of where I had been when I was asleep. There had been a chase and a struggle and a fence too high to leap in a field of dead grass. That's all I could remember. The unicorns gazed at me from the shelf where they had guarded me all night. I got out of bed, shook my mane to free myself from the dream web that clung to me and became an ordinary girl, arms and legs too long for this plain face and torso. I chose a pink t-shirt with yellow flowers because they made sparks fly out from my heart. My mother would say it was a silly design that a child would choose, because she couldn't see the sparks anymore. Downstairs, I loped around the dining table to prove that I could outrun anything in a dream that might try to get me. The beauty of daylight outside made me snort and paw at the air. In this small moment, when no one was looking, I let go of the gangly arms and legs that trapped me and raced in a full gallop around the furniture, a graceful horn guiding me.

"It will take five minutes. Just come in here to my office and look. You'll know right away if these are unexhibited photographs," Daddy said.

"I'll look when I get back. Those damn photographs aren't going anywhere. Are they? If we deviate from her routine, we'll never get out the door."

"That's what this entire remodel is. We have to deviate. Just look. Please. You're the only one in the world who could say where these were taken. Daphne's memory is unreliable."

Their words kicked and twisted when they talked about Daphne. I closed my eyes so I couldn't see this, and thought about the way the ocean moved, collapsing and expanding. The phone shrieked at all of us, and I bolted away from the clamoring. My mother talked and Daddy folded his arms and listened.

"But Nick, today is the day we agreed to start," Mommy said.

Nick was the name of the man was going to fix our not-broken kitchen. Daddy held out his hand for Mommy's phone.

"This isn't acceptable," Daddy said and now my mother folded her arms and listened. I trotted out of the room and loped through the blue kitchen, its old surfaces worn and familiar, but I could not get away from the unhappiness and argument in the next room. When Daddy finished yelling, he gave the phone back to Mommy.

"He'll be here in half an hour," he said.

The tones inside their fighting words made my silver horn recede, made me stop moving. Daddy snapped his laptop shut and put his coffee cup in the empty kitchen. Mommy followed and took his cup back to the pretend kitchen she had made in the dining room.

Something was about to happen, a man named Nick was going to invade our house, which made me start racing again. All those men who had come to the house to talk about kitchens had been loud and clumsy except for one with curly blond hair and tan skin. Sun and ocean had soaked into him and he moved like gentle water. Because of that, I stepped into the living room when he was here talking to Mommy and Daddy. It was as if he had come up from the water to walk around on land. I had sensed this from the doorway and stepped closer to understand where he came from. My parents watched me then, quietly speaking to each other with their eyes. The man smiled at me, turned back to my parents to say something. Still, I didn't run like I had from the others who'd stomped through the kitchen and talked about tearing it up. I came close enough to sniff the ocean in his hair, but Mommy stepped between us and stopped me.

He was the one, Mommy told Daddy later. He had to be the contractor they hired. And he was going to arrive today.

"Hello sweetheart," Mommy said when she saw me, her words full of smiling but not her eyes. "Remember that today is when the contractor comes? Remember Nick?"

The microwave and coffee pot made a new kitchen on the bookshelf. I wanted to play house with her today, stay here where it was safe, not go to school.

"Just take a look and call me," Daddy said, before he went out the door.

My mother made a fist around her car keys and pointed to the garage door. "Audrey, time to go to school."

Not school. Not when the sun was light yellow and the sky was endless blue.

"Audrey, stop running around the house," Daddy said. "Get in the car."

But I did not obey.

"There is no magic path," I said, breathless from avoiding capture.

"There are no flower petals today," Mommy said, putting two fists on her hips. "The irises wilted from your party and I threw them out."

"There has to be a magic path," I said.

"Okay, okay. Here."

Mommy gathered an invisible fistful of flowers from an empty vase, and for a tiny moment the three of us could see the petals pulled from her bouquet as she sprinkled them on the floor. Sometimes, even if it didn't last, my parents could see pathways made of petals. It never lasted for them, but I had to keep trying to show what they couldn't always see. In that moment, we were peaceful. But then Daddy let out a huff and I hurried to follow the purple path before it disappeared, lifting my backpack from the chair, strong against the weight that tried to make me collapse. Then we were out the door and in the car and moving fast down the street. Tangled thoughts about coefficients and variables darted at me when I wanted to think about the horse I'd read about last night, the one with wings who made water come out of the ground where his hooves struck the earth.

"What are you thinking?" Mommy asked.

But I had to be quiet so that I could be able to get out of the car without whining, which was for two-year-olds, Mommy said. A river of students flowed in the same direction and poured into the entrance of the school. I didn't belong in the river, in the churn and swirl of unhappy faces that tried to pull me under. I would not be able to swim. I did not get out of our silver carriage when my mother stopped.

"Go ahead," Mommy said. "You're not late." I fluttered my lips and tossed my head because I did not belong here. "Audrey, none of this. Just go. You can do this for a few hours."

I pulled the latch slowly. The car door swung away and I fell forward. A piece of curb jumped up to grab my foot. The sidewalk came at me but I sprang forward and found my balance before the pavement could bite. My mother shook her head, did not see how the concrete tried to claim me. I started walking, but the scent of someone's lawn on the morning air made me prance toward it.

"Audrey," my mother shouted. "Be careful."

I shook my head once more and then moved into the river like everyone else. Except I held my breath. My beautiful mother drove away in her silver chariot as the long bridle of rules and ridicule swung toward me.

"Find anything good to eat at the mall?" Madison Moncrief asked, pulling away from the mouth of the boy hovering over her.

Her skirt hugged her hips and her shirttails were pulled out. She pressed up against the wall while the boy pressed up against her, holding half a donut in one hand. I didn't speak and the boy moved his mouth back to Madison's, which made me shiver, stare straight ahead and keep walking. The sting of someone's laughter faded as I moved into the hallway.

I fought until the metal locker released the textbook I needed and went to class. Then the worst thing in the world happened; I stepped between Madison and her best friend Mitzi. They went everywhere together and I had stepped between them. No one was supposed to do that. I wished I were dust, powdery soft grains that could float away in the breeze. But I was still me: arms and legs and stupid. A new boy in a long-sleeved flannel shirt with bangs that hid his eyes asked loudly if it was time for lunch, because he saw a sandwich he wanted to eat. I didn't see any sandwich, but a wave of laughter rolled toward us as everyone in the classroom turned to stare at us. More students howled in the hallway. My face went hot.

For a moment, the new boy pushed his bangs back and saw that I was trying to disappear.

"Take your seats. All of you," Mr. Ross said.

The boy raised his hand. "Take them where?"

More laughter rolled across the room. The class turned from me to him. Mitzi and Madison shoved me away and I was glad for the boy's dumb chair joke.

"Today we mere mortals are going to visit the world of gods and goddesses who continue to be larger than life."

Mitzi and Madison sat down next to each other. My seat was next to the new boy.

"Can I borrow a pen?" he asked.

I didn't know him, and he wanted my pen, but it wasn't just a pen so I couldn't give it to him. I flipped the pages in my book like I was looking for something. Like I couldn't hear. But I could feel him staring. Mr. Ross fired off a question about Persephone and the reason for winter. The words on the page became disconnected and made no sense the way they did last night, when Demeter had to make a deal with the gods to get her daughter back.

"Audrey," Mr. Ross said as he moved toward my desk. "Can you tell us what was going on?"

My skin stung with invisible pinpoints. I shook my head, unable to move my tongue. My heartbeat pulsed in my face. He would move on if I kept my head down. Mommy had talked to all of my teachers and explained that I was shy and might be far inside myself but I could not get far enough inside right then. All I had to do was wait. After Mr. Ross moved on, Mitzi and Madison smirked, punched at each other and fluttered their lips like horses. Small bursts of laughter fired around the room, and it took several minutes for Mr. Ross, veins rising in his forehead, to make the students quiet. I pushed the point of my pen into my thumb, dimpling the flesh, making it white and unfeeling. Then the boy with the long bangs started talking.

"Persephone was a babe. Not just any high school whore," he said turning briefly toward Mitzi, who held up her middle finger. "She could make the gods stop breathing when they saw her. Except the dude in the underworld, he wanted her. He was poisoned by her beauty. What the fuck was his name?"

"Language," Mr. Ross said.

"Hades," I said in a whisper to my book.

"Hades. He tricked her into coming to his place and she made a mistake there. She ate an apple."

"A pomegranate," I whispered again.

"A pomegranate," the shaggy boy said. "Demeter was pissed. Made it winter all year until the gods rolled over. But since Persephone, you know, swallowed, she belonged to Hades. So she has to go back every year, for part of it. And that's why we have winter. Because one god's lust is another's weakness."

He turned to me and stared for a long time, long after Mitzi and Madison threw wadded up notes at him.

"Thank you very much, Mr. Bixby," Mr. Ross said, causing the kid to jerk up out of his seat.

"Oh shit. Is my dad here?" He looked and sat back down. "Dude, I'm Lucas," he said, tossed his hair from his eyes and held out his hand to me. I touched his fingers with mine like a quick handshake, like grown ups do, and then I stared at my desk until the bell rang.

After class, Mitzi and Madison trapped the new boy and the three of them walked out together, but the back of my neck could feel his eyes following me.

Lunchtime meant I could visit my patch of grass under a small tree whose trunk had been scarred with hearts and swear words. I sat down and brushed the blades with the palm of my hand. They tickled and teased to try and make me feel better. The rest of the lunchtime herd moved past, exchanging calls and responses of ohmygawds and fuckyous. I lifted an apple to my lips, its smooth surface cool and perfect. I refused to be lost. Everyone was trying to be like everyone. All those faces passing by questioned my not being them. I took a bite of the apple, but it was mealy, and the softness of it made me gag and spit it out, which ruined everything.

The rotten bite lay in the grass, whose tiny barbs tickled my legs, making me want to roll around on them, but the apple bite said no. I plucked at the blades with my fingertips as if my hand were a soft muzzle and lifted a single blade from the mouthful in my hand to taste it. Madison and Mitzi strolled past with the new boy. They talked to each other and laughed. Mitzi reached over to put her arm in his but he pulled away. I sprinkled the rest of the grass on my leg to hide me from predators who might be near. I tossed the apple at the trashcan. But I missed because I was not a sports girl. Someone behind me snorted.

"Later. I just found my next meal," he said.

Mitzi and Madison walked away, glancing back at us a few times. He lay down next to me, reached over, picked up the apple and bit into it right where I had bit. His mouth touching where my mouth had touched made me shiver.

"Yum. Applesauce," he said.

I laughed because I knew the apple was bad but I didn't have time to tell him, and now he knew it too. His face looked unhappy but he made himself chew and swallow as if it were good. When he offered the bitten apple to me, I squealed, jumped up and galloped across the quad.

"Wait," he called.

But I was already far away. A dozen students pointed and laughed and shouted giddy-up. I slowed to a trot and walked like a girl on two legs like Mommy told me to. Like everyone else, even though all of us wanted to run.

Eve 4

A beat-up white truck blocked the driveway. A young man leaned against its rear tire well. He was more handsome than Eve remembered. She parked on the street and got out. He nodded at her but continued to talk on his cell phone even as she approached. Lanky, in his late 20s with a baseball cap turned backwards, Nick looked more like a boy. A twinge of regret spasmed in Eve's chest. He'd only recently completed his contractor's license, and while he was more affordable than all the others, which appealed to Carl, he was less experienced. When he broke down his estimate, Audrey had stayed in the living room instead of running off in a panic like she had from the others. He quietly explained the ways in which the kitchen could be updated, making them all envision the picture window he described, the sunlight it would let in, the island that would integrate all elements of stone and tile and wood. He had glanced over at Audrey but only quickly as if, it seemed to Eve, that he sensed the delicate nature of her temperament. But there was something gentle and kind about him, something genuine. She and Carl exchanged a look, and had hired him on the spot. No discussion, no "we'll get back to you."

Eve approached Nick, but he continued to press the phone against his curly hair and spoke in a tone that suggested a technical problem, a crisis of some sort.

"Would you estimate an anterior dimension of three to four feet? And would that be a right-hand lateral? Okay. I understand. I'll have to get there right away," he told his caller.

A surfboard shared the back of his truck with a wheelbarrow. Overhead, the sky was cloudless, which meant the coastal zone would climb into the upper 80s later, warm for October, but good weather in which to remove a wall of your house. Unless excellent surf conditions prevailed. Eve knew this because her past had included a few surfers.

Nick ended the call and extended his knuckles to her. She hesitated and then pressed her knuckles to his.

"Bad news," he said. "My crew is on another job. I'm gonna have to delay the start."

"I figured the right hand break was cresting at three to four feet," Eve said.

Nick laughed, throwing his head back and offering his dazzling grin to the sky. He shrugged helplessly and nodded. He was stunning, young. As if he could tell what she was thinking, he looked her up and down.

"We scheduled this months ago, Nick. Isn't there some way to start?" she asked.

"This isn't a one-man job," he said, shaking his blond hair. "Unless we want to get day laborers we don't know from the hardware store."

Eve was supposed to turn this down like a demure housewife. But days could become weeks that turned into months.

"Let's go man-shopping," she said.

Nick grinned again, gazed at her, then gestured to his truck. The paint job was chipped and the body was dented. Eve climbed in. The thick metal door took effort to pull shut. The dashboard was strewn with receipts, paper cups and surf wax. Nick got in on the other side and inserted the key into the ignition. The engine turned and stalled three times before the motor struggled to life. She was riding shotgun in this young surfer's truck to go pick up more men. Eve had to look out the passenger window to conceal her pleasure.

A queue of brown-skinned day laborers lined the sidewalk next to the cheap warehouse architecture. Some sat on the curb in the modest shade of juvenile trees. Some stood, but looked as if they wanted to sit. Dressed in sweatshirts and baseball caps, jeans or white painter pants, they eyed the truck as it approached. When Nick pulled over, several men moved closer.

"Do they know you?" Eve asked.

"Not these ombrays. But I'm telling you, it's better to have a relationship with someone you bring into your house. Otherwise it's like a one-night stand. Could be unforgettable. Could be someone you never want to see again."

She stared straight ahead. "Dating is going to take too long."

"Okay. Who would you put the moves on, Mrs. Tilden?"

She got out of the truck and slid to the ground, dwarfed by the height of the cab. The men stared. She must be a rarity on the day-labor sidewalk. But there were no low whistles or rude remarks. Mostly the men smiled, smoothed their hair, and tried to make themselves desirable. They wanted work. Eve surveyed them quickly, came back to the truck and shrugged, empty-handed.

When Nick got out, the men on the sidewalk surged toward him. He looked up and down the line, and pointed to two different men. They eagerly approached and he spoke to them with a clunky gringo accent to ask their names. She understood the older one was Isaac. The younger one called himself Fred. Isaac and Fred exchanged a few more words with Nick, who pantomimed a sledgehammer, and they nodded vigorously.

"Kwantos kwesta?" Nick said, who also seemed to understand everything they said.

They reached an agreement, a number, and Nick turned to Eve to translate what she would have to pay. "They want twenty dollars an hour. Each," he said. She shrugged and nodded. "That's too high," he added. "You have to knock the first offer in half at least. Fold your arms and shake your head no."

Eve did what he said, and he turned back to the men, telling them that the señora said it was muy alto.

"Ocho," Nick said.

But Eve knew they had families. She nudged Nick. "Twelve," she whispered.

They finally agreed on ten dollars an hour. Nick motioned to the back of the truck and they climbed in.

"Why those two?" Eve asked as she got in the cab.

"Wedding rings and crucifixes. If they're married, they're more motivated to do well. If they're religious, they'll put in an honest day's work."

Eve studied them as the remaining line up of hopefuls stepped away and gravitated toward another truck pulling to the curb. Perched next to the surfboard in the back of Nick's truck, Fred and Isaac grinned, the breeze rearranging their hair. These two men were about to invade her household. These three men.

Nick explained to the workers about window removal and demolition of the wall as the three of them laid cloth down on the dining room floor. The plan was to take out most of the west wall, add a huge window, redo all the cabinets, and install an island with a counter. This meant all new appliances, and almost everything had been figured out except how Eve wanted to finish the walls. Not wall paper. But not paint either. Despite looking at dozens of kitchens and dozens of photographs she had not yet found what she wanted. It was pointless to brainstorm with Carl. He was leaving it entirely up to her.

Fred and Isaac worked together to move the refrigerator to the makeshift kitchen Eve had created near the dining table. A rectangle of beige dust outlined where it had stood for years, along with two bottle caps that had run away and managed to keep themselves a secret until now. Eve retrieved the broom and started to sweep the dust into a small pile. But Nick grabbed it from her, his hand on hers for a brief moment.

"No need. It's going to get worse before it gets better. We'll clean up at the end of every day."

She nodded, moved out of the kitchen unsure what to do. With a quick glance she dismissed Carl's office and the photographs he wanted her to look over. Not right now. Later. She listened as Nick explained some other tasks to the men, told her he had to run out for some supplies and that it would be wise for her not to leave them alone. Then he hurried away, making a call on his cell phone as he sprinted to his truck. Within the hour, they had removed the windows and fresh air flooded through the gaping holes. She checked on the progress, but there was little else she could do. Near the entrance to the kitchen, a sledgehammer leaned against the wall, its handle smooth with use. Eve reached out to touch it, closing her fingers around the wood. She wanted to lift it, feel its weight make the muscle contract in her arm.

"Señora," Isaac, the larger of the two men, said. "¿Quiere usted?"

He picked up the hammer, held it out and tapped the wall where she should land the first blow. She took it and almost dropped it to the floor before she found the strength to hold on. This was not a new sledgehammer. It had to be older than Nick. Polished with sweat and wear, the wood handle was slick, the iron head dumb with heft. She doubled her effort, hoisted it behind her and swung, but it arced down toward the floor like a golf club and barely dented the hideous wallpaper. She frowned and leveraged the weight of the hammer above her again, took a second swing and this time lodged the iron head into the surface of the wall. But she only made a dent. Three more blows barely sank themselves into the flat surface. With her face pink from the effort, she rested the hammer on the floor as muscle burned against ligament and tendon. Isaac took the tool from her, lifted, and swung with far more power and aggression, lodging the head into the wall then pulling chunks of plaster and paper off as he yanked it back out to swing between the two-by-fours that supported the roof.

Her home was a piñata. Eve backed away, went to the temporary food-prep area in the dining room. She could not escape the rattle and crack of iron against plaster, the way each blow shook the house. Audrey would have been hysterical, and in the pit of her stomach, Eve understood why. For the rest of the morning, violent demolition splintered and crunched wall into chunks and pieces.

It would be lunchtime soon and Eve debated whether she was supposed to feed the men. Nick had not left instructions. She stood in the temporary kitchen, which suggested playing house, and the housewife put her hands on her hips, folded her arms, then walked away. A cordless saw whirred and screamed. Ragged sections of daylight found their way in through the broken wall, illuminating mess and debris. While Isaac destroyed the wall, Fred filled a wheelbarrow and rolled it through the hall to the front yard. Eve followed anxiously to see where he was depositing pieces, and there on the driveway, a pile of broken kitchen began to form.

Across the street, aging Mr. Holmquist stepped out his front door and observed the pile at Eve's feet. She waved and smiled and shrugged the way Nick did, but the old man only frowned and retreated into his house. There was little Eve could do. She couldn't deliver those boxes of her unwanted items to a thrift store. She couldn't run to the market.

By one o'clock, Nick had not returned and Eve grew increasingly concerned that the men must be hungry. She foraged through the produce in the refrigerator and assembled salads of organic baby lettuce and brown rice pilaf. She carried the two beautiful plates of food into the destruction zone. But Isaac and Fred had left the kitchen. After managing to open the front door without dropping a plate, she stepped outside and was about to call to them when she saw that they were sitting in the shade of the eucalyptus tree. They got to their feet before she said anything, but it wasn't because she came bearing organic salads.

"Ombrays, tengo lunch," Nick sang, emerging from his truck, holding bags of fast food.

They hurried to him, nodding and smiling with gratitude. Eve stepped quickly back into the house, lowering the plates from sight, embarrassed at the effort she should not have made. Nick had grabbed the broom from her earlier, and she had made lunch like a fool. Like a housewife. Her mother's accusation flared again. In the temporary quiet that descended on the house, she returned to the kitchen to examine the missing wall and windows that exposed this home to the outside world.

Nick was suddenly next to her, his arms full of plastic sheeting, tape, chocolate bars, and a huge boombox splattered with paint.

"Want the extra burger?" he asked, but he followed her glance to the salads lined up on the dining table.

She shook her head. "Want some organic salad?"

"Totally. Righteous."

He sat down and devoured what she had prepared, responding to the first bite with a nod and a hum. Watching him eat felt intrusive but gratifying, and he didn't seem to mind. When Nick finished the salad, he dug into the bag, unwrapped the factory-slaughtered patty imbedded in a white starch bun, and devoured it with just as much gusto.

"So what happens to the pile on the driveway?" Eve asked.

He explained that a dumpster would be delivered, but that he was holding off on it because of the cost. It would be more efficient to create a pile and then move it into the dumpster when they were ready to make a run to the landfill. Maybe he did know what he was doing. The smell of hamburger and fries distracted Eve from her salad. Nick nodded and pushed the fries toward her, but Eve declined, left the table, and walked back through the Ground Zero her kitchen had become.

"You might want to invest in paper plates for a while," Nick said, suddenly close to her. "Anything that makes a remodel easier" He captured her with his boyish gaze. "I'll be back around four," he added.

She watched him walk out the door. She wanted him to stay, but she couldn't figure out a way to make that happen. Fred and Isaac returned to the kitchen, smiling, nodding. Eve carried her unfinished salad and Nick's empty plate to the bathroom and knelt next to the bathtub to wash dishes.

Audrey 4

The last bell yelled at us, disrupting the pristine shape that came out of the point of my pen. Everyone gathered binders and books, but I finished drawing in the margin of my book where a unicorn emerged. She wasn't supposed to be there. Nothing was. But she insisted on making me draw her. She looked away from the geometric picture of the insides of molecules. Why could everyone believe in molecules without ever seeing them and not unicorns? That's what made me put a unicorn in the book.

In the hall, lockers slammed and bodies headed toward the exit, merging and touching and shoving. So I waited. I pretended to study the books in my locker like I was trying to make an important decision. Someone snorted as they passed, but I acted like I didn't hear. When the hallway was empty, I closed my locker, but it would not latch. I shoved it hard, and the metal slammed together, which scared me and I pawed at it. Mommy told me to not act like I felt at school. Sometimes I couldn't help it.

Outside, the air was clean and I inhaled as much as I could. Today, I could walk home. I loved to walk home, but Mommy was afraid sometimes, so she usually picked me up. But today she said I could if I came straight home. Because of the men at the house working on the kitchen, Mommy needed to be there. I looked down at the sidewalk sliding past my feet. There were too many lines to count and I tried to step over them, and finally I swerved onto patches of lawn. Soft grass, springy under my feet, invited me to lope. I took off my shoes so I could feel the lawns that were like small fields. I zigzagged and circled back in all directions. The further I got from the school, the quieter the street became. Noise from the hallway and parking lot became chirping birds and a distant leaf blower, until finally it was safe enough to lift the pen in my hand and hold it to my forehead. The shadow on the grass outlined a tiny horn, too small for the rest of my body. I held my breath, watched myself be what everyone thought did not exist.

Somewhere behind me a serpent whispered danger, hissed louder as it got close but turned into skateboard wheels on concrete moving toward me. That new boy grabbed my arm and spun around to stop but fell off his board and landed on the sidewalk.

"I meant to do that," he said, getting back onto his feet.

My arm hurt where he had grabbed me and I covered his invisible handprint with my hand but I scratched myself with the pen I'd used to make a horn. A blue line marked my skin. The line didn't belong. It damaged me. The pavement buckled under my feet.

"I didn't mean to do that. Wow. Awkward. Sorry."

I bent over to keep my stomach from jumping out of me, and looked away from the ink that stained my arm.

"Hey. Sit down. You don't look so good."

He moved me to the gutter, sat down, and patted the curb for me to sit next to him. The gutter had a small river in it filled with dirty water.

"It will wash off. Really."

I told my eyes not to spill but they didn't listen.

"Here, you can make a mark on me. Okay?"

I shook my head.

"I want you to."

He took the pen from me, just pulled it right from my hand, then rolled up his sleeve and offered me his inner arm. Freckles became the points of constellations. After a minute, I could see how they connected, how they created shapes on his skin.

"Please," he said. "Can I get your phone number?"

I sat down, took the pen and wrote ten numbers along his wrist. But further up his arm, two dots wanted to be connected. Then more dots wanted to be attached. Orion's belt. Then the point of his sword. Figures in the sky had been hiding in his inner arm until I traced their ancient forms. They nodded to me in thanks. I had set them free. We both looked at what I'd found, Andromeda, Ursa Major, the Pleiades, a cup with a long handle.

"Whoa, shit," he said. "The fuck?"

His words made the constellations turn into ink stains on skin, ugly and wrong. I had made a mistake. I felt awful. I'd ruined his arm, so I jumped up and ran as fast as I could. When I looked back, Lucas was still sitting on the curb staring at his inner elbow. Just staring at his arm.

I stayed on the concrete until it brought me home, did not wander onto lawns, did not waste time, as Mommy said. But when I got home, my house was ruined. Pieces of kitchen lay helplessly on the driveway, cut up, broken, torn apart with some kind of weapon. They bled dry bits of themselves on the concrete. I stopped at the curb and listened, sniffed, and took cautious steps closer. There was agony and pain, the rip and pull of being harmed and broken. I took several more steps, smelling the strange chalky flavor of pieces that were not wall anymore.

"They will take some of the kitchen out," Mommy had explained many times. "They will put in new walls and counters. It will be beautiful."

What lay at my feet was not beautiful. A short man came out of the house pushing a wheelbarrow of more broken kitchen. He grinned at me, his sharp teeth flashing, and then he dumped everything out. More pieces of wall complained and clattered at my feet, which made me kick and bolt toward the house, calling for Mommy.

"Come see," Mommy called to me from the dining room, her excitement confusing my fear as she motioned me to the kitchen doorway.

The house was destroyed. Gaping holes had been torn into the wall. Windows had been pried out and taken away. A wood skeleton was exposed like naked bones. Dust and chunks of wall covered the floor.

"Where are your shoes?" she shouted at me.

An older man swung a large weapon into the wall and pulled out pieces of it, tore off the broken sections that came apart under each blow and exploded into dust. A pain in my ribs made me scream. The air bled tiny bits of wood that spewed from the broken sections, particles that came at me to invade my lungs.

"No!" I screamed.

It didn't matter where I ran or if I covered my nose with my hands, I could not get away. My mother ran after me but I was fast. A howl from deep in my lungs pushed out the dust, grew louder, and made me run in circles through the ruined house and followed me no matter where I went. But Mommy caught me, locked her arms around my shoulders. The smell of tree insides went in and out of me with each breath, and I tried to cover my nose and ears, but the toothy man parked the wheelbarrow and made a power saw scream into what was left of the cabinets.

I pushed and pulled to get away, but my mother was strong and told me stop stop stop. Mommy said it was okay, but the noise and the pieces of house outside and strangers with screaming tools were not okay. I gave up and collapsed to the floor. Mommy collapsed with me, holding me, protecting me. The warmth of her embrace dissolved the swarm of panic and pain. The two of us lay on the carpet, my mother's body pressing me to the floor.

"Stop," Mommy yelled once more but this time not at me.

The horrible noises in the kitchen stopped. The floor held still and no longer vibrated or moaned. I could hear my own fast breathing and smell Mommy's lavender perfume and feel her breath against my neck. On the other side of the forest made by dining chairs and table, two men came out of the kitchen and stared.

"Be still," Mommy said. "You're safe. We are going to get up and go to your room. Do you understand?"

Mommy let go slowly, releasing me little by little to see if I still needed to be held or if I could be still. The two men watched. My mother got to her feet, held out her hand and helped me up. She guided me to my room.

My room.

My unicorns.

My beautiful posters.

Everything was where it should be.

"You stay here. You're safe. I'm going to go back down to talk to them," Mommy told me.

I went to the bookcase and stood near the herd.

"I'll come back very soon," she said, and she closed the door and left.

All the unicorns remained calm about the complaint and protest from the kitchen that started up again. I breathed hard, but they were not scared, so I did not run.

Then the kitchen went silent. The house stood still. Mommy had stopped the destruction downstairs. But a rumble grew from outside, came closer, made me tremble again. An old white truck pulled up and parked. A man got out wearing a towel around his waist. I pressed myself against the wall, my heart bouncing against my insides. I took a breath and leaned over to look quickly, then moved back. After a few seconds, I leaned over again, this time longer.

The man pulled a t-shirt down over his head and he couldn't see because he didn't put his arms through first like you were supposed to. When he finally got his arms through the sleeves, he pulled the fabric over his naked chest and shoulders. Then he took off his swim trunks without the towel falling down, which would have showed his private parts. I started to hide myself beside the window, my face hot because of him naked under the towel, but I stopped. He did not see me. Did not know I was looking. He put on a pair of jeans without dropping the towel, then threw it into the front seat of the truck, shoved his feet into some shoes, combed his hair with his fingers and became Nick, the man from the ocean who came to the house to destroy the kitchen.

I put my hand over my mouth to hold in a shout. A laugh. A squeal.

He walked into the house. I leaned against the wall and felt the front door close. He stood inside, just under me. Tiny hooves ran across my shoulders. The herd on the shelf snorted. They had been looking too and then hurried back to their places. Each of them resumed their poses, showing off their special beauty.

Grinding and screaming started up downstairs, which the herd did not like, but they nodded to me that I was safe in my room. I went back to the window to see the white truck still parked at the curb, and the sight of it made a shiver run up my back and down shoulders all the way to my fingers. I looked to see if there were constellations hidden in my arms.

Eve 5

Audrey refused to go near the kitchen or dining room all that evening or the next morning. Eve had brought her toast, got her dressed for school, and Audrey held onto her tightly as she ushered her out the front door before the workers came, avoiding any hysteria. This would have to be their routine until the kitchen became a kitchen again. By the time she returned from dropping Audrey at school, the boombox was spilling lively music out of the missing wall. The men showed up on time and got right to work. For a regular crew, Nick had chosen well. She raced upstairs, brushed her teeth and hair, and then checked her reflection in the mirror. A middle-aged woman in a sweater looked back. She frowned, turned sideways, modeled her hair up, let it back down again then hurried down to see Nick.

But he wasn't there.

"¿Dondé está Nick?" she asked when she entered the demolition zone.

Both men spoke, their rapid words and gestures colliding. Isaac pointed to an invisible watch, indicating the hour Nick would return. He must have gone out to catch a morning set, but since the two men were working hard, it seemed pointless to object to this arrangement. The paint-splattered boombox on the floor spewed happy happy lyrics about heartbreak or love that she couldn't translate.

"Tejano," Fred told her.

"I like it," she said. "Es bueno."

He nodded.

These men were kind and honest and hard-working. She wished her high school Spanish had not evaporated so she could explain about Audrey. But she barely had that vocabulary in English. Asking the men to end their day at three o'clock to accommodate her daughter's sensitivity would prolong the construction. She would discuss this with Nick when he got there.

Isaac and Fred maneuvered the stove away from the wall, positioned it on a dolly and struggled through the doorway to wheel it to the driveway. The only place to cook would be the toaster oven and microwave on top of the bookshelf. Confronted by demolition and dust, Eve wandered through the house trying to take sanctuary in rooms that had four walls. Everywhere, stuff they had accumulated over the years confronted her, making her want to box the clutter as she had done with the kitchen. On the coffee table, a tennis ball, stacks of holiday cards now eight months old, two candles in ceramic holders that had never been lit, and an empty crystal vase could all be boxed up and no one would miss any of it. Eve opened a drawer where she found miles of video footage from Audrey's infancy and childhood. If she ever found the time to convert it to digital and edit, which she never would, she might find her baby girl looking solemnly at the camera, trying her first spoonful of food, stacking blocks, or taking her first steps. Somewhere in there was Audrey, with round eyes, breathtaking softness and promise, before she'd been taken hostage by unicorns.

Eve studied the door of Carl's office. The recently discovered photographs he wanted her to see were on the other side of the door. She could not summon even a mild curiosity to take a look at them, the fact of them in her house sending her upstairs instead. She stopped at Audrey's door. Her daughter's empty bed directly across from the doorway made her long for Audrey's return in the afternoon. She stepped into the room and faced the shelf of unicorns. They stared at her, frozen by her unexpected arrival. The herd had grown in size. Daphne had started this with the first white one. Now there were twenty.

They all had names. She couldn't remember who was who, this circle of friends that stood in for what didn't exist in Audrey's world. A single sweep of her arm could destroy them all, smash and break their fragile legs and horns into pieces. Something on the shelf drew her toward the figurines. A piece of apple grooved with Audrey's teeth marks, brown with exposure to the air, had been placed in the middle of the herd. Last week there had been a sugar cube covered with a dozen ants. The week before that, a piece of carrot. Audrey had been feeding them. They had talked about that. Eve thought she had made it clear that she couldn't leave bits of food on the shelf.

Two explorer ants emerged from behind the mother unicorn lying down with her colt, traveling along an invisible path toward the piece of apple. Eve reached over quickly and squished the ants with her thumb. Otherwise they would bring an army. The Sawzall in the kitchen screamed as it cut into wood and shook the house. She picked up the rotted fruit and flushed it away in Audrey's bathroom.

In her own room, she stumbled on a shoe lying on its side. The bottom of it was covered with rainbow stickers Audrey had pressed there.

"So I can walk on rainbows all day," Eve said.

Adrift in her house, just as Audrey must feel adrift in that sea of high school students, Eve wished it were three o'clock already.

Fashionable pants and jackets and dresses in her closet defined women who shopped at Bloomingdales and boutique stores; women who went to yoga with make-up on. Her clothes echoed her mother's accusation of housewife.

"Where did you go?" Daphne had asked.

"I went where you were afraid to go," Eve said to the empty sleeves.

The cardboard box of her old t-shirts invited her to sit. The flaps of the box released that musty smell again. The shirts needed to be washed. But what was the point unless she was going to wear them?

She sat on the carpet and lifted up Heart again.

Arena acoustics bounced with anticipation. Fans poured in, populated the floor, exhaled the gossamer haze that filled the air. Sound check sent feedback across the crowd. Metal beams wove a sky of catwalk. Excitement for what was about to be unleashed on stage ran through everyone like an electric current.

Sitting in a closet in the middle of the suburbs, she could still recall that sensation in her arms and legs, like muscle memory.

She could imagine the lights going out, the crowd howling at the dark. Follow spot searching the universe for deities; Anne and Nancy.

Ladies and gentlemen.

Wolf & Rissmiller presents.

Bill Graham presents.

Don Kirshner presents.

The first downbeat released a deafening roar. Guitar chords rang from the Marshall stack. The crowd, the music, the revelry erased the lonely world in her mother's apartment. She became part of the euphoria. She could laugh with a stranger at accidental closeness. A magic man. A barracuda. She might speak into his ear. Intimacy in a crowd, everyone swaying or shimmying. They came to rock, to compare notes on the last show, the last tour, the last venue. True fans, tethered by the band. When she turned, caught that stranger's eye again, he smiled back, couldn't believe his good fortune, shared the magic of the moment at the foot of the stage. Danced with her.

London was calling further down in the box. She dug out The Clash t-shirt. This was no reissue. This was the real thing. This was the concert that changed everything. Her first lover. She had been so young. Too young. She hadn't been ready. Not really. But what did it matter? It didn't. If it had, Daphne wouldn't have been on the other side of the world. She'd told him she was eighteen. He was already inside when he realized he was her first, but she assured him this was what she wanted. And it was. It was. Night turned into morning and breakfast in Venice Beach. He stayed through the weekend. His name was August but everyone called him Gus, the equipment manager. After the second show, he brought her backstage, introduced her to the band, let her watch the entire production shut down and pack up. The next night was the last show before the tour moved on, and Gus secured her a place at the foot of the stage. Afterwards, he invited her to travel with him to the next town.

It was summer. There was nothing to hold her back.

She had stayed with Gus for three weeks. They ran it out as far as they could, and the end of the tour became the end of the line for them. Beautiful, harmonious, no expectations. Before things had a chance to become anything else, she left. Just like that. Disappeared from his RV early one morning. Used the cash she had brought with her to catch a bus home. They never crossed paths again. Didn't need to.

It had been so long since she'd thought about any of this, since she'd opened this box of t-shirts.

At seventeen, she left high school for a job with a rock promoter. She'd been Audrey's age now. It was hard to imagine Audrey ever being so bold, so independent. She worked for Rick Samuels for the next fifteen years, and he became her family she supposed. At first she was just office support, but she knew so much about backstage logistics that Rick had her travel to venues to be his eyes and ears on the ground overseeing productions. She enjoyed the travel, the adventure, and the sequential euphoria she shared with different lovers. Her adventures weren't all perfect. Once in a while, she woke up in her hotel room next to a man who couldn't see further than having made a conquest of her. He would leave, a grin on his face she didn't share. Some guys turned out to be selfish in bed, and she learned to spot them. Some refused to use condoms. End of evening, game over. Only twice did she ever have to call hotel security.

One night, her mother walked into their apartment where Eve and a lover were entwined on the living room floor. A single candle flickered on the coffee table as the apartment door opened suddenly. They had only each other to cover themselves.

"You have company," Daphne said with a hint of amusement and surprise. "I'll come back another time."

It could have been a dream, except for the fact that Eve's lover had jumped up and gotten dressed. Daphne slipped out first, and didn't return for another six months.

The cash tucked in the shoebox reminded her she was here in this house, in this marriage, by choice. She didn't need escape money. Behind her, an audience of Carl's empty suits hung unresponsive. Her own side of the closet offered linen suits and Italian knits, disguising the fact that she had once defeated loneliness inside the armor of her concert t-shirts. Carl's law practice and earning power made her own paycheck working for the concert promoter seem pointless. Then there was the worry that something was wrong with their beautiful baby girl, who barely talked, stayed so far inside herself. Other girls her age babbled. Eve left the job to be home with Audrey. This was supposed to bring their quiet daughter out of her wordless world. But it was Daphne who did that when she gave Audrey her first unicorn figurine. That unicorn unleashed full and unsolicited sentences from Audrey at the age of five.

"Out," Audrey had said. "She wants to go out."

The porcelain figure filled her small arms as she cradled it. They took the creature outside and let her stand in the grass. More sentences came.

"It's sweet. The grass. She likes it," Audrey told her.

Eve was grateful for the breakthrough, and encouraged by the special connection between Daphne and Audrey. Audrey could talk, and Daphne could nurture. If she were in town. Those porcelain creatures had given Eve a way into Audrey's world. Audrey could talk of nothing else, but at least she was talking. Eve tried to lead by example, dressing like the other mothers in the neighborhood, participating in play dates and conversations that were a thin guise for competing their kids. But Audrey played alone, ran sand through her fingers, conversed with clouds and trees. She moved further and further away from other girls at playgroup activities. Her imaginary world did not recede, though she mastered the process of going to school, doing homework, and passing tests, with the exception of math.

Eve dedicated herself to Audrey, gently offering social activities from time to time, and constantly checking on Audrey's well being. Maybe this was what Daphne had been asking when she asked where Eve had gone. Eve had left herself in a cardboard box. She'd gone from independent kid to groupie to housewife to mother.

She touched the hem of a pant leg that hung near her. Black silk. Expensive. Tailored. A tug brought it to the floor. A beige-colored dress that said nothing worth listening to came down next. Piled next to the stack of concert shirts, these expensive clothes looked distressed.

"Señora!" one of the men called. A string of words followed, and all she understood was his panicked tone. Eve pushed the box back into the corner and hurried toward the stairs.

The kitchen wall was entirely gone, and part of the floor had been removed. It seemed, for a moment, they had cut too much of something that would not grow back.

"Señora, aqui por favor," Isaac said, pointing to a dark stain where the adjacent wall ended.

But it was not a stain. It was a moving, living mass. Eve stepped closer to understand and Isaac held out a protective arm. An angry colony of black ants swarmed up from the exposed flooring, crawling out of where they lived quietly without anyone knowing. A shiver ran up Eve's spine. Panicked by the ruin, this colony carried small white eggs, frantically trying to save the future. How easy it had been to squish those two ants on Audrey's shelf.

Several ants crawled onto her arm and neck. Eve jumped back and brushed her skin to remove them, but there was nothing there. Fred arrived with a gallon container of paint thinner and issued a stream of words to her that ended with a question.

Did she want him to light the house on fire? She was pretty sure that's what he asked.

"Es okay," Isaac tried to reassure her.

Fred took the cap off the paint thinner, placed two fingers over the top and sprinkled the toxic liquid over the swarming ants. They writhed as they drowned, and after a few moments the colony was almost completely wiped out. A few stragglers, not comprehending what had just happened, still struggled to save their eggs, but Fred and Isaac swept up the colony with rags, gathering the outer most survivors first.

The fumes engulfed Eve, clutched at her throat as she stepped away. The rags that the men refolded were covered with dead ants. Eve shivered again. She put her hand over her mouth and nose and left. The colony of ants had been destroyed in a matter of minutes after living inside the walls of their house for years or possibly decades without conflict or invasion. Carl would have smirked at her concern, waved it off as unimportant. Audrey would have run in panic, screamed at the toxic injustice.

Outside the front door, Eve sat down on the porch. The ground rumbled as if her thoughts had summoned the surviving colony, but when Eve looked up, she saw Nick's truck pulling to the curb. It coughed and sputtered and convulsed when he shut it off. Relief flooded her. Then a huge sixteen-wheeler pulled up behind him. The truck angled into the driveway with a racket of beeping and finally stopped. The driver lowered a forklift and unloaded the massive amount of lumber, which he positioned next to the pile of old kitchen. She could smell the freshness of the wood, earthy and clean.

While all this went on, Nick strolled over and sat down next to Eve, his ocean-colored eyes greeting her, leading her to the wisdom behind them.

"Hey," he said.

"Hey," she said. "My house is missing a wall."

"Who would walk off with a wall in the middle of the day?" he answered.
They both grinned. The tension in her shoulders melted.

"So how do we do this?" he asked.

"I hope you're not asking me how to rebuild the wall."

"No. I mean, I need money," Nick said, and laughed. "I mean they do. I
mean, you need to pay him for the materials."

His arms were lanky but muscular, a surfer's arms dipped in California tan.
His inexperience when it came to talking about money was charming. Thirty
years ago, when she wore concert t-shirts for armor, she would have seduced
a young man like him. She shivered again, not because of the ants. He smiled.
She nodded, and went back in the house to get the checkbook.

Audrey 5

My Saturday morning bed was warm and safe, and I could stay curled in it for a long time, but thoughts of the kitchen that had been torn from our home kept stabbing at me, would not let me find my way into a dream. I opened my eyes, stared at the ceiling and knew what I had to do. Each day this week, I had come home and raced straight to my room as more and more kitchen had been ripped out. Windows, walls, cabinets. Mommy had made the men stop with their awful sounds when I got home, but I could not find the courage to go near the pain that came from the kitchen. So I stayed in my room. But today, our house was quiet. It was resting. Trying to heal. If I went downstairs, I might be able to understand.

It is your turn to protect us, the herd told me. Go see, then come back and tell us.

I held my breath and got out of bed. The smell of dust and wood told me a monster slept where the kitchen used to be. Then I saw the beast attached to the kitchen, still sleeping. Its opaque skin draped from ceiling to floor where there was once a wall. The monster breathed, expanding and contracting its skin. I could almost see through it to the light outside, which turned from gray to yellow. Where there had been a cabinet, there was an outline traced in glue. Where there had been an unmovable sink, a stub of pipe poked out of the floor. I moved further into the sleeping beast, my heart clattering inside my chest. It did not wake, did not know I was there. Cold had invaded the house overnight. I crouched in a corner of the kitchen, tucked my thighs against my chest under the tent of pale roses my nightgown made. Three large nails and some sharp crumbs of old wall threatened my bare feet. Near them, a beat-up gray tool box lay open, a mean hammer with a red wooden handle next to it, waiting to hit and hurt. I sniffed the emptiness, and the creature that swallowed our kitchen answered with a deep rumble. Plastic skin rustled, bones clattered from the outside. The hammer could protect me, maybe, so I reached for it.

The beast's skin shook violently, stirring to life, lifting away from the kitchen as it woke. Then the top of a ladder poked up from under the sheet. I held the hammer tight, could not scream, like in a dream when I have no voice. Curly blond hair and a pair of shoulders rose from the lower edge of the plastic.

It was Nick, climbing up into the kitchen after being eaten. My throat became tight. I wanted to talk to him but nothing came out. He shifted from the ladder to the kitchen floor. But something by his boots made him stop and stare. He did not stand up or see me in the corner, but took a screwdriver from his tool belt and jammed under the turquoise linoleum to pry it up. I held the hammer tighter, clutched it to me.

"Motherfucker," he said.

My eyes went round. "Hi," I yelled.

He jumped and fell off the edge of the house.

I screamed as he went over. He grabbed the plastic sheeting and managed to hold onto the ladder and the floor. Three nails still threatened to stab me if I moved to help him, but he pulled himself back into the kitchen. When he stood up, he put his hands on his hips as if I had played a trick on him. I hid the hammer behind me.

"Let's pretend that didn't happen," he said.

But it did. So I laughed.

Then he laughed.

Which made me laugh again. I held my breath to stop, but I did not dare to stand up and leave the corner. He smiled, ran his fingers through his hair. His falling and scrambling seemed like a cartoon. I had to laugh again, could hardly breathe from giggling.

"Is everything okay?" Mommy asked.

She surprised us and Nick and I jumped, then looked at each other and laughed all over. Panic pinched her face as she looked from me to Nick. I wrapped the hammer in the folds of my nightgown, and started to tell about Nick falling out of the house, but I could not speak because I was hiding his hammer. Nick explained to her that he knocked the ladder over, but he hid the part about me surprising him and falling out of the house. This man with his heavy boots and big tool belt shared something with me that my mother did not know about. And I had something of his that he did not know about.

"Audrey, you okay?" he asked.

My face became warm when he looked at me.

"I'm okay," I whispered.

Mommy looked from Nick to me.

"This is amazing," she said. "The demolition has been so upsetting for her, but look. She feels comfortable in here. Wait! There are nails." Mommy pulled me away. "Let's get you out of here. Watch out for the nails," she said, and guided me out of the kitchen.

The hammer remained hidden. I could not let go of it, and I did not want to hand it back. I held my breath so I wouldn't laugh, but Nick winked at me, and my laughter sputtered out again.

"What in the world is so funny?" my father asked as he came down from upstairs and tightened his bathrobe around him. "You're freezing," he said, rubbing my arms and holding me as I disguised the hammer in the folds of my nightgown. "Go upstairs and get dressed. The house will be cold until they rebuild that wall."

He reset the thermostat on the wall and air rushed into the house. The skin of the monster rustled again and I screamed because Daddy did not see how it moved toward him.

"Jesus, Audrey. Upstairs. Now," he ordered.

"Carl, you can't run the heater with a wall missing," my mother said. "That's wasteful."

"It's fine. Did you look at those photographs, yet?" he asked.

I leapt away, and lunged up the stairs. When I was in my room, I slammed the bedroom door and leaned against it. The herd froze, listening for danger. I told them with my thoughts that the creature's skin that covered the kitchen was only a piece of plastic. I brought out the hammer, sniffed its smooth handle, and then looked for a place to put it. I shoved it under my mattress just before my mother opened the door and came in.

"I'm going to get dressed, and you're going to get dressed and then we are going out. Do you understand?"

I nodded.

"Audrey, it's okay. There is no danger."

Two men's voices argued downstairs. My mother opened the door a slice and the voices became clearer but not enough to know what they were saying.

"Let's go somewhere special," Mommy said, stepping into the hallway.

"To see Daphne?" I asked.

"Get dressed, beautiful. That's all you and I have to do," Mommy said, and then she went to her room.

I remembered Nick falling out of the house and I laughed into my hands. But I had to use them to open a dresser drawer, and the laughter that had been in my palms jumped onto the pink flowered t-shirt on the back of my chair. I put it on. Mommy would be mad because I had worn it yesterday, but it made my heart skip in circles. I visited the herd to tell them that Nick had been funny and I had been brave.

But I had a new feeling about him I did not share with them. Because I didn't know what to tell them.

My mother opened the door a tiny slice. "Why aren't you dressed? What's going on?" she asked.

I skipped over and showed her the pink flowered shirt.

"Audrey, sometimes you're a young woman and sometimes you're a little girl."

"Aren't you sometimes both?" I asked her.

She started to say something but couldn't find any words and that made her face change into a handful of different expressions until she sighed, hugged me and left again.

When I came down to the kitchen, Nick raised a piece of floor for my parents to see, but it made my mother take a step back and cover her mouth and nose. I wanted him to look at me again. I wanted to show that I would not laugh.

"Is it dangerous? Should you be handling it?" she said.

Ice needles poked my skin. Nick tossed the piece of floor at his feet and wiped his hands on his pants. He was serious and did not look at me.

"Only when it becomes exposed, when the particles of asbestos move around in the air. Have you seen my hammer?" he asked, looking around.

"Jesus, Carl. This isn't safe. Those men who were here working, and us. Audrey, how long have you been standing there? You shouldn't be here. It isn't safe," my mother said and pointed to make me turn and leave.

"But Mommy, you said it wasn't dangerous."

"Well, now it is."

"I thought I left it here on the floor. It belonged to my father."

I felt bad and had to turn away from Nick so he wouldn't see that I knew where his hammer was hiding.

"I expect you to honor your quote," my father said, making Nick give up the search.

"Carl, he couldn't have foreseen this," my mother answered, folding her arms then covering her mouth and nose again like she forgot for a moment.

"He knew the kitchen was from the 1960s. That must indicate some probability of asbestos. It certainly isn't our job to know that."

"Look, Mr. Tilden," Nick said, "I'm sure there is a way we can—"

"No, you look. Do whatever is necessary to have it properly removed without increasing what you charge us."

I looked from my angry father to my helpless mother to Nick who stood between them. He raised his palms to show he had no weapons.

"But Carl," Mommy started to say.

"Audrey, out. Now," Daddy yelled.

"Carl this is unreasonable," Mommy yelled.

His words unleashed the herd. A stampede carried me around the dining table two times before taking me to the living room in a wild storm of frantic hooves. Slashing hooves. Fast feet. Nowhere to go to escape the yelling.

Eve 6

Nick held the front door open.

"Don't let her out," Eve yelled.

But Audrey responded instantly to the shrill whistle he had already let out, and ran past him into the daylight. Eve followed, her limbs surging with adrenaline as Audrey headed for the street. Leaping off the front porch, Audrey sped toward the asphalt, not looking at traffic. Eve yelled. Audrey flew into the air, clearing the low shrubs, and kept going. But just before the curb, she stopped, turned back, and circled the olive tree. Eve approached cautiously and placed a hand on Audrey's shoulder, which she pushed away.

"You screamed at me," Audrey said.

"You were about to run into the street."

"You said the kitchen was safe. Now you say it's dangerous."

"It was safe, but it isn't anymore. Just for a little while. I know this is confusing. Nick will fix it."

Audrey looked back at the doorway where Nick stood.

"There's glue under the floor that has to be cleaned up and taken away. It's dangerous glue. Do you understand not to go in there?"

Audrey continued to stare at Nick, her face pink from running. Eve hugged her but Audrey stiffened, did not yield to Eve's affection. Nick went into the house.

"Let's get away from here. I'll take you somewhere special today. Some place you've never been."

Audrey still stared at the door. "What kind of place?"

"A place where people bring the things they no longer need and leave it for others who might."

"Is there treasure?"

"I guess you could say that."

Audrey followed Eve back to the house. In the dining area, Nick struggled with masking tape and a large plastic sheet in an attempt to seal off the kitchen doorway. Audrey hesitated, pressed herself against the wall to observe him.

"Today," Carl boomed. "We don't want that material in our house any longer. If you can't do the job, I need to find someone who can. And I want the doorway sealed off."

Carl crossed his arms, the image of a man protecting his home and family.

"This requires abatement equipment," Nick explained.

"If you need to subcontract, then do it. But not at my expense."

"I can handle it. But I need to rent some of the machines. That's all. If you can give me an advance, I can start today."

"No advance. We have an agreement."

"What's wrong with an advance?" Eve asked.

Carl held up his hand for her to be silent.

"I'll find a way," Nick said, "No worries."

The roll of tape shrieked as he tore a strip off it. The plastic sheeting rattled and crunched as he grabbed it and sealed the doorway. Audrey snorted.

"Audrey," Eve said. "Go up to your room and wait for me there."

Audrey sniffed at the kitchen, lowered her head, and backed away.

"I'm concerned about removal if a professional crew doesn't do it," Eve said.

"I have a buddy I can consult," Nick said. "I just didn't factor in the cost."

"I'm sure there's a way to work this out," Eve said to both Nick and Carl.

"Can I see you a minute?" Carl asked her, dismissing Nick and walking toward his office.

Eve followed. He closed the door behind her and stood firmly in front of it.

"He gave us a quote. Every time he finds some additional problem, he'll change the total. Do you understand that? We can't set a precedent. It will never end."

"Carl, none of us knew what was under the floor."

"But we all knew it was a kitchen from the 1960s. Why are you taking his side?"

"I'm not. I feel bad that he's going to take a hit on this."

"What about the hit we're taking on the whole damn thing? His expenses aren't our problem. Agreed?"

There were no words to accurately argue why she felt they should extend themselves to Nick. And Carl was right. They should not have to open their wallet every time Nick found something. But her unease did not leave despite the sense she saw in Carl's thinking. Eve nodded, hoping to excuse herself from this powerlessness in the presence of his desk and computer and files. He earned their living while she spent it. Housewife. She fingered the hem of the t-shirt she had put on that morning and studied this man with whom she had built a life.

"What's with the Van Halen t-shirt?" he said.

He hadn't noticed The Who yesterday, and The Stones the day before. Van

Halen held her in a snug embrace like an old friend.

Carl smirked at the t–shirt. "That thing must be 1,000 years old."

"1978, actually. Before I knew you."

"Great tour. You must have been a baby."

"I can claim that Eddie Van Halen was my babysitter."

Carl studied her shirt, then her.

"Hey, can you take a quick look at Daphne's photos?" he asked, lifting a black portfolio from his desk. "Tell me you've never seen these before."

He opened the cover and gently lifted three photographs from the card stock folder.

They were exquisite. A study of a stone fence made from huge slabs of metamorphic rock, each slab a section of fence. A triptych from three different angles created a tangible sense of the divide between viewer and hill beyond. They could have been taken anywhere, except for the small villa that sat almost unnoticed on the ridge. Rich shades of black and white on matte paper had locked this rock fence in time, capturing both the effort to erect it and the division it created. Eve's heartbeat pulsed in her ears. She had mapped her mother's travels since she could remember, knew where she was from the postcards that arrived in the mail, the one thing about Daphne's travels she could count on. Ireland, Prague, North Africa. Every photograph of a fence that became important in Daphne's oeuvre corresponded with a postcard from the country where she'd taken the picture. But Eve could not link the fence in these three photographs to any postcard she'd ever received.

"I don't know where this is," Eve whispered.

"But they're her work. They have to be."

"I suppose. She could have taken a trip I didn't know about. Why not?"

"This is big," Carl said, pacing past his desk where the photographs lay. "These are going to put us on the map. Put her on the map. Again. People will pay attention to unseen work from Daphne Delfin. Do you have any idea where these might have been taken? Or when? She has no other triptych. Why now? Why this fence? I'm thinking Europe."

The past threatened. Eve's blood slowed and her arms grew heavy. The air went out of the room. If she wasn't on guard, she could still be left behind. Carl kept talking, but she couldn't make out what he was saying.

"Why couldn't she take me with her?" she asked, waiting for the room to level out, for her vision to stabilize.

"Hey," he said. "You okay? I know this stuff isn't easy. Why would she keep these in a drawer for so long? Evie? You okay? Look, I'm sorry for yelling about the kitchen. I sound overbearing when I'm just trying to avoid costs we shouldn't pay."

Carl opened his arms, the father of her child, her partner in the creation of their domain. He offered up a man who understood his limitations and hers. Eve stepped toward his affection and let the history of their intimacy encircle her, restoring peace in a house filled with disruption. She chose him. Chose this. He spoke over her shoulder, his deep voice vibrating from his chest to hers.

"You miss that other life, the one with Van Halen and the Stones. What if I get you some concert tickets and backstage passes? I can see who's touring."

"Would you?"

"I'll see what I can do."

"And passes?" she asked, holding him harder.

She started to tell him about the t-shirts, about what made her want to wear them, but Audrey's shrill laugh from the dining room made them both leave his office.

Her wide-eyed daughter pressed herself against the far wall of the dining room. Nick freed himself from a length of tape he'd been trying to make hold plastic sheeting in place. The tape grabbed the plastic and would not let go. He wadded everything into a sticky ball and tossed it at Audrey. She shrieked, then squealed, then laughed helplessly.

"Audrey," Eve called.

Audrey picked up the ball of tape and threw it back. Eve turned to Carl to see if he had seen her playfulness, but he was bent over the photos on the desk, his back to the rest of the house. She needed to get Audrey away from the asbestos, out of harm's way.

"Sweetheart," Eve said. "Can you help me carry these boxes to the car?"

"You said we were going somewhere special."

"We are. We need to take these with us on our adventure," Eve explained.

Audrey didn't move. Eve waited for her to become agreeable, this bundle of daughter that fused frustration to joy.

"I can give you a hand with those," Nick said.

"That would be great."

"I can give you a hand with those too," Audrey offered, following Nick empty-handed as he maneuvered his way to the car with a stack of boxes. He made two more trips with Audrey shadowing him, finally helping when he handed her a box to carry. Eve made space by taking out a bag of jumper cables, emergency blankets and water, and loaded the boxes into the trunk and back seat. After the last box, Nick explained that he was headed out to rent the removal equipment. He got in his truck, but the engine wouldn't turn. It complained and groaned a few times, then gave up completely.

Eve walked to the street, to the open window of his cab. "Sounds like the battery," she said, holding up the jumper cables she'd removed.

He grinned. "Cool t-shirt," he said. *"Beautiful girls all over the world,"* he sang.

"You know Van Halen?"

"My parents play classic rock."

Her affinity for 70s rock made her as old as someone's parents.

"What's wrong?" Audrey asked.

"He needs my car to help start his car. Let's help him." She and Audrey got in the car, and pulled up alongside his truck. He raised the hood of her car.

"I have to do this two or three times a week," he said, attaching the red cable. "The battery isn't holding a charge."

Eve turned her engine, and he did the same. The truck rumbled to life. He hopped out and removed the cables. She got out, and blocked from Audrey's view by the raised hood, she handed him a hundred dollar bill.

"Hey," she said. "Get a new battery."

"You don't have to do that."

But he let her put the bill in his hand.

"It will help you move quickly on the asbestos," she said.

"True," Nick said and got back in his truck.

She dropped the hood and blew Audrey a kiss through the windshield but Audrey's attention was fixed on Nick.

Audrey 6

Boxes full of lonely had no more room, could not hold the lemonade pitcher and salad bowl that bulged out of the top in the back seat. The soup pot had been taken hostage. Unwanted clothes tried to reach for the car door, to escape from the garbage bags they'd been stuffed into. The sadness of things plucked from the kitchen weighed down the car.

"There is sadness in the back seat," I said, trying to breathe out the abandonment that traveled with us.

Mommy glanced in the mirror.

"The thrift store will be their home until they become someone else's new treasure," Mommy said. "We aren't throwing these things away."

But we were. We were casting off our stuff because we didn't see any of it as treasure any more. How could you love a wooden lamp one day, and the next decide it was ugly and worthless? What made that happen?

We stopped in front of a tiny shop that stood apart from the rest, surrounded by new while it was old. Like it had been left behind by the rest of the street. I got out, walked toward it and touched the peeling gray paint to feel if it was rough and scratchy or powdery and delicate. The window, cluttered with the insides of other people's homes, made so much noise. Behind the glass, an old street sign had no regard for a set of TV trays. A stack of blue metal bowls ignored the quiet complaint of a metal ironing board. Everything shouted a story, so it was impossible to hear each one. Crowding and criticism made me want to wait outside, but Mommy needed help carrying in the bags and boxes.

I held the clothes she gave me, trying not to upset them, trying for one last minute to let them feel a pair of arms around them, but the weight of their sadness made me lurch forward and I let go of the bulky sack. It fell to the ground and several sleeves came out, sprawling across the sidewalk in a get-away attempt.

"Mommy," I shouted, even though I wanted her clothes to hurry off and hide.

"It's all right," Mommy said as she put her box on the sidewalk and forced the shirts and pants back into the mouth of the garbage bag. But the clothes were not garbage.

"You're not garbage," I told them.

Mommy gave me a look as she handed me the captured clothes. The bell on the shop door tinkled a magical sound as I walked in. Maybe there was treasure here. But inside, more unwanted belongings crowded each other on the tables and shelves. No one came out to answer the pretty bell, and I waited by the door. Mommy walked further into the shop. The smell of someone else's relatives filled the room, like old people no one wanted to visit. Clothes and shoes and shelves of unwanted dishes and books packed the walls. I tried to understand each thing; lonely teacups, mismatched saucers, and an electric yellow-and-white popcorn maker tried to tell me about the homes they used to have. Books on cancer and a collection of empty vases tried to tell me a story that didn't make sense. My stomach became small and made my feet want to go outside.

Mommy carried her box to the glass counter and sat it down next to an old register. I followed with my bag of clothes, placing it on the floor and tipping it with my foot so the clothes could have one more chance to run. But they had given up. Behind me, the noise and chaos of everything grew. I turned to a round rack of clothes that sent clashing voices out in all directions. The colors fought with each other, infecting everything. I covered my ears just as a woman emerged from a back room. Her long white-black braid swung out as she turned to talk to Mommy and the length of it went down to the back of her knees. She wore wire-rimmed glasses on her smooth face that looked younger than her hair.

"Kitchen items, maybe. But I can't take any more clothes. I don't have the room," the woman said unsmiling.

"These are very nice clothes. They won't be on the rack for long," Mommy answered.

"I'm just not getting the customers."

Mommy and the woman pulled legs and arms from the bag, and I backed up without meaning to get so close to the arguing rack of clothes. Can't you stop? I wanted to shout. And they did. Like they could hear me. Then they pleaded with me to step between their fabrics into their circle to help them. The rack of clothes around me started shouting and fighting again, and I didn't know if they would let me back out. Before I could scream for help, an unfamiliar chirp silenced them. Somewhere a mechanical bird sang until I realized it came from my pocket. I took my cell phone out and opened it to answer a call that wasn't Mommy or Daddy.

My hands trembled with a stranger in them.

"Hello," I said.

"I want to know what the fuck you were drawing on my arm," a gravelly voice demanded. "I can't figure it out."

It was the boy with the constellations inside his elbow.

"Maybe Orion," I said quietly.

"The dude in the stars?" he asked, roughness fading from his voice.

"Maybe the Pleiades," I told him. "I have to connect the dots to find out."

He didn't say anything and the clothes began to murmur again, resuming their arguments. Sleeves of different colors that had been shoved against one another. They didn't belong next to each other, they complained. I turned in the circle and gathered four pink items and hung them together, which calmed them.

"You see constellations in my arm. That's cool," the boy said.

"Lucas," I said because I thought of his name.

"Yo," he said.

I smiled when he said that, and then I gave my smile to the rest of the pinks I had gathered, including the corals and dusty rose colors. I grouped them together on the rack. But the other colors didn't like that the pinks all got to be together, so I collected the oranges and put them together next to the pinks.

"That's what you were doing. Connecting the dots," he said.

I nodded even though he couldn't see.

"Would you connect all my dots?" he asked, which made a flock of birds rise from the branches of my arms and legs and take to the air.

"Audrey?" Mommy's voice called for me, her panic jumping on the edges of my name.

I waved to her and she frowned at me. Who? She mouthed silently. I acted dumb and kneeled down in the circle of clothes, but just as I did something blue on a far shelf caught my eye, something made of glass that captured a beam of sunlight in it. I stood up again. There, in a beam of sunshine, a unicorn glowed in the tangle of stuff in the window display.

"I have to go," I said and ended the call.

I started toward the creature that balanced on its two hind legs. It reared up between a porcelain lady with an umbrella and a scary clown. This was a special unicorn. He was completely made of blue glass and balanced on his two hind legs. His head and neck turned toward me, his front hooves pawing at the air. The look in his eyes asked me if I could help him.

"Mommy!" I couldn't hide the excitement in my voice as I gently made the unicorn's acquaintance, picked him up in one hand, and brought him to her. "Look who I met. His name is Blue."

Mommy rolled her eyes. "Audrey we agreed no more."

"Mommy, you said there might be treasure. And there is. I can't leave Blue here. He needs a home. Our home. Please."

I didn't mean to whine. Mommy hates the whining, but the creature became afraid when Mommy said I could not have more. Tears welled up in me and turned into a sob that escaped from where I clutched the lonely unicorn against me. I ran and hid again in the circular rack of clothes. The woman behind the counter stepped toward the rack, her braid swinging as she tilted her head to study the rainbow in the room.

"This is nice," she said. "I never thought to hang the clothes by color."

She pulled out a skirt that was green like new grass, walked around the circle and ended on the other side of me. I stood up again and watched how her long braid hung down her back.

"Can I touch your tail?" I whispered.

"Audrey, people don't like strangers touching their hair," Mommy said.

I shrugged, lifted my shoulders up to my ears and held them there.

"I've been growing my hair out since I was seventeen," the woman said. "And no one has ever asked me if they could touch my tail."

"I'm seventeen," I said.

For the first time, the woman smiled. She looked at the unicorn I held, then pulled her braid from behind her back and offered it to me. I stepped out of the clothes. With my free hand, I stroked its coarse, woven texture, and ran my fingers up the length of it.

"I'm Lydia," she told me.

I lifted Lydia's braid to my face and sniffed it, touched it with my lips.

"Audrey, enough," Mommy said, staring until I let go of the braid. "Do you know where else I can take these clothes?" she asked Lydia.

"Are these yours?" Lydia asked my mother.

"They were."

"They don't really go with the Van Halen t-shirt. You were probably too young to have actually seen that concert, but I was there."

"I was there," my mother said.

"It was magic."

"It was an incredible show," my mother agreed and the two of them smiled. The shop bell tinkled and two women walked in.

"Dance the Night Away," Lydia said. "I think I have the album here."

"Don't sell it if you do."

Lydia stepped over to a table full of crates and sorted through the cardboard squares in them. "I thought I did."

My mother looked too, pulled out an album with a picture of a cow's udders on the cover, slid out its disc and turned it over.

"I wonder if they're touring," Mommy said. "Want to go to a concert, Audrey? Loud music, flashing lights. You'd probably hate it."

I didn't say anything. Lydia didn't say anything. They kept searching through the cardboard. Then she slid something out of one.

"What are these?" I asked, touching the shiny black disc.

"The fact that you have to ask is proof that I'm a failure," my mother said.

"Most kids don't know what albums are," Lydia laughed.

"I haven't taken an album out and played it since she was born," my mother said.

Lydia handed me the disc, which was shiny and light, but also sinister and black.

"What does it do?"

"It makes you younger," Lydia answered.

She and my mother laughed. "It plays music," Mommy said.

"Music comes out of this?"

I looked across the fine texture of tiny lines that went round and round.

"Does it speak to you?" I asked.

"Absolutely."

"Like my unicorns speak to me," I said.

My mother put the album back in its sleeve. "Not like that."

"I guess I could put these on the five dollar table," Lydia said, reaching for a bag of clothes on the floor.

"These will sell for more than that," Mommy told her. "Look. Armani. And here, Betsy Johnson."

The two women who entered the shop approached the rainbow in the middle of the store. Their conversation stalled as they sorted through each color. I stepped back and watched them go around the circle of clothes.

"This coral would look good with that beige skirt," one said to the other.

"You have to try them on," her friend replied.

Lydia looked from me to my mother.

"The unicorn does need a home," Lydia said. "She can have it if she finds a place for all these in that rainbow," she added, winking at me.

I pranced in place, excited to arrange more colors.

"You don't need to give her anything," Mommy said.

"I insist. I have hangers in the back," Lydia said. "I'd appreciate your help with the pricing since I don't usually get designer clothes."

"I can do that," Mommy said.

She held up her palm for me to high-five, but I pressed my hand against hers instead, and held it there. She pulled me to her and kissed my forehead.

"No!"

"Sorry. I forgot. Please, Audrey."

Lydia handed me an armful of hangers before I could be upset about my silver horn, and I started hanging all Mommy's clothes by color, which made them feel they belonged. The rainbow grew.

"Is that Armani?" one of the customers asked me as I hung up a soft gray suit.

"Yes, and there are more," Mommy answered. "That suit is fifty dollars."

"Fifty?" Lydia protested.

"I'll try it on," the woman said, taking it from me as she headed for the dressing room made of fabric.

Now it was Mommy's turn to give Lydia a wink. The rainbow of clothes hummed a chord that everyone knew. When Mommy was on the other side of the circle, Lydia whispered to me that I could come back and help her any time I wanted. I held the glass unicorn against my heart and loped around the rainbow of sleeves and skirts, even after Mommy told me not to.

On the way home, my mother remembered to ask who had called.

"When you were in the clothing rack. You got a call," she said.

"Oh, that was a wrong number," I said, to see if keeping this secret from her would be funny like when Nick and I had a secret.

But it wasn't.

We returned to our home where things we loved still got to be with us. My mother went to get the mail, and I hurried ahead to introduce Blue to the herd. But the sound of a large vacuum cleaner roared in the kitchen. Then an awful scraping sound started as if something was being torn apart. I held Blue close, told him to be brave. Our house was supposed to be a better place for him but loud and dangerous sounds filled every room. I approached the kitchen doorway. An opaque piece of plastic had been taped across it, sealing everything off on the other side and making it blurry. My heart thudded as I unpeeled the tape and pulled back the plastic.

A spaceman in a white suit moved across the empty kitchen, shoving a pole with a metal blade hard under the linoleum. Pieces of the old blue floor peeled away. I did not scream but my heart raced around inside. He did not see me. He had no face, only a pair of goggles and a mask made of blue filter over his nose and mouth. White fabric covered his head and shoes, and his hands were gloved. Each piece of floor he tore off was stuffed into a black garbage bag just like the ones that held Mommy's unwanted clothes. Powdered sugar floated through the air and was sucked into the roaring machine.

"Audrey, get away!" Mommy yelled, startling me.

I jumped.

Blue slipped out of my arms.

He dropped to the floor.

And broke.

His horn and front leg broke off.

"No," I wailed, kneeling down, reaching for his limbs. "Mother," I said, as if the word could undo the damage.

"Audrey, I'm sorry," she said. "I didn't mean to make you jump, but the kitchen isn't safe. You have to stay out of there. We talked about that."

She went to the plastic sheeting to tape it back down, as if there were no damaged creature that had been ruined.

"He's broken. I didn't help him."

I laid Blue down, a sick feeling in my stomach. The hum of the machine shut off, and the spaceman approached the sheeting that covered the kitchen doorway. I shrieked at the danger Mommy didn't see behind.

"Stay where you are," she yelled to the spaceman.

I bolted and raced out of the room, away from the machine in the kitchen, away from the frightening man wrestling it, away from my mother. Halfway to my room, I realized I had left Blue back there. Dread and regret grabbed at me as I leapt up the stairs, snapping and trying to bite until I was in the safety of my room. The herd stared at me. They knew I had abandoned a broken creature. Breathing breathing breathing, I paced then stood still. The scraping and humming started again, the machine sucking the very air out of the kitchen, maybe even sucking up the broken glass that was once a unicorn.

Eve 7

Nick worked past dark, and while the thought of poisonous fibers floating and escaping distressed Eve, she was glad he was there taking care of it. Downstairs was off-limits, so Audrey amused herself in her room, and Eve found herself back in her closet, examining her clothes. They were not her. Not really. She began shoving them into garbage bags until two overstuffed lumps of her former self lay by her feet. Arms and legs of high-quality fabrics pressed against each other. Merino wool crushed silk. Linen wrinkled against cashmere. She put the last of the upscale wardrobe into a fourth garbage bag and dropped an emergency blouse and black vest into the t-shirt box, covering up the shoebox with four thousand dollars in it. The larger that box of cash became, the more it reaffirmed that she did not have to escape. She was here in this house, in this marriage, because she wanted to be here. She had the means to leave, but chose not to.

One by one, she hung her rock t-shirts on padded hangers. She had washed and dried them on the delicate cycle, and now her side of the closet reflected the authentic Eve, the person she used to be, wanted to be.

The kitchen worklight fought against dusk, which had filled the rest of the house with purple and gray. Eve turned on a lamp just as Nick emerged from behind the plastic sheeting, his toolbox in one hand.

"Sorry about the horse. Super glue will fix it," he said.

Eve followed him to the front door.

"Audrey has dozens. She doesn't need another one."

"She seemed pretty upset. I should be able to finish removal tomorrow. Maybe we could go out tomorrow. Just for a little while."

Was he asking her if he could take Audrey on a date? Her face flushed.

"The two of you?"

"I'm sorry," he said. "I meant maybe you could take her out," Nick corrected himself. "So I can finish."

"Oh," Eve said. "Of course."

When they got to the porch, he kept walking. Eve stood in the doorway and waited until he got in his truck. The engine turned and faltered. Turned and faltered. And again. Nick got out, opened the hood and poked around

with a flashlight. She waited. Then he slammed the hood and tried to start
the engine once more.

She walked to the curb, a chill in the evening air making her hug herself.
The two of them spoke simultaneously.

"You didn't get a new battery."

"I used the cash for the asbestos vacuum."

"I see."

"If you don't mind, I'll just crash in the truck."

"I gave you money for a battery."

"It isn't just the battery. It's the distributor and the transmission. I had to
rent an industrial vacuum. The vacuum won. It's no big deal. Sometimes I
sleep in the truck. I didn't want you to wonder why it was still at the curb."

"You haven't had dinner. You've been working since Audrey and I got back
this afternoon," she said. "I realize the asbestos removal has set you back, and
the truck will too. Can I ask a direct question?"

"Sure."

"Are you homeless?"

He laughed. "I live in those bungalows on Ocean Park near the pier."

"Just south of the pier? The gray cottages with the white trim?" she asked.

She knew those bungalows. If she hadn't been there, she'd driven by so many
times it seemed like she had. Surfboards crowded the porches and wetsuits
hung on a line in the courtyard. Knowing where he lived made her feel better.

"Nick, you're welcome to stay here," Eve said. "In the house. You don't
have to sleep in your truck."

"I don't think your husband would dig it."

He was right. Having spent very little time around Carl, Nick could already
predict that he would come home later and banish Nick to the curb, citing
a precedent for freeloading on the couch. An understanding passed between
them.

"If you need anything, just come to the door," Eve told him.

She went back to the house, to her makeshift kitchen, disappointed for
some reason. Audrey surprised her, standing by the living room window like
an intruder.

"You scared me," Eve said, putting a hand on Audrey's shoulder. But Audrey
remained silent and kept peering into the dark.

Eve walked toward the kitchen to let Audrey stare out at the night. The wall
where boxes of kitchen junk had been stacked was now empty and clean. This
was the simplicity Eve wanted for the rest of the house. They had accumulated
too much. Clean lines and open surfaces calmed her, and she thought about

how to slowly restore the entire house to that state.

Just then, the front door opened.

"Audrey, where are you going?" she called.

But it was Carl coming through the door.

"Hello, beautiful wife. Van Halen I understand, but what's with the Sex Pistols?" Carl asked. "You hated them."

"I did. The ultimate in a dysfunctional band. Vicious, rotten music. But I was there. Winterland, 1978. No fun."

"It might be worth something on eBay," he said, and started to embrace her.

"The measure of all value." Eve pushed Carl away.

"He still working?" Carl asked, indicating the kitchen.

"His truck won't start, so he's going to sleep in it."

Carl shrugged. "Cheryl Moncrief returned my call. She's free tomorrow," he said. "For lunch." He glanced up from the incoming messages he held in his phone. Cheryl Moncrief owned an art gallery. Carl was angling for a photo exhibit.

"Did you hear the part about Nick?" Eve asked.

"Yes. Did you hear the part about Cheryl? I offered to meet with her but she wants to have lunch with you."

Eve clenched her jaw. Cheryl's daughter, Madison, was one of those girls at the mall who'd laughed at the mannequin and pronounced it frigid. Madison and Audrey had almost been friends, but that was long ago. Carl should have lunch with her, not Eve. Before she said something she regretted, she stepped back into the living room where Audrey still cupped her hands to the window to see out.

"I don't like that he's going to sleep in the truck," Eve called back to Carl.

"There's remodeling and there's freeloading," Carl said, right next to her. "He said you would say that."

"He did?" Carl looked out the dark window, too. "Will you have lunch with Cheryl?"

"Will you go out there and invite him to sleep on the couch?"

They stared at each other with faint smiles until Carl opened the front door and stepped outside.

"But leave the Sex Pistols at home," he said as he walked away.

Lunch with Cheryl Moncrief to discuss her mother's brilliance in exchange for her contractor sleeping on the couch. How was this a victory, she wondered.

"Done," Carl said when he returned. "But I'm not making the bed."

"I'll make it," Nick said, stepping into the house. "This is really cool of you."

Audrey ran circles around the dining table then raced upstairs, forcing both men to step out of the way.

"Audrey, you okay?" Carl called. "I'll go check."

Eve collected sheets and a blanket to arrange on the living room couch. Nick grabbed an edge of the sheet in Eve's hand.

"Let me help," he said.

The two of them parachuted the sheet and landed it on the couch. She placed a pillow at one end.

"Thanks again, Mrs. Tilden," Nick said.

"Eve, please."

"Night, Eve."

He went back to the couch as she made one last pass through the house, turning off lights. Deep in the night, she heard Audrey's soft footsteps moving down the hall, down the stairs to the living room. But when she followed, there was no one out of bed spying on the man who slept on the couch. No one except Eve.

Audrey 7

Darkness came for me, spreading from the corners of my room until it covered everything. Footfalls moved past the door, my father's steps fading as he went downstairs, then silence, then the open/close of the front door. Then silence again. I rolled away from the direction of his leaving and looked at the floor. Emerging from the warm cocoon of my covers, I pressed my ear to the carpet but heard nothing that could tell me about the man in my house or the kitchen he took apart.

In the living room, sheets draped over an empty couch, their folds a riddle about where Nick's body had been. I knelt to touch them and felt the warmth he left behind. Someone moved around in the dining room and I stepped away, quiet as a cloud. Nick's hair was tangled with sleep, his eyebrows gathered in concentration. He held the broken blue unicorn, and my throat clenched inside my neck from the thoughtlessness, and injuries, and damage. Nick handled it carefully, turning upside down, holding the broken stump of a leg to the light as if it might float from his fingers. Then he placed the broken piece of leg back on the unicorn, held it firmly, and gently blew on it, which made my leg tickle.

"Count to ten," he told me, not looking up.

One, I breathed, looking toward the kitchen's ruin. Two for the stillness that settled. Three because sunlight wrapped itself around this new day. When I got to ten, Nick let go and the broken creature had four legs again.

"Here," he said, offering a small tube of glue and the fragile horn to me. "You glue it on. It's okay."

I hesitated, and then fumbled with the tiny piece of glass. He closed his hand around mine. Steadied me, guided my fingers so broken glass met broken glass.

"Just a drop," Nick said, and helped transfer a teardrop of glue to the end of the broken horn.

My hand felt safe and protected in his but it was hard to breathe. I seated the narrow piece of glass on Blue's forelock.

"Turn it until it feels right," he said.

The two surfaces matched up. I could feel them fit. I started to shout, to pull away in excitement.

"Don't let go," Nick said. "Count to ten again."

My knees turned to candle wax and I looked at his face instead of at the unicorn. I inhaled. Ocean, sky, the moon in the middle of the day. He was close enough to feel the warmth of his cheek, close enough that I could put mine against his.

"You're not counting," he said.

As he counted each second, I forgot about the glass and only thought about our hands. Then suddenly the horse without a horn became a unicorn again. Up close, the small cracks on its legs were visible, but from further back they disappeared.

"Thank you," I said, and threw my arms around Nick.

When he pulled them off I captured him again, pouring my gratitude against his arms and chest, inhaling his t-shirt and its earthy, salty scent.

"Audrey!" Mother blurted at me.

I let go and Nick stepped away, went through the doorway and taped up the plastic behind him.

"He fixed Blue."

My mother gave a quick not-happy smile for the creature that was able to stand once again, whose unique dignity had been restored. I lifted it from the table and hurried upstairs to introduce Blue to the rest of the unicorns, but my thoughts kept trailing back down to the kitchen, to the hum and scrape I could feel through my feet on the floor. Nick was down there, his hands pushing and pulling and tearing. All of that noise might be from causing damage, but he could also repair. The fractures that were now part of Blue would always be there. But they would make me think of Nick's hands, of his face close to mine. I took my math book from my backpack, but it had grown heavy. The quadratic equation teased me because I could not make sense of its symbols and letters. I glanced at the unicorns, at Blue rearing up with the joy I wanted to feel. The danger downstairs reached its long claws through the house to trace my skin and make me shiver. A dark shape full of gloom and lifelessness passed my door, a shadow there and gone. The shiver on my skin turned cold. I shut the book and ran to my mother in her closet. If the monster gave chase, she would protect me.

But it didn't.

I waited. Nothing came for me.

I collapsed, a puppet with broken strings. Mommy hummed to herself, not knowing that I had narrowly escaped something that would wait for another chance.

"Hey, sweetness. I want to show you something," Mommy said.

Her clothes were all different. The ones we had taken to the treasure shop had been replaced with old t-shirts that hung limp and thin on her hangers. She explained that they were from when she was my age, and that she had forgotten them for along time. Each t-shirt had strange names and words, graphics I did not understand. There were no flowers or joy. My mother smiled and smiled and held the fabrics to her. She lifted a black shirt to give me. I took it with my finger and thumb, touching it with as little of me as I could.

"Try it on. You'll be the coolest kid at school," she told me. "This could change everything for you, sweetheart."

I did not want to put it on. Mommy insisted. My bare shoulders crawled up toward my ears. I crossed my arms over myself. That monster downstairs could find me like this. I would have to run out of the house and down the street. With no shirt. And it might catch me.

The dark fabric closed around me. I held my breath as Mommy dropped my bouquet of pink flowery shirt to the floor and made me look in the mirror. A girl in black stared at me, lifeless, unfriendly.

"What are The Ramones?" I asked.

She tried to make me see a stage, lights dimming, the way she was pressed against by a crowd like an ocean moving behind her, and I tried to picture a dark surface made of water, swelling and falling. As she talked, I crawled under the sleeves of Daddy's shirts, and looked up into the tunnels of their cuffs. There was no one inside where his arms were supposed to go. There were many tunnels to choose from, all of them leading away, into darkness, to some place where I was too large to go.

Mommy sat down on the floor and scooted in next to me.

"What are you doing under here?"

I shrugged.

"Are you hungry?"

I shook my head.

"I have to go out to lunch with Cheryl. Remember her daughter, Madison?"

The mean, laughing girl who went everywhere with her friend Mitzi.

"We used to be friends when you two were little."

I had been little but now I was too large to crawl through the fabric tunnels hanging above me.

"You'll be home by yourself, but only for a couple of hours. Are you okay with that? Will you stay upstairs? The kitchen is off-limits. You're safe up here."

The machine grumbling in our kitchen filled the silence of my answer. A small part in the middle of me wanted to be home alone. With Nick.

"Would you rather come with me?"

"I don't want to go."

"Me either," Mommy said.

I laughed because she had to go to lunch.

"But I'm going to take the Sex Pistols along." She stood up and changed her shirt, then leaned over to kiss my forehead.

I froze.

She stopped her kiss. "No kisses there. I know. I'm sorry Audrey," she said, and placed a kiss next to my eye. "When I get back from lunch, I'll find that Ramones album and play it for you."

She agreed with her second self in the mirror and walked down to the noise that destroyed our kitchen. I moved further under Daddy's shirts to hide from the angry sounds my mother left me with. But I wanted to go down there too. Because Nick was making those angry sounds. The smell of old t-shirt choked me. I was trapped here between wanting to go down and staying, between shirts and smells, unable to fit through the passageways in Daddy's sleeves. I lay on the floor, making myself flat against its plane so I could become part of the geometry that turned nothingness into the walls and floors of a house. The wind once blew here, the sun and rain left their footsteps, and now a house surrounded the family in it. But the rattle and grind coming up through the floor took part of that house away. I put my ear against the carpet and listened to the floor rattle and vibrate.

Then it stopped.

Nothing.

For a long while, I lay there listening for the hum and rumble to start again. But it didn't. The house sighed. Curtains sucked themselves against the screens of my parents' windows as the house exhaled. This rest, this relief, this pause in the destruction, could be a trick. I crept to the hallway and looked toward the stairs. Quiet filled my ears with weight. The strain of listening for clues made me move closer to the source of silence. My heart rang like a bell. My own silence matched the deceptive quiet as I advanced. At the bottom of the stairs, I glimpsed quickly toward the dining room, toward the plastic sheeting that covered the kitchen's doorway. I crept to the plastic doorway to spy on the blurry shape of a spaceman.

But no one was there.

No spaceman.

No machine.

I moved like white fog floating silently through the trees, then put my finger on the plastic, my hand trembling, my legs prepared to run.

"Don't be afraid. I'm right behind you," a voice said, soft and calm.

I turned and the spaceman stood close enough to touch me. My heart screamed. My legs froze. I had no voice. I could not move.

"I'm going to take off my mask."

He reached up slowly and pulled off the blue insect head that covered his face. Then he was Nick, smiling.

"You're a spaceman."

"One giant step for man, one giant leap backwards for his bank account."

I wanted to run, but I also wanted to sniff his hair. I stayed still.

"How is your unicorn?" he asked.

My shoulders dropped, my heart sank through the floor. "He is cracked. He will never heal."

"But he's a unicorn again. With four legs, right? And a horn."

He walked out to the deck, peeled of his space suit and the paper socks covering his shoes, and stuffed them in a garbage bag like the ones my mother used to take away her clothes. When he came in, he looked all over the kitchen and through his toolbox and around the dining room.

"Have you seen my hammer?" he asked.

"No," I shouted and ran away.

I closed my bedroom door and leaned against it. All the things I could see were the same, except for what was hiding under my mattress. I shoved my arms under it and felt for Nick's hammer. Metal and wood hid under the softness where I slept. I wanted to go back downstairs, but the unicorns wanted me to stay.

"I'll just get you an apple," I told them.

I went down. For them. To get them a treat.

A blurred figure beyond the plastic sheet taped on the kitchen doorway pushed a mop across the floor. This time, I watched Nick's distorted shape push and pull the mop, moving as if liquid and not dust surrounded him. Again, I found myself next to his gray toolbox, which gaped at me. The yellow handle of a screwdriver caught my eye, like a jewel among the heavy metal objects in the box. This was what he had used to pry up the floor. I crept closer, hid myself to one side, and crouched down to touch it. Nick stopped moving and I froze. Then he started again and I gripped the yellow handle. Keeping it tucked against me, I raced away before he came out.

In my room, I sat on my bed and tried to look through the plastic handle. The world should have been all sunny but everything was distorted. I put it next to the hammer under my mattress.

"Oh," I said. "I forgot your apple. I have to go back and get it," I said.

Again, I went back downstairs, breathing all huffy like I didn't want to go, but instead of getting an apple, I lingered by the kitchen doorway and watched Nick through the plastic, pushing a mop across the floor. I looked around, ignoring the wooden bowl full of apples, and moved closer to Nick's beat-up toolbox. This time, I chose something silver and heavy. Its handles looked like long bird legs and it had a bird's beak on its round head. Nick continued to push the mop with his arms as I walked past. I took the silver bird back upstairs and hid it with the screwdriver and hammer under my mattress, tucked in the soft darkness where no one could find them. Except me.

Eve 8

Feeling displaced among the pairs and trios of women having lunch, Eve waited for someone to seat her when, across the room, an armful of gold bracelets jangled and waved. It took a moment to realize Cheryl Moncrief was flagging her over to a small table by a sunny window. A choice location. Cheryl's straight blonde hair hung down to her shoulders. She was beautiful, polished, confident. Hugs, a brief clasp of hands. Like best friends. Eve lowered herself into the chair that had been pulled out for her by a waiter who placed a napkin on her lap. Instantly, Eve became half of a duet doing lunch. She straightened her shoulders and let her blazer fall open.

"God Save the Queen," Cheryl said on cue. "Winterland, San Francisco. 1978."

"Were you there?" Eve asked.

Cheryl shook her head. "My brother was. I was too young. My parents wouldn't let me go with him. Truth be told, I wasn't really a fan."

"Me either," Eve smiled.

"That was a million years ago B.C., before children," Cheryl laughed. "How is Audrey? Has she taken an interest in boys? Or is it still horses?"

"It's never been horses."

Cheryl stopped buttering her bread and looked intently at Eve. "I remember horses. I wonder why that is. I asked Madison if she sees her, but I guess they run in different circles. I told her to be a friend now and then."

"How is Madison?"

"Her boyfriend made a woman out of her last month. Well, she was hell bent on losing her virginity. Girlhood into womanhood. It changes everything."

"She told you?"

"If I'd known what sex was going to do for Madison, I would have paid someone to make this happen. Otherwise, if it happened at college, I wouldn't get to be there if she needed me. Does Audrey know where she's going?"

"She's taking a gap year," Eve said, lifting the menu like a barricade.

"That's what I think Madison should have done. Travel Europe. But I'll tell you, discovering her sexuality has expanded her maturity and confidence like I've never seen before," she said. "If I could bottle that, I'd be rich," she added.

"You are rich," Eve said, more loudly than she meant to.

Cheryl laughed. "I am. Thank you for reminding me to be grateful for what I have. Where did all the years go? I miss your humor."

Cheryl's eyes were kind. Eve put the menu down.

"Audrey has no interest in boys or her sexuality. She tends to follow her own path," Eve said.

Cheryl put her hand on Eve's.

"If there is one thing I've had to master as a parent," Eve added, "it's respecting who she is."

Eve tried to imagine Audrey in a boy's embrace, close enough to share a kiss, but she was a million miles from that, from going to college, from leaving childhood behind. It was hard to imagine how Audrey might react to a boy's advances. It was hard to imagine a boy making advances without unleashing a colossal stampede. Only this morning Eve had narrowly prevented a scene when Nick glued the glass unicorn and was too close to Audrey to understand that he'd almost sent her into panic mode. Audrey was so far behind Madison in this realm.

"I admire that," Cheryl said.

"And I admire that your daughter talks to you about sex," Eve said.

They both smiled. "God," Cheryl said. "My mother never talked to me about sex. Did yours?"

The question filled Eve's arms with ice water. Cheryl could not know what she had just asked, and there was no reasonable response. Eve picked up the butter knife and severed a floret of butter. The waiter, an older gentleman, approached their table at the perfect moment. Salad. Dressing on the side. Iced tea. Cheryl ordered the same thing.

"How is your mother?" Cheryl said.

Eve tried to think of the lyrics to "God Save the Queen," but could not remember them. *Don't be told what you want.* She should get out all her albums, play them for Audrey. At least Nick would appreciate the music.

"She's comfortable," Eve said. "She's taken care of."

"That's important. Her work is important. Daphne should not be forgotten. My god, for a woman to succeed in photography when she did. It was a man's world. Carl tells me there's exciting news. Three photos no one has ever seen. But you've seen them, yes? A triptych. Is that true?"

"Three shots of a stone fence. Huge stone slabs. I'm not aware of her having shown these, ever."

"This could be big. I may have an opening. For a solo show. My featured sculptor had a paranoid spell and won't let his work out of his studio," she went on. "If we put up Daphne's new work, along with a retrospective, it may get some considerable attention. It could increase the value of everything. It might mean New York."

That would be ironic; Daphne's work traveling long after she couldn't. The waiter placed their salads before them. Cheryl had been amicable over the years, even when friendship between their daughters drifted. But ultimately, that had gotten in the way.

"These three photos, I'd love to see them. I don't know what to do about identifying them to be sure they're authentic. Is Daphne capable of that? Carl wasn't sure, but he thought you could reconstruct enough of her past to figure it out. He said you saved things, kept track of her."

"She sent me postcards from every location, every place she went."

Trying to figure out which postcard went with that triptych's landscape might not be precise. She'd have to visit Daphne, talk about the past, see if Daphne could remember where she'd been. "On the other hand, Cheryl, isn't part of the appeal not knowing everything? If someone came out and told us all why the Mona Lisa is smiling, wouldn't that diminish her allure?"

"That's true. But it would also make me want to see the artwork again with my own eyes. The value of Daphne's work could increase. Carl said that might help with the kitchen remodel."

"He told you about the remodel?"

"There's nothing quite like having your home ripped apart, is there?"

Cheryl pressed the linen napkin to her lips to remove the residue of salad dressing and smiled. All Eve could think about was the fact that Madison had had sex and could talk to her mother about it. And Cheryl could mention it so casually as they had lunch. Audrey was far behind. When Eve had her first sexual encounter, she was living on her own, not even street legal. Cheryl lowered the lipstick kiss on her napkin to her lap, but didn't see the napkin fall to the floor like a flirtatious message from a different century.

Eve returned home anxious to get away from all topics of conversation with Cheryl, eager to see Audrey, to find out how she had fared upstairs by herself, if she was curled up in a ball in the corner of her room, hands over her ears, sobbing. As Eve turned onto their street, her pulse raced. Nick's truck was still parked at the curb. She was eager to see what he had done, changed, removed. But instead of going straight to the kitchen, she made herself go check on Audrey.

Kneeling at the side of the bed, Audrey had both arms tucked under the mattress.

"What's this all about?" Eve asked.

Audrey jerked her arms out and stood up.

"Sorry if I surprised you," Eve said. "The door was open. You okay?"

Audrey nodded rapidly.

"Everything went okay while I was gone?"

Audrey smiled. "Fine."

"Did you go downstairs?"

"Watch me," she yelled, and ran downstairs. Eve followed.

Nick was pulling down the plastic sheet that had taken the place of a door.

"All done. All gone. No more asbestos." He grinned at Eve, his eyes alive and a little bit dangerous.

"Do you see me not running? Look at me," Audrey shouted.

"Yes, wow. I see you."

"I'm going to take off as soon as the tow truck gets here," Nick said.

"Tow truck?"

"It's hopeless. Not even jumper cables will help at this point," he said.

Audrey dropped her head and stood still.

"Apparently that's not happy news," Eve said. "I think she's become comfortable with you here. You should just move in until this is all over," she laughed.

"Right. Let me know if you find my hammer and screwdriver. They've both gone missing. They have to be here somewhere, unless they're in my truck."

He looked around, then headed to the front of the house.

Eve walked into the kitchen and surveyed its empty surfaces. Audrey put a toe in the kitchen but did not step all the way into its barren space. When Eve stepped back out, Audrey followed. When she sat down on a dining chair, Audrey followed again and sat on her lap. A teenager one moment, a child the next. Her weight was too much. Eve felt trapped under the embrace Audrey wrapped around her. But she let her stay.

"Are you feeling better about Nick being here?" she asked.

Audrey nodded without lifting her head from Eve's shoulder.

"He's nice," Audrey said. "He's good."

Eve nodded too, but Audrey's weight had become painful and she nudged her to stand up.

"You are holding me," Audrey said.

"But it's too much."

"Then I will run away."

Audrey stood and then loped around.

"Aren't you going to chase me?"

Audrey opened the door. But Eve didn't give chase. She sat, immobile in the chair, trying to determine what had triggered her sudden dark mood. A flash of yellow light pulsed through the windows in the living room, announcing the tow truck's arrival.

"Mommy," Audrey called, panic laced through her voice.

She got up and went to the front of the house where Audrey hovered by the olive tree, a safe distance from the tow truck. The sun had dipped to the horizon as the planet tipped away from its bright star. The earth spun away from the light, but houses did not slide off the street. Gravity held everything, nothing shifted except the front wheels of Nick's truck lifting off the pavement. Ribbons of pink and orange sky clashed with the yellow flash of tow-truck lights. Nick spoke with the mechanic as Eve watched from the driveway and Audrey retreated behind her.

"I won't be back tomorrow. The truck, my weekend."

"I understand. You did a lot," Eve said.

"Have you seen my vice grip? It's silver. Long handles."

He searched the pile of debris on the driveway, lifting pieces with the toe of his boot.

"That's three tools missing," Nick said.

"Do you think one of the workers is taking them?" Eve asked.

Nick looked uneasily back at the house, and when he glanced at Audrey, she suddenly ran back indoors.

"They're good men," he said. "The tools will turn up."

After Nick left, Eve's heart sank into shades of dusk like the evening light. She had grown used to his intrusion, and Audrey seemed to have acclimated as well. Now there would be a delay, two days or more. After the tow truck drove off, Eve was drawn back to the sanitized kitchen. In a matter of two days, cancerous fibers had been erased. There was satisfaction in having the asbestos removed so it could no longer threaten her home. The vacant space was a blank canvas. The plastic, draped over the missing wall, would become a large window. An island would give her family a place to gather. But Nick's absence meant the kitchen would remain unfinished. She would concentrate on the color and texture to use for wall coverings. She would contend with drawer pulls and hinges for her kitchen cabinets.

All through dinner, Audrey sat quietly, pushing a collection of baby carrots around her plate. Carl shoveled his food, barely breathing between bites. It seemed absurd to remodel a kitchen when two-thirds of the household didn't really understand how to enjoy food.

"Audrey did really well staying home by herself today," Eve said, watching for her daughter's reaction to the praise and the topic.

"That's marvelous, Aud," Carl said, beaming at her. "Tell me about lunch with Cheryl."

"Don't call her Aud, Carl."

"Eve, you read too much into that. Tell me about lunch."

"We sat by the window," Eve told him. "We both ordered salad and iced tea."

Carl nodded and ate his dinner, concentrating on these details as if they were valuable clues.

"And a sculptor had to be institutionalized, so she has an opening in two weeks."

Carl dropped his fork and looked up with delight.

"That's so soon. I thought it would be longer. But that's great. We can figure this out. I wonder how many prints she's thinking? I'll need to get Daphne to remember where the three new ones were taken."

Eve's knife scraped against the plate.

"I may have to borrow some of those photos I hung in her room, but just for the exhibit."

Audrey leaned her elbow on the table and stroked her cheek with the back of her fingers. Unaware that Eve was watching, she kissed her fingers with a tender kiss meant for someone's lips, practicing with an imaginary boy. She'd never shown any interest in boys, and suddenly her lips were pressed against her hand in an exchange of tenderness meant for someone else. Maybe her afternoon alone with Nick had inspired this somehow.

Eve darted her eyes from Carl to their daughter and back, but he didn't understand what she wanted him to observe. Then Audrey dropped her hand into her lap and kissing practice ended. She yawned, rolled a carrot around and finally bit it just as the doorbell rang.

"Nick," Eve and Audrey said at the same time.

"I know who that is," Carl said, slapping the table and rising to get the door. "Audrey, go get your homework. I hired a math tutor for you."

Audrey's eyes flew wildly from the front door to her father to Eve.

"He's a nice young man who can help you."

Audrey's feet did not move.

"Get your homework," Carl said, looking to Eve for backup.

"Carl, we never discussed this. You didn't prepare her. Who is this tutor?"

"It's worth a try, Aud," Carl said.

"Could you not call her Aud?"

Still silent, Audrey retrieved her backpack and hoisted it onto the dining table with exaggerated difficulty just as Eve cleared the dishes and went to place them in the tub. The young man who Carl led to the table was too old to still have acne, and had grown a whisper of a beard in an effort to conceal it. Carl seated him next to their thin, graceful daughter and made the introductions.

"Samson, this is Audrey."

"Just Sam," the young man stammered.

Samson had pencil-thin arms. He wore a plaid shirt tucked into pants that were held with a belt. Eve was relieved to see that he did not have a pocket protector. He peered at both Eve and Audrey from behind his black-framed glasses, which tilted forward and back as he nodded. His eyes were dark brown when the lenses didn't fill with the reflection of the chandelier.

"Eve, could I see you outside about the house?" Carl asked, opening the sliding door to the deck.

She was reluctant to leave Audrey, reluctant to cooperate with Carl when he had never bothered to bring her into this decision. When they were outside, Carl nudged her, grinned and looked back at the two of them curled over Audrey's algebra book.

"Where did Samson—Sam—come from?" Eve asked.

"Remember Roger from the office? He gave me the number. Said his son's grades have jumped dramatically."

From outside, Eve watched as Audrey pulled the cuff of her pink fleece sweatshirt over her hand and covered her nose, a response she could guess was Audrey's reaction to the young man's bad breath. She needed Eve to rescue her. Eve closed her eyes, breathed for her daughter.

"She's beautiful," Carl said. "I think she's finally noticing boys."

In the night sky, a soft moon dressed in a thin layer of fog floated above her, obvious and beautiful like the answer to a question she was supposed to ask.

Audrey 8

I leaned away from the tendrils of bad breath that curled from Samson's explanations of exponents and variables. I did not want his odorous vines to wrap themselves around me and invade my skin and eyes and nose. When I fell off the chair, he laughed, which released more vines from his mouth and forced me to crawl under the table and hold my face in my hands. He knelt next to me, put an icy hand on my shoulder. There was no spark in the darkness that filled the underside of me when he touched me. Instead, I shivered from his claw fingers. He tried to apologize, but I didn't want more words from him. I wanted him to go away. He did not have the beauty of sunlight in his face. He knew how to read math but he did not know how to read me.

The sliding door to the back deck opened and my mother and father walked in.

"That's probably enough for the first time," Mommy said.

She knelt down under the table with me, which made Samson go away. Thank you, Mommy. I watched his feet walk toward the door, my father following and joking and laughing even though nothing was funny. I wanted to crawl over to Mommy, to inhale her lavender perfume, but I planted my face into my knees and stayed where I was until I heard the front door close. My father came back and looked over the notebook where I had written out the squiggles and letters that meant math. He was pleased by symbols I didn't care about.

"I think this was helpful," he said. "No need to hide under the table, Aud."

I crawled out, and hurried upstairs to brush my teeth because I could still smell Samson's words as they came out of his mouth.

In the morning, on the way to school, I saw a pink balloon float up and away from the rooftops and telephone lines that could not trap it. I became that pink balloon on the walk from the car to the entrance of the school, which took exactly forty-four steps. But each step made me heavy with invisible weights on my shoulders and neck, and I had to give in, droop like everyone else, and make my silver horn recede into my forehead. When I remembered I would see Nick after school, I loped through the halls. Giddyup someone said, and I hurried from the scratchy weeds of their words.

Lucas' chair was empty all through English class, and I kept looking at it while Mr. Ross talked on and on about Pandora and what she let out of a jar.

My hand shot into the air and then my words. "If hope was the last thing left, then hope is evil too," I said, without waiting to be called on.

I had silenced the class. I never talked, and I don't know why I had said all that. My face went red and I looked into my book because everyone turned to look at me.

"Miss Tilden brings up a very insightful point. Who here has experienced hope as anguish?"

That empty chair wanted me to explain. Mitzi and Madison nudged each other. Again, all eyes turned to me, but I escaped by turning into a porcelain unicorn.

"It isn't hope that causes anguish, it is the expectations that hope makes us feel," Madison said. Then she lowered her voice and spoke to me. "Like when you want someone you don't have."

"But you have the expectations because of hope," another student added.

"Hope sucks."

"Bullshit. Hope is the only reason we carry on," Mitzi smiled at me. It was a warm smile. I wanted to smile back but I was a statue.

"Maybe we shouldn't carry on," someone added, which made Mitzi stick her middle finger up at the back of his head when she thought no one else saw.

"Maybe what we imagine when we hope is better than what is real," Madison said.

"Like unicorns," Mitzi said. "Or boyfriends."

The class laughed but then they talked and argued. Mr. Ross glanced at me with a question in his eyes, but I said nothing more. I wrapped my feet around the skinny legs of my chair, which held up the surface of the seat to bear the weight of someone or sometimes to just hold up the plastic. At lunch, I sat on the grass and ran my palm across the tips of the blades. A shadow blocked the sun as it passed by. But then it stopped. Mitzi and Madison stood above me. I swallowed hard and looked up.

"My mother asked me to say 'hi' to you. So, 'hi'," Madison said.

Both girls started to walk away.

"Wait," I said. "Do you want to eat lunch with me?"

I had done what my mother asked, too.

Their elbows went out to each other at the same time. I thought they would laugh next and point and keep walking, but they lowered themselves to the grass.

"Why do you want us to eat lunch with you?"

Neither of them had brought anything to eat. I looked in my sack, found something wrapped in shiny foil and opened it.

"I have sugar cubes," I said.

"Are they illegal sugar cubes?" Mitzi asked.

"I doubt it," Madison said.

"All sugar cubes are magic," I told her.

Mommy had put them in my lunch, a shiny white treat.

"Sugar cubes are a unicorn's – are my favorite food," I explained. "Here." I held out four sugar cubes, even though I wanted them all to myself.

"Crazy," Mitzi said to Madison. "I think she's still into that whole unicorn phase," Mitzi snorted.

"You used to have a whole bunch of them," Madison said. "You used to bring them to the park, but you wouldn't let anyone play with them."

They each took a white cube from my hand. My heart jumped around.

"So you keep looking at Lucas Bixby's chair. You like him?"

I shrugged. "I already have a boyfriend."

"Who?" Madison asked, a clump of hair falling across half of her face.

I didn't answer.

"Maybe it's a pretend boyfriend she gives pretend blow jobs, like you used to do, Madison."

Madison stuck her middle finger up at Mitzi then put it in her mouth, which made them both laugh and look at me.

"Blow jobs?" I asked.

"Head. As in, give him head," Madison said.

"Holy Jesus," Mitzi said. "She has no idea."

"Blow job? Head? Aw, hell," Madison said.

"Suck his dick," Mitzi said.

"Dick means penis," Madison added.

They laughed all over again into the air, not into their hands. Their mouths opened wide and I could see bits of sugar cube.

"Is there anything else you want to know?" Madison asked.

"There is."

The sun forced me to shield my eyes as I looked at the girls next to me, but even under the shade from my hand they were obscured by brightness and glare. They knew words I didn't know but wanted to know.

"No, wait. It's our turn," Mitzi said, using a finger to wipe under her lower eyelashes. "Is that V on your forehead permanent?"

There was no V on my forehead, but I touched it anyway and looked at my fingertips.

"V for virgin," Madison explained.

"That answers that question," Mitzi said. "Virgin and unicorn all in one."

Both girls laughed again. The wind picked up the plastic sandwich bag from my lunch and floated it across the concrete with unchecked delight. I did not get up to chase it or put it in the trashcan where it was supposed to go.

"Okay, one last question," Mitzi said. "It better be good."

"Do you want to come over after school?" I asked.

No one was home. I brought Mitzi and Madison over and took them straight to the kitchen to see Nick, but no one was there.

"Hello?" I called out, but no one answered.

"No boyfriend. I didn't think so," Madison said.

"He's not here right now. He'll come back."

"Let's go to your room," Mitzi said.

She went first, didn't need me to show her the way. I followed them like this wasn't my house. The first thing they did was to go to the herd on the shelf. A quiet filled me. I couldn't tell if they understood the enchanted world of unicorns, whose delicate features and shapes were unlike anything in this world. I hoped they wished for this kind of beauty in their rooms and in their lives.

Mitzi picked up Sapphire Jones.

"They don't like to be held," I said.

She turned my most special unicorn over and over. "What's her name?"

"Sapphire Jones. Put her back. Please."

When she handed her back to me, she almost dropped her, and I screamed.

"I'm kidding," Mitzi said. "Wow. You really have a thing for these."

I put Sapphire back on the shelf where she was safe. Madison sat on my bed. Mitzi kept looking at the herd.

"What the fuck?" she asked, reaching for a sugar cube I had left for them two days ago. "What's up with you and sugar cubes?"

"They love sugar cubes," I explained.

"So you still play with them? Do they like talk to you and stuff?" Mitzi asked, sitting down next to Madison.

I nodded, relieved that she had moved away from the shelf.

"Then that really is a magic sugar cube" Mitzi said, and gave Madison a look.

Madison shrugged. "She likes unicorns. You like things with dicks. So what?"

Mitzi punched Madison, but Madison dodged her and jumped up from the bed. Mitzi chased her around, swerving into the shelf even though Madison wasn't near it. Everything rattled. The herd lost their footing and wobbled, but none of them fell over. Mitzi said uh-oh and made her eyes really wide, but I don't think she was really worried. She stood near the shelf, nudging it with her arm, making the unicorns tremble.

"You have to be careful around them," I said.

"You're the same as second grade," Madison said. "Even your furniture is in the same place. Your bed has always been right here."

"Where your mom can see you when she walks by," Mitzi said. "Hey, let's move shit around," Mitzi said, stepping away from the shelf again.

"But not the shelf."

"Not the shelf," Madison said. "What if we put your bed on the other side of the room."

Nick's tools rested in the dark under my mattress, and I didn't want them to fall out. I could not explain this to Madison and Mitzi.

"Then I can't see my unicorns."

"But they'll be closer," Madison said, which made Mitzi laugh.

"Plus, you'll have more privacy," Mitzi said and shoved hard to dislodge the bed from the wall. "I bet your mother looks in every time she walks by. Right?"

How could Mitzi know that?

"Help me," Mitzi said.

Madison grabbed one end and the whole thing jerked out of place. I held my breath but the tools did not fall out. We slid the bed to the other side of the room with a scraping noise that hurt the wood floor. Then the bed caught on something, maybe one of the tools. I froze.

"There's something underneath," Madison said.

Mitzi got down on the floor on her knees and elbows and she pulled on something. A dusty book came out as she fell over against me. Madison laughed and sat down on my other side, and they opened the yearbook from last year.

"Let's see Madison's picture," Mitzi said.

"It isn't pretty."

They both howled and laughed at their pictures. Then they found me, a small face trapped in a rectangular box, my mouth covering the braces I had to wear that year.

"Fucking braces," Madison said.

"Let me see," Mitzi said, grabbing the book. I was afraid of what she would say about me.

"Everyone has a picture like that," Madison said.

Her words made me feel less afraid.

"So, are you going to wait until you're married to have sex?" Mitzi asked.

A flame glowed under my face but I shrugged.

"If Lucas Bixby likes you, we can find out," Madison said. "Then you could like him back and have a real boyfriend."

"And give him a real blow job," Mitzi snorted.

"I bet no one's ever said blow job in your room before," Madison said, looking up at the shelf of unicorns.

"Or dick," Mitzi said. "Or penis."

"Or fuck or shit or cunt," Madison said, reaching over to slap Mitzi, who punched her back and forgot about the shelf.

"Or fucktard or dickwad or cum or cock or balls," Mitzi added.

This string of new words wove itself around the three of us. "Or three-way or sixty-nine."

The math numbers sounded like code for something and I felt stupid for not knowing.

"Why did you invite us over?" Mitzi demanded.

I didn't know. This felt like a dream where I have to please the monster so it won't harm me.

"Because I need a makeover," I said.

They turned to each other and then to me.

"It could be kind of fun. A community-service project," Mitzi added.

"She needs more than a makeover."

"She needs to get laid or else I can't look at her anymore," Mitzi said, socking Madison in the arm.

"Virginity is a fucking ball and chain," Madison added as she lay down on the bed. I didn't want her on my bed, but I didn't want them to leave either. "The first time isn't great anyway."

"Mine was," Mitzi said, stretching out next to her.

Madison looked at her. "Bullshit. You told me it was painful and you didn't come. Come means orgasm. Aw, hell, Mitzi. You get to explain orgasm."

There was no room for me on the bed, but they made room and pulled me down between them, like we were all part of the same herd. They were my friends when they made room for me. They propped themselves up on an elbow and leaned in.

"What's your favorite ice cream flavor?" Mitzi asked.

"Rainbow sherbet."

"Makes your mouth do somersaults, right? Orgasm," Mitzi said, "is like eating rainbow sherbet. Except it isn't your mouth that does the somersaults."

"Whoa," Madison said. "At least start simple with a kiss, you perv."

"Fine," Mitzi said. "Make your mouth do what my mouth does."

Eve 9

The search for paint or wallpaper was fruitless. Every model, every display of samples, every salesperson lacked the answer to her question about how to finish the walls. The city, with its traffic and sprawl, didn't help. It conspired against her, kept her from getting where she wanted to go, which was home. Exhausted, Eve finally made it back to the house and went directly to the unfinished kitchen. Perhaps she had missed something. Perhaps seeing the kitchen now, after seeing everything that didn't work, would reveal a solution. Paint and wallpaper were too traditional. Too predictable. She put her hand on the rough plywood surface of the subwall Nick had put in place. Cheap, raw. But still better than anything she'd seen during her search.

She could consult Carl, but she already knew he'd tell her whatever she liked was fine. Nick had taken today off after working through the weekend, but maybe she could call him, ask about other materials she hadn't considered. What about corrugated tin? She looked at her phone and saw his missed call.

"It's Nick. I need to be away until Wednesday. Hey, Eve," he said. Then a long pause. "Thanks for understanding."

She sat down on the couch. Played the message back once more. "Hey, Eve." Then that long pause. She looked down at her denim jeans, at the V her thighs made.

Her mood darkened. Frustration from searching without results, from not finding the perfect solution for the walls. If Nick were here, it would help. And now he'd be delayed. She played the message a third time.

"Thanks for understanding." He had been about to say something else before that, but changed his mind. She could hear that much in his voice.

The weighty sound of furniture being dragged across the floor upstairs made Eve jump up and hurry to Audrey's room. She opened the door without knocking. Two girls with low-cut clothes and makeup lay on Audrey's bed, which had been dislodged and moved halfway to the opposite wall. One of the girls straightened up from bending over her daughter who lay across the bed. A vapor trail of secrecy marked the room.

"Hi," Eve said.

"Hey," said the girl closest to the shelf.

It took Eve a moment to place her. Mitzi something. The other was Madison Moncrief, Cheryl's daughter. Audrey did not speak, did not introduce them, did not even look at Eve.

"Madison," Eve said. "I just had lunch with your mother."

"How funny is that," Madison said, but it wasn't a question and it wasn't funny.

"And Mitzi. Last time I saw you both, you were still in elementary school."

"Good times," Mitzi said, glancing at the unicorns.

"Audrey, you have friends over. That's great," Eve said. "And you've moved the bed?"

"Audrey wants to rearrange things. Or did she need to ask permission first?" Mitzi said.

"Of course not. Can I get you guys a snack?"

"A snack?" Madison repeated. "Like juice and cookies?"

The two girls laughed. Audrey motioned for her to leave. The wordless gesture pushed her out of this inner sanctum where these girls were having fun with Audrey, with her furniture. She should be elated. Her daughter was finally having friends over. But instead, she felt excluded. Why had they moved Audrey's bed? She stood there listening, feeling stupid because a play date was exactly what she had wished for. But Audrey did not indicate any need to be rescued. Snickering exploded just as one of them closed the bedroom door completely. She listened from her own room until the scraping of chair and desk stopped. Those girls were popular. How had Audrey managed this?

Eve retreated to her closet. To The Police, The Bangels, The Pretenders, to the t-shirts that were souvenirs of conquering loneliness.

Except for Joan Baez.

This was not hers.

This was Carl's, and it had managed to join Zeppelin and Van Halen. She flicked Joan Baez to his side of the closet.

Muffled laughter floated from down the hall. She argued with herself whether to get up and check on them or stay where she was. This was not how she imagined it would be. They should all come downstairs, hang out in the living room. She could play them her old albums.

How pathetic. They didn't want to hear her music. They wanted to spend time with Audrey. She should be glad about that. But the silence from Audrey's room drove Eve to her feet, to her daughter's door. A hush consumed the house as if the girls sensed her presence on the other side and refused her any information. She moved away quietly. She'd talk to Audrey later that evening.

But Audrey offered nothing about her adventure. Carl was working late, so she and Audrey had dinner together at the dining table. Eve ate the microwaved pasta, but Audrey only rearranged it on her plate. Eve's prompts and questions provoked nothing. "They seem nice. Did you have fun? What made you decide to move your bed?" All of this was answered with a series of shrugs until Audrey looked up, smiled and announced that she was going up to her room.

Eve stood in the corner of the kitchen where walls of plywood angled from behind her in perpendicular directions. A blank canvas. She unfolded her arms and pressed herself against one wall as if someone held her there. "Thank you for understanding," Nick said in his message. And she did. She understood. He had other jobs to attend to, other bids to place. But she wanted him to focus entirely on her counters and cabinets. Right here, in this kitchen.

Vertical wall became horizontal mattress when she climbed into bed. Cotton sheets against her bare skin teased her. She stretched her arm across Carl's empty side of the bed, and later when he climbed in, he became a stranger whose curly hair and body heat were finally in reach. He murmured and rolled toward her, compliant as she slipped off his briefs. Then she was on him, under him, above him. Her face to the ceiling, her eyes closed. This, and now this. Here, another hidden pleasure discovered. Given and taken. When her heart begged for recovery she rolled off, but an insistent ache remained. She kissed Carl's wrist, turned onto her side, and lay in the dark, free for a few minutes from the habit of marriage.

In the morning, Carl made no indication that their escapade had taken place. She dressed, made coffee, stood on the deck and pretended that she had just stepped out of a gray-and-white beach bungalow, the morning light brilliant on the ocean. This hurt no one. This was not betrayal. She was entitled to her own mind, her own thoughts, her own surprise and satisfaction.

At the market, her step was light, her smile ready for everyone. In the produce aisle, strawberries seduced her with their deep red flesh, peaches made her reach again. She was helpless against the flood of sensual sensations that possessed her. This lust, harmless because she would never act on it, had been absent from her life for too long. Nick brought it all back. Her t-shirts brought it all back. It had been so long since she felt this alive. Even the motion of loading groceries into her car was infused with fluid choreography. The vast blue sky bent close to whisper against her neck, and she had to steady herself. At home, she parked in the driveway, next to the pile of lumber, and a low ache demanded to be acknowledged. As if telepathy could shout, Nick pulled up and blocked her. He'd come back early. Helped her unload the groceries and carry them into the house without a word. Their hands touched briefly, electrical charge leaping across fingers. When she looked back, only her car and a pile of lumber occupied the driveway.

Audrey 9

It had been days. But finally he was back. In the kitchen where I could hear feel sense him.

A slice of my mother flashed by as she passed through the hall, holding a t-shirt up to her body. I darted across the hall, closed the bathroom door and ran water in the sink so the sound would excuse me from hearing her.

"Audrey? Audrey."

I did not answer.

My mother called again to the girl in the mirror, a pale animal with a single horn on her forehead tracing arcs in the air with a silver point. One variable could define another if you subtracted it from the first; a creature of mystery, minus the voice in the hall, could equal footsteps finally walking away. A shiver ran up to the top of my head and left a frost of white crystals. I wanted to be downstairs closer to the kitchen. I was not afraid. But my mother and her music had built a fence.

I lifted the bouquet of flowers on my shirt and pulled it over my head, removed the white bra, then made my lips into a kiss. But it was missing its other half. Something stirred, some creature lurking in the dark not shaped like the unicorn that lived inside me.

The girl in the mirror unzipped her pants, pulled them down and took off the cotton undies with butterflies. Exposing that hidden furry patch made my hand draw to its delicate curls. I had pulled away from Mitzi when she kissed me, which made her laugh. Then Madison held my head in place for the second kiss, which made something down below in me ache, but not with pain. I leaned against the towel rack and closed my eyes. When I opened them, the wild eyes of a unicorn flashed from the mirror at my nakedness and I pulled the towel from the rack and covered myself. I dressed and went to my room and lay across my bed. Madison and Mitzi were right. No one could see me here on my bed when they passed in the hall, even with the door open. From where I was, I could no longer see the herd because the shelf was next to the bed instead of across from it and I had to get up to say hello.

They did not speak. They wanted quiet. So I sat back down.

Then I knew what to do with one of the things under my mattress.

I took the screwdriver downstairs, holding it against my side, and then I placed it on the floor near a wall, half of it tucked behind a bookcase. My mother's music rang out with its screaming, whining plea. I sat on the couch and covered my ears. From here, I could sense Nick working in the kitchen, moving back and forth. When he finally saw me, he winked. I motioned for him to come out, then pointed and stood up.

"Were you looking for this?"

"My father's screwdriver. Oh, man. Oh, wow. Thank you."

He grabbed it from the floor, kissed it, then put his arms around me and kissed my cheek. Except I turned so that my lips met his. We stepped into the doorway of softness our lips made together. Then his tongue pushed passed my lips, inviting my tongue to come play, which I did. Warm, dark, close. I could not breathe.

Then he stepped away and looked down at the floor a moment as my mother walked into the room. The doorway that Nick and I had created to this other place disappeared. My mother looked around, trying to see it.

"Hey, there. What's going on?" she asked.

"I found my screwdriver. Audrey found it," Nick said, holding it up.

"Why is it special?" I asked.

"It belonged to my grandfather and then my father."

"Did they teach you how to use it?" I asked.

"My dad did."

"Is it a weapon?" I asked.

"No."

"But you use it to pry up floors."

"Not usually. It drives screws into wood."

He looked from my mother to me.

"Want me to show you?"

"Yes!"

"Be careful," my mother said.

He led me into the kitchen and my mother stayed back, pretended like she wasn't watching but called out for me to be careful again. Nick gripped the long yellow handle, and made it turn the threads of a screw down into a piece of wood. That piece of wood became part of the house, strong and unmovable.

"Check it out."

I pushed on the wood but it was fixed in place.

"My turn?" I asked, and put my hand on his hand and looked into his ocean colored eyes. A thousand birds flew up from the tree that grew inside.

"Audrey, that kiss. I didn't know—"

"Me either."

I chose a silver screw from the blue-and-yellow box, its sharp spiral winding to a point.

"This could be the horn of a unicorn," I said.

"I'll start. You finish," he said.

The tip of the screw sank into the wood, which made room for it each time he turned the yellow handle. Then he handed it to me. The handle was warm from his hand. I fit the metal end into the slot and turned. It took more strength than I started with, but slowly the threads began to wind down into the wood the same way he'd made them sink in. But I could not make the top of the screw flat with the wood like Nick's. He finished for me like it took no effort. I stood back and looked at how two pieces had been joined together, at the fact of having built a piece of something, creating it where there had been nothing.

"I built a wall," I said.

"Sort of," he said. "But this is how you really build a kitchen." He picked up an orange power drill, squeezed the trigger and it whined as he sank a screw into the wood in three seconds.

I shrieked but did not run away even though my heart tried to make me. The speed and power of the drill made me laugh and shiver. But I knew it would not try to get me.

"Can I try that too?" I asked.

"That's enough," my mother said, intruding on us. "Let him work."

His hand closed over mine when I handed the screwdriver to him. "Thanks again," he said.

The insides of my legs turned from bone to liquid. I wanted to rest my face against his face. But we walked away from each other, stretching against a force that tried to pull us back together. He took the screwdriver with him and I took a kiss with me.

I wandered upstairs to where the hammer and silver thing remained under my bed, laid my head against the bedspread, and tucked my arms underneath the dark mattress where the lost became the hidden. When I touched the hard objects, my bones became liquid. Downstairs, Nick moved through the house, working, pretending that he did not want to go through that doorway we had found. I could feel him thinking of me, of our kiss.

His footsteps came up the stairs. Approached my room. Stopped outside my door.

My heart raced.

"Good evening, sweetheart," Daddy said, stepping in, flipping on the light. "What's this?" My father stuck his head into my room and looked at the furniture's new arrangement. "Time for a change?" he asked.

I nodded and caught the kiss he blew, but I didn't know what to do with it so I opened my hand and let it fall to the floor. Later, after I got in bed, I couldn't sleep. My eyes circled the room, settling into the right angle where the wall joined the ceiling. Perpendicular planes, connecting so that they shaped the room I was in and tricked me into thinking there was nothing beyond these four walls. But I could picture telephone poles and clouds outside running across the sky. I could imagine ice skating rinks with flat floors of white cold. There was a world beyond this house where my parents slept in their room while I was awake in mine. The shelves in my bookcase made right angles where the herd stood and listened to the night. The house creaked, sending secret messages through the floors and walls. What is it? The wounded kitchen. It was trying to tell me of the night that poured in through the open wall where a window belonged. Trying to tell me that outside, the stars whispered to each other in the sky.

I got out of bed, started to take Blue and Sapphire Jones from the shelf but put them back. Instead, I knelt by the mattress and reached in for the hidden hammer and vice grip. As quiet as a shadow, I moved through the hall, went down the stairs, walked toward the kitchen. It was still. The wooden beam I'd helped put in place remained fixed. I sniffed its wood, raw with newness. Night pressed against the black glass in the dining room, called me to it. I undid the latch and pulled it so slowly it didn't look like it was moving. Cool air wrapped itself around me. I stepped into the night, my bare feet on the damp wooden deck. Splinters folded back to kindly let me pass. Below the deck, dark grass blades waited with their icy tips to tickle the soles of my feet. I knelt on the grass. The color of my parents' bedroom window above me did not change. No amber light appeared and they slept and dreamed, not knowing I had left. Night air made my skin tingle like peppermint. A breeze blew and the plastic skin of the kitchen rustled and whispered for me to lie down and listen to the stars.

I placed the hammer near my head and the vice grip near my feet then lay inside the constellation I'd made with Nick's tools, protected from the rustle in the leaves and the creak in the fence. This silver world made of moonlight was a kingdom of ancient shapes that the stars above me traced.

Guided by a silver compass, I search for the moment when light and shape become beauty. Nighttime shadows lean away from the house. I find the apricot's fold, a smooth seam hidden in my long limbs that bend into knee and elbow, and angle against the cold grass as I turn on my side. I face no one. My flesh curves like the hills. The breeze whispers across my landscape. I want to run, but I must wait for someone. For who? I press into the tight knot down there that insists on touch. I want a pair of arms to wrap me in the shapes made by the stars. I want a kiss that makes me tremble. This is not a unicorn on the grass. I obey a different animal's will. I move against my fingers, my palm, the earth to release her. When she no longer needs me, my fingertips are damp. Is she weeping in gratitude for this brief freedom?

The stars pulsed above me. In me. Dawn crept across the sky, bringing the color of concrete. I pressed my hand against my cheek and felt my icy fingers. These belonged to someone else, something else.

If Mommy could see me, she would run to get a sweater and shoes. I touched my lips to feel if they were blue but I didn't know what blue felt like. The moment I entered the house, I heard footsteps above me, someone walking across the floor. I hurried to my room and crawled into bed. Just as I closed my eyes, my mother knocked and called to me that it was time to get up. But I said nothing. The herd said nothing. I opened a drawer to choose a t-shirt for school. A shirt of silver daisies on lavender fabric might erase the concrete color of having to go to school and of having to show my mother silence. The spray of daisies reminded me of the grass and stars and last night's adventure, which lived entirely inside me. And only me. I put on the daisy t-shirt and stepped over the Guns N Roses t-shirt my mother had placed outside my door.

Downstairs, my parents turned to see the bouquet of shiny flowers on my t-shirt. Neither of them could speak because of my bright, new beauty.

Eve 10

The sliding door to the back yard was wide open, the sign of an intruder. Eve stood still. Fine hairs on her neck rose in alarm. She was sure she had closed and locked it last night. She moved cautiously to the living room, to the dining room, to the kitchen. But there was no intruder. There was no one.

"Nick?" she called through the open door.

No indication of forced entry. The lock had never been latched, the door never closed. Or it had been opened during the night.

"Nick?" she called again.

No answer.

"Is Nick here?" Audrey asked, thundering down the stairs.

Carl followed behind her. "What's going on?"

Audrey searched the kitchen, then the yard, then the living room. "Is Nick here?" she repeated.

"The door is open," Eve said.

"Look at you," Carl turned to Audrey. "Ready for school without a single word from me or Mom."

"Where is Nick?"

"I'm sorry, sweetheart. I called his name because I thought he was here. The door was open. Carl, did you leave it open?"

Audrey's face fell. Her shoulders wilted. Her fresh, eager mood turned dull and resigned.

Carl shrugged, already lost in his email and messages. Audrey hugged her backpack to her chest, arms wrapped around it, cheek resting against its canvas.

"I'm late. Bye, sweetheart," Carl said. Audrey did not respond. "Hey," he said, kissing her forehead.

"Not there," she wailed. "No one kisses me there."

She writhed and squirmed away to protect the delicate horn no one else could see.

"Sorry, Aud," he said. "Sorry, Audrey," he corrected himself and shrugged helplessly at Eve.

"I think this door was open all night."

"So was the kitchen wall. What's the difference?"

He hurried toward the front door.

"Wait," Eve called after him. "Will you remember to get me concert tickets?"

"What concert tickets?"

"You were going to see who's touring. Remember?"

"Oh, right."

Then he was gone, late for the deal, the meeting, the traffic.

Progress stopped. The kitchen remained in its state of unfinished mess for two days. Audrey moved through it and then slowly moved into it. Each time Eve passed, she caught a glimpse of her daughter exploring it, hovering at a safe distance from the unplugged power saw or pressing her ear to the two-by-fours that framed a place for the large window. Later, Audrey spread her homework across the floor and sat in the corner, leaving only to bring back the blue glass unicorn to keep her company.

Darkness fell. Color drained from the kitchen and long shadows engulfed the room. Carl and Eve sat down to eat at the dining table. Audrey took her plate of take-out back to her corner and disappeared into the gray light.

"Come on out," Carl said. "You can't just sit in the dark."

"This is where we want to be," Audrey said in a quiet voice.

"Who's we?" Carl murmured.

He got up, went to the garage and returned with an orange extension cord. When he plugged it in, a beam of light shot out from the work lamp. He held it up, making shadows grow and swing. Then he hooked the lamp to Nick's ladder.

"Thank you, Daddy."

He was a caring father. Eve smiled at him, touched by his gesture. She'd chosen well. She'd given her daughter a father, and become the mother that she never had. Bathed in its yellow glow, Audrey rearranged the papers around her, flipped through pages in her book, appeared to be doing her homework. But Eve saw her gaze float up to the ceiling and across the kitchen's construction to the empty rectangle where the window had been. Something besides unicorns occupied her thoughts. Or someone.

"Maybe we shouldn't finish the kitchen if it helps her get her homework done," Carl joked as the two of them ate. "I've never seen her work like this."

Sitting amid the construction, Audrey placed Nick's tools on her homework like paperweights, then stared into the middle distance.

"Let's all go visit Daphne this evening," Carl sang out, loud enough for Audrey to hear. "We can bring the photos. Maybe she'll talk about them."

Eve pressed her lips together. Audrey, who would never refuse an opportunity to see the fragile old woman, shook her head.

"I'm going to stay here," Audrey said quietly.

Carl and Eve exchanged glances.

"Are you okay?" Carl asked her. Audrey nodded and smiled like she had a secret. "This isn't like you, sweetheart," he said, kneeling down. "Come on, Audrey. Go with us. You always put Daphne in a good mood. You can help pick out the photos we'll put in her exhibit. You're good at that, too."

After a hesitation, Audrey shook her head, folded her arms, and settled further into the corner, into what could only be proximity to Nick, Eve thought. He had repaired her broken unicorn and she had found his grandfather's screwdriver. This was a crush, that's what it was. It reminded her of her own girlhood passions; harmless infatuations that reverberated like an echo in her mother's empty apartment. Eve's home was a victory over her mother's empty apartment. A crush on Nick might be proof that she was unfolding from girlhood, even as she crouched like a child in the corner.

Carl shrugged. "C'mon, Evie. Let's you and I go."

"Maybe I should stay here," she said, indicating Audrey with a tilt of her head.

"You can go," Audrey said.

Eve looked at the glass unicorn next to Audrey. The prospect of visiting Daphne stretched itself out into a long moment that waited patiently, like a cat sunning itself before the impulse to pounce.

"Can this be quick?" Eve asked Carl.

"Absolutely. We'll be back in an hour," Carl said to Audrey who was looking at the world through the transparent yellow handle of Nick's screwdriver.

"You sure you're okay?" Eve asked.

Audrey nodded. "Give Daphne a kiss for me."

"Sure," she said.

"Will you really?" Audrey asked. "You, and not Daddy?"

Eve knelt down. "How about if you give me the kiss you want to give her?"

Audrey tilted her face to Eve's and pressed her lips against her cheek, her arms wrapped around Eve's neck like when she was a small girl. Eve inhaled, did not want Audrey to let go.

"Here's one for you, too." Audrey kissed Eve's other cheek. "Mommy? Love shouldn't make you cry," Audrey whispered.

Eve stood up and wiped away an unplanned tear with the hem of her Graceland t-shirt.

"It's the dust," she said.

"Hey, speaking of dust," Carl said. "Did I tell you I found my Joan Baez t-shirt?"

At the care facility, Carl rushed into Daphne's room, embraced her, sat on the edge of the bed and held her hand.

"You look lovely," he said. "What have you done differently? Is it your hair? I can't figure it out. Radiant. That's the word I'm looking for. Like there's a light inside you."

His stream of compliments and questions circumvented protest or confusion from the old woman.

"One of the nurses brought me a new moisturizing lotion," she said.

Carl raised her arm to his nose and inhaled. Eve had never thought to bring her new lotion, but a nurse, someone who wasn't family, could show her this kindness. Tightness grew around Eve's throat.

"Lavender? Lilac?" Carl asked.

They played a guessing game while Eve stood in the doorway like a child afraid to venture into the room and disturb the white queen.

"Don't I get a kiss?" Daphne asked, lifting her face.

She should have stepped in and lightly delivered Audrey's kiss, and maybe one of her own, but her feet were stuck, her legs refused to move. Carl did what she could not; he leaned down and kissed Daphne's forehead. She reached for him, embraced him, a benign exchange of affection between helpless and helpful. With her arms still circling Carl's neck, Daphne stared over his shoulder at Eve, a cold unknowing gaze, a look that asked, "Who is she?"

"Daphne, I found some prints of yours," Carl said, releasing himself from her. "They were in this folder at the bottom of a print drawer."

He lifted the three prints from their protective black folder and held them up one at a time for Daphne to see. "Where were these taken? Why have I never seen them? I'll bet you can tell me."

She lay back in her bed, expressionless as each section of fence was presented to her. She said nothing.

"They are yours, aren't they?" he asked.

"They're mine," she answered sharply. "It was Greece."

"Greece. Would that have been 1984?"'

"Lovely people there. And the food. There is no better food. Certainly not here."

"You traveled a great deal," Carl said. "I suspect you were in the southern part? Though these hills make me wonder if it was north."

"Wine, too. Nothing comes close. California has its wine, but Tuscany weather does something to those vines."

"You said this was Greece."

"The only place that rivals Italy for wine and food is France. They know a thing or two."

Carl bowed his head.

"Daphne," Eve said, stepping into the room. "You went many places, but none of them had a stone fence like this. Maybe there were other features built out of this kind of stone? Maybe castles or homes?"

"What do I care what homes are made out of?"

"I'd like to have them framed," Carl said.

"We could hang them up here and you might remember where this was," Eve added.

"Who is she? Why is she in my room? Is she the one who's been taking my things? Hand me my camera. First my hair brush, then my lotion. Hand me my camera before she tries to steal it."

Carl handed Daphne her Nikon, which she clutched to her as if someone were going to rip it from her hands.

"How does this thing work, anyway?" Carl asked.

It was a standard question that always brought Daphne back to the room. She might mix up the past and all the places she'd been, but she could still tell anyone about f-stops, aperture, the kind of lens that worked best for shooting landscapes filled with fences. Carl nodded and listened and asked questions to keep her going. It was a dance they did, a routine he led her through to prove that everything was fine.

"Your brush is over here on the dresser," Eve said. "No one is taking things."

Carl interrupted. "Let me pour you some water."

"What I need is a martini."

"Where was the best martini you ever had?" he asked, shooting Eve a look that told her not to interfere.

"Best gin martini I ever had was in the south of France, would you believe? It had champagne in it and a twist of lemon."

He had distracted her back into the past, away from this accusation of theft that was somehow linked to Eve. The only thing Eve had ever taken from Daphne was the cash she would find on the counter when Daphne left town. But Daphne had left it for her. Still, there was some connection in her mother's mind between Eve and stealing. Nothing made sense, unless Daphne saw Eve as someone trying to steal Daphne's livelihood, her pursuit of photography. But time had done that. Carl carried on with Daphne about martinis and France, not noticing that Eve had turned and gone outside.

Not much later, Carl came out of the building with his arms wrapped around two large photographs.

"Are you stealing those?" Eve asked.

"I told her I was going to have the glass cleaned. She won't remember, but I couldn't have a rational conversation about borrowing them for the exhibit. She was starting to fade. She couldn't recall anything specific about the location. It's unfortunate"

"So you're just going to make something up about these? And come back and take her other photos until you have what you need for Cheryl's show?"

"Is that bad?"

"Not until she has a breakdown and blames me."

"It's sweet, you know. You do care," Carl said, pulling off his sweater to pad the photographs he placed carefully in the trunk.

"I shouldn't."

"Some part of her cares. I'll take my chances that she won't notice. I'm sorry I made you go with me. I shouldn't have."

"I'm a grown woman."

Carl put his arms around Eve. May this never end, she thought, but it had to. Wordlessly, they got in the car.

In order to get Audrey to go to bed, Eve told her that Blue, the glass unicorn, could stand guard, bring a message in case there was news about Nick's arrival. Then she hated herself for it. If she wanted Audrey to stop living in a world full of unicorns, she needed to stop contributing to the fantasy. But it worked. It always did.

In the morning, Audrey went directly to the corner and held the glass creature to her, listening for some telepathic message.

"Audrey, it's time," Eve said.

Audrey followed her out the door for school, but before they could get in the car, Nick pulled up in his white truck. He waved and smiled, then got out of the truck. There was a casual confidence in his gait. His body was breathtaking, his smile electric. Eve wanted to put her hands on those shoulders, explore the contours of those arms that pulled him through the surf when he lay against his board. Eve sequestered her impulses, but Audrey dropped her backpack and galloped to him. He'd hardly closed the driver's door when she wrapped herself around him and grinned and shouted, "It's you, it's you, it's you."

"Hey," he said, peeling her off, one arm at a time. "What a welcome. Audrey, come on. But you gotta let go, now."

When he freed himself and stepped back, she lunged at him again, grabbing him with fierceness this time. She could lose control at any moment, act on any impulse. Horror pulsed across Eve's arms and shoulders. Fred and Isaac got out of the back of the old truck, coughed and looked away.

"Audrey," Eve said. "That's enough. He asked you to let go."

Nick jumped out of her reach when she started toward him a third time, making this a game.

"The house is open," Eve told Nick, putting her hands on Audrey's shoulders to steer her into the car. "I'll be right back."

Audrey flinched, broke away, and locked an angry gaze on Eve. But she also complied and got in the car. Then she twisted in the front seat so she could watch the house as long as possible.

"Why isn't he happy to see me?" she asked.

"He has to work, the way you have to go to school," Eve said.

When Eve returned, Nick was lifting a length of lumber from the driveway that would be cut and shaped into a kitchen island. He balanced the wood on his shoulder and moved with grace toward the back of the house. Fred and Isaac also picked up beams and followed. She wanted to trail behind, hoping for an audience with Nick alone. But she went into the house, instead. Audrey's schoolgirl embrace played itself out again in her mind.

Before the boombox started up, she dug through the far reaches of the living room cabinet and pulled out a stack of albums, dusty with neglect. These relics belonged to a window of time when she was younger and had no clue that she was living in an era that would one day fade. But the music could take her back there, even if she was stuck in the middle of this suburban neighborhood, far from the loading ramps and sound booths. What had Lydia said? It could make you younger.

Surrounded with album covers laid out on the carpet, she became part of a collage of cover art that evoked a sweet sense of loss. Black vinyl slipped from the album sleeve with a zeppelin going up in flames behind a group of WWI pilots whose faces belonged to the band. Eve tilted the record to the light to see the fine grooves in the vinyl spiraling inward like an ancient hieroglyph. She placed Led Zeppelin on the turntable. God, did it still work? She powered up her old analog stereo. When she moved the arm over and lowered the stylus onto the spinning surface, sweet rumble and pop filled the living room. Then guitar exploded through the house as Jimmy Page's guitar ripped into the morning.

"Whole Lotta Love" pulsed. Robert Plant's vocals blew through the missing wall into the neighborhood, flared across the rooftops. You need coolin' baby I'm not foolin,' Plant sang. She flattened herself against the carpet and closed her eyes, searching her memory for the lyrics.

A second voice sang along, knew the words. She opened her eyes, and Nick leaned against the doorway keeping up with every lyric. The tool belt that hung from his left hand set off a tremor, and desire race from her shoulders to knees. This feeling was once her compass, pointing her intuition toward the magic of a lover's companionship. The needle spun, the room tilted.

Nick stepped closer. Something that hadn't been allowed out in many years stretched and rose to its feet as he held out his hand and pulled her up.

"You've been learnin,' and baby I been yearnin,' all them good times, I been discernin'. Baby, baby," she sang with him.

They got to the chorus and she had to laugh when he let his vocals rip off-key, but deadly serious. The power of the chords and words and passion fused. There was revelry and daring and delight in his rendition. She tried to drop back in and they howled together right through the ending, sustaining the word "love" along with Plant.

The song was over. They were breathless. He was close enough to kiss. Flame surged, desire consumed and destroyed every objection in its path. She wanted to feel the heat and pressure of his body against hers, wanted to drop to the carpet with him and redefine everything.

"Rock 'n' roll," he shouted, and she laughed again.

He picked up the album cover and turned it over.

"Hey," Eve said. "I'm sorry about Audrey's outburst."

"Don't be. I like that her emotions are so completely honest. She doesn't hold back."

She considered the distance to the ground and the powerful force of attraction that fired through her limbs.

"I'm glad you're here. Audrey missed you," she made herself say. "She stayed in the kitchen all day, all evening next to your toolbox."

Nick stepped away, retrieved his tool belt and strapped it around his waist.

"On Sunday, she kissed me," he said. "I guess I kissed her back."

So there had been a kiss.

Audrey's first.

Eve's internal compass spun. She should have seen this coming, should have been able to predict it, but she had no idea about the kiss until now. This man in her kitchen had already become something to her daughter. He was attractive, Audrey was comfortable around him. This explained her hovering in the corner near his things, looking for him when he wasn't there.

That unspoken desire that had almost seduced Eve had also made itself known to Audrey. It had come for her. Maybe it could take her away from childish obsessions. Nick cared enough about Audrey to be honest with Eve. Her attraction to him flared again, made her restrain herself when he ran his hand through his hair. He was maybe only ten years out from his own boyhood, from his own first kiss.

"Thank you for being honest," she said.

"I shouldn't have done it."

"I'm glad it was you."

"I didn't mean anything by it. It won't happen again."

His last words were meant as reassurance, like he was apologizing for having betrayed his attraction to Eve. The needle found its way into "What Is and What Should Never Be." Eve turned the volume down.

The faded fabric of his jeans, the outline of a wallet in his back pocket; these textures and contours made Eve's heart skip. If she were Audrey's age, she would have already made her move. But Audrey didn't know how. Not without someone to teach her.

Audrey 10

My English book was a shield in the Battle of the Hallway. A daily riot that never made history. I held the shield to protect me from the shoving, the sharp laughter, the sudden change of direction from someone ahead of me. I made my way to class, but what I really wanted was to stay home with Nick, to be near him, to help him work. The clock above the chalkboard stopped moving whenever I looked at it.

The yellow pencil I rolled back and forth across my desk reminded me of the handle of his screwdriver. A shiver ran across the back of my shoulders as if he had entered the classroom.

"You miss him?" Mitzi asked.

I nodded at the vacant air near the ceiling of the room.

"We've thought it over, and we have a proposal. We are willing to take you for a make-over. A real one."

I sat up, turned to them. "You would?"

"This isn't the kind of make-over you get at the mall."

"It's the kind where you'll get to see your boyfriend."

How did they know about Nick?

"Interested?"

"Yes."

"Let's go," Madison said. "Before Mr. Ross gets here."

They both stood up.

I had never left school when I wasn't supposed to, but I picked up my book and walked out of the room. Some girls called to me as we left, whistling low with admiration and danger. We hurried down the empty hall, slipped into the cafeteria, and walked out a side door to the place where trucks pulled up to unload. Then we were out on the sidewalk, laughing in the sunlight, all three of us hysterical that we had just gotten up and left. For all these years, I had never done that, then I just walked out. It was easy. I snorted and leaped over nothing.

"Neigh," Mitzi said.

"Moo," Madison answered.

I stopped, alarmed by their animal words, listening to see if they meant harm in the fun they made.

"Hey," Mitzi said. "Look what I brought."

She reached into her pocket and held out two sugar cubes, their small white shapes pure and sweet in her hand.

"Mitzi, what the hell?" Madison said.

"It's fine. It's part of the make-over."

I took both cubes.

"Only one," Madison shouted.

I popped one in my mouth, its sugary taste spreading across my tongue. The grainy edges of the other one pressed into my hand, and I decided to save it for the herd.

"These are magic cubes," Mitzi said.

"Magic?"

"Your field trip today is going to be educational. There will be a quiz later so take notes about what's real and what isn't."

"But we're going to my house, right?"

"Not yet."

Mitzi laughed, pulled Madison by the arm and I followed. We walked four blocks to a bus stop. The school grew smaller and smaller behind us. Then we ran across the street without waiting for the light because the bus was coming. It exhaled its dark breath on me and opened its doors.

"I can't," I said to them, my heart fluttering up into my throat.

"You scared of the bus?"

"You ever taken one?"

I shook my head. "It's like a monster."

"Come on," Madison said.

"We're gonna teach you how to ride a bus," Mitzi smiled.

They climbed up the bus and stood inside, motioning for me to join them. The bus driver didn't have all day, he said, so I stepped up. Mitzi dropped some coins in a machine that tinkled and the doors closed behind me. I screamed as the bus lurched and they pulled me down the aisle. The three of us wobbled to empty benches at the back. The bus lurched again, and I screamed. But then I laughed because I had been afraid and there were just regular people in their seats who had not been devoured by a monster. They were only bored.

"Never sit in the back of the bus," Madison said, choosing a seat in the back.

Mitzi took a separate seat so I did too. But when a dingy man in raggedy clothes got up and sat down next to Mitzi she raised her arm and pointed at another seat.

"You have to move. Now," she said to the man.

His grin faded and he hurried out of her seat. The driver watched in his mirror until the man sat somewhere else.

"That's how you handle freaks you don't want to sit with," Mitzi said. "Just like talking to a dog."

I counted five other people on the bus. They looked out the window and I looked too, to see what they stared at. We were so tall above the rest of the cars. The world outside swung by like a movie on a screen, the lines on the road flying past, outlining our direction. Two parts of me separated. One sank down inside while the other flew above me. My heartbeat pulsed through me in rhythm with the phone poles that strung the wires across the sky. I turned to Mitzi and Madison just as they each reached for a sugar cube from a small metal mint tin. They popped a cube into their mouths.

"You're ahead of us," Mitzi said. "But we'll catch up."

I laughed because they were sitting right behind me. I wasn't that far ahead. Mitzi took out her phone and made a call.

"We're bringing you a gift. We want some product in exchange."

She hung up, smiled at Madison who smiled at me, but there was something sad in her eyes.

A beautiful man wearing only his underwear watched me from the billboard where he posed. He stared right at me and my face went warm, thinking of Nick and the kiss and his tongue in my mouth. Palm trees towered along the boulevard, their goofy hats dancing at the ends of their skinny necks. Red light, green light; traffic stopped to let us pass knowing we were special. We were a tall procession of bored people and naughty girls who ran away from frozen clocks and rows of desks. I waved at the drivers in their cars, stopped at a red light. They sat patiently behind their wheels and looked straight ahead. They didn't wave back, and only stared at whatever was ahead. As the bus traced a broken white line on the asphalt, the city became quieter. The painted line ticked alongside me, stitching together a grid of streets that had flattened out into warehouses. Behind the warehouses, towers of glass rose into the air. Downtown tried to scrape a sky that could never be touched. The warehouses we passed did not have many windows, and the ones they did have were covered by bars, like a birdcage, except they were too wide to keep a bird inside. Unless it was an ostrich.

"Are there ostriches in those buildings?" I asked, turning around to Madison and Mitzi. My question made the three of us laugh.

Their faces turned pink and they shoved each other to stop. Madison opened her mouth to say something and feathers of every color came out: aqua, pink, dark blue. They floated out the bus window and sailed away from behind us. I watched them as long as I could until Mitzi stood up and pulled me out of my seat.

"Our stop," she said.

One more feather fell out and we stumbled through the accordion door. The bus roared away and I turned around, unafraid now, and roared back. Mitzi and Madison roared with me. Then the three of us were alone on an empty street where the lampposts drooped toward the concrete, each doomed to stare at nothing with their Cyclops' eye. I looked down at the sidewalk to see what they saw. A small flower surprised me, growing out of a crack in the sidewalk. I knelt down to keep it company. The lampposts leaned nearer to watch over it. Its yellow buttonhead beamed at me, a tiny sun in this colorless world.

"You triumph," I told it.

Mitzi and Madison knelt down too, and we worshiped the beauty of this flower's determination. Then Mitzi reached over and ripped it out.

"Why did you do that?"

"It's a weed. No one likes these."

Liquid inside me became solid, as I turned into a piece of metal that couldn't move.

"It's a dandelion. You can make wishes on them. Dent de lion," I said. "Teeth of a lion." My jaw kept moving. I needed to keep talking.

"It doesn't even look like a lion," Mitzi said, twisting and shredding the yellow flower in her fingers.

"The leaves," I showed them. "They are the lion's teeth. But you've killed it and it was trying so hard to make a life here in the middle of nothing."

Sadness gathered and spilled out my eyes, and I was sure my tears would be silver drops. But only one fell, staining the concrete dark gray like a drop of rain.

"Harsh, Mitzi. What did it ever do to you?" Madison said, and put a hand on my shoulder. "She's not all bad. Not as bad as she used to be."

"Fuck it. C'mon. We're almost there," Mitzi yelled as she ran from us.

"Where?" I asked.

I wanted to be back in class, and my stomach felt jumpy, which made my neck and jaws wiggle.

"There." Madison pointed to a pale gray warehouse with black writing someone had sprayed along the bottom, writing I couldn't read. "Lucas's kitchen. You're our meal ticket to no-man's-land."

"What do those words say?" I asked.

"'Danger lies this way.'"

They laughed. I followed them around the back, past some dried weeds that had not been allowed to grow. A large metal bin leaked a smell that made my throat jiggle, and the dirty ground rose up and dropped quickly beneath me.

"You okay?" Madison asked.

I nodded. But I felt wobbly. I felt afraid of Mitzi and the way she'd grabbed the flower and destroyed it. I felt afraid of the gray metal colors on every building.

"This is a strange place for a make-over," I whispered.

"Think of it as a magic kingdom," Mitzi said.

She knocked, then pushed a white metal door open and shoved me inside. Darkness swallowed us. I stumbled as I stepped from bright daylight into the chamber of a hollow kingdom. I took three steps and stopped. My footsteps rang out with an empty song that was interrupted by the clang of the door as it slammed shut. A chemical smell attacked, and I covered my nose and mouth. There could be an endless canyon in front of me, or a brick wall. There was no way to know. I held my other hand out to feel for something in front of me and did not move except for my heart, which raced to get out. I could not find my voice to protest. My stomach twisted. My arms rose in front of me to protect me. I felt for Mitzi's arm and grabbed onto her. Where was my silver horn? Where were my four hooves to carry me away?

"Yo," she called into the darkness, braver than me.

A beam of light switched on and spread across the floor in the shape of something that my math book had tried to tell me about. The shape spread away from a flashlight that lay next to what might be a mattress. We walked toward it on the illuminated concrete.

"Yo," a voice called from the mattress.

"We brought you human sacrifice," Mitzi hissed.

My eyes adjusted, and I could see shapes overhead, rafters that stretched across the ceiling.

"Say something," Madison whispered.

"Tell him you want a make-over," Mitzi said, yanking hard on my arm.

My legs shook. I didn't want to breathe the darkness and that other smell. Paint thinner. I had smelled it in our kitchen when one of the workers poured it on a cloth to clean his hands. Thunder drummed around my heart.

"I can't breathe," I said. "I want to go home."

My voice came out slow and strange, like I spoke through a long tube full of cotton. My English book fell to the floor as I realized I had carried it all this way. I fell to my knees, bent forward, and without a silver horn to guide me I pressed my forehead to the cover as if that contact could open a doorway out of here.

"Leave her," a male voice yelled as it came toward us.

A stampede rose up inside, hooves striking dead earth where nothing would grow. I had to obey the swiftness trapped inside my body that surged in circles until I released it. I ran into the dark. I didn't know which way to go, where I could turn. I ran blindly. The flashlight tried to follow me but I doubled back and escaped its light. But it found me again. I turned, stepped on something that rolled under my foot, and twisted my ankle. The concrete came up fast as I fell into blackness.

Floor became ceiling.

Time slowed.

I could not move, could not get up. I needed to run, to find a bus with its ugly cloud of exhaust. I knew the ocean was far away and I wanted to be at the beach in the light. But I could not move, except to slide back down into darkness.

"Leave her," the voice yelled.

Alone. Lost in that dream where I call out for help, for my mother. No one comes. I am trapped and no one comes. Don't leave me, I try to say but my voice won't speak.

Don't. Leave me.

There are no words, no sounds I can make. No one to help me.

A serpent slid across me, waking me, breathing on my cheek. If I held still, it might think I was dead. Maybe I was. The serpent's cold skin draped itself across my forehead, made me flinch and open my eyes. A city skyline towered above me, a jagged row of deep greens and purples, defined by a heavy black outline. Then it changed from a city to a maze of pipes and conduit and machinery, as beautiful as it was grotesque.

Six flashlights balanced on the floor upright, lighting the wall where this city had been painted. The boy from my English class sat next to me on the mattress. This made no sense. The two of us floated on a raft, passing a city made of paint. For a moment, we were the only people in the world, and this was all that was left. Shadows in the rafters replaced the stars. Concrete replaced the ocean. He reached toward me, pulled a snake from my forehead that became a wet cloth.

"And we're back," he said.

A smile flashed from his eyes hidden behind his shaggy hair. I was not alone. My eyes pooled with relief.

"You wake up, find me and it makes you weep. FML."

"Is this your kingdom?"

"I don't have a kingdom. I am not a king. I'm an amateur."

Lucas picked up one of the flashlights and pointed it at the wall. Spray-painted buildings became bulging letters of words I could not read. Nordic gods emerged, frowned down on me; a warrior face became the side of a building above a freeway that blossomed into jagged waves that rolled into an underwater world of skate boarders whose hair floated away from their faces and whose limbs swerved through small silver bubbles that rose and collected in the limbs and muscles of Neptune who pointed his trident toward the top of a dark sky that disappeared into the ceiling.

"You painted this?"

He nodded.

"You see other worlds," I whispered.

"You see unicorns," he whispered back.

I tried to sit up, to stand, but searing pain shot up my leg.

"Don't move. I think you twisted your ankle," Lucas said, hurrying back to me, stumbling over a pile of metal cylinders that scattered across the floor.

"What's wrong with me?" I could barely breathe. "Where are Mitzi and Madison?"

"I ran them off. What exactly did they give you?"

I pulled the last sugar cube from my pocket. Lucas took it from me.

"Fuck," he said, and threw it into the darkness.

The word rang out from his mouth into the dark, a word Madison and Mitzi had made me know.

"Fuck," I said.

There was power in that word.

Lucas got up and kicked a metal cylinder away. It knocked into others all around the floor making empty cans of spray paint collide and roll until they settled. Lucas became quiet for a long time. Something he had let out to run wild came back to him. He sat down on the end of the mattress, and curled over his unlaced sneakers like a boy on a curb who'd lost something down a storm drain.

I didn't want sadness to descend on this little boy of him, but I was afraid of how he kicked the cans.

"Audrey, why do you hang out with them?"

"I don't have any other friends," I whispered.

"You can do better," he said. Then he slapped his forehead. "Idiot! God. I sound like my dad, telling you how to pick your friends. You choose who you want. Okay? Promise me that?"

I wanted water. I wanted to go home, but home felt like it was a million miles away and I had no idea how to get there. I'd never find the right bus.

My mouth turned to paper, and the rest of me became dust. Without Lucas seeing, I moved my hand to my cell phone, tucked in my pocket. My mother would come get me, but I couldn't tell her where I was because I didn't know. And she might never let me walk home from school again. She might never let me go to school again. I would probably never have another adventure with Mitzi and Madison. And there would be horrible tutors at the dining table.

Then Lucas leaned over me, his face moving toward mine. I stopped breathing. I closed my eyes. He put his lips on my forehead where no one had ever kissed me because of my horn.

But I let him. His lips were soft. Warm. My heart did not race. It stood still and listened. When he sat up, I could still feel gentleness where he left a kiss.

"Come on. I'll take you home," he whispered.

Home wasn't what I wanted anymore. I wanted to stay on this raft and float below his painted city. He put his paint-covered hand on my arm and pulled me to my feet.

Eve 11

Something heavy slammed to the kitchen floor downstairs, violence reverberating through the rest of the house. A beam, a body, something with mass had crashed in an unintended way. Eve listened for sounds indicating injury or accident. But she only heard Nick whistling.

"Whole Lotta Love."

She turned to the mirror, catching a glimpse of the red asterisk punctuating the black cotton t-shirt she wore. Chili Peppers. The choice had been a conscious one when she pulled it from the hanger that morning. Would he respond to this, or to what she was about to ask? She lugged two more bags of clothing to the front door. Lifeless suits from her former career in concert promotion lay at her feet. Downstairs, Nick built out the cabinets, filling the house with an overpowering hum, making her long for sounds of an arena sound check. Audrey's longing glance toward the kitchen when Nick wasn't there gave her away. Eve understood the anticipation, that thrill, of the excitement he ushered into their house. Other girls, like Cheryl's daughter, were already exploring their sexuality, changing their worlds. Chances of Audrey doing that on her own were slim. Eventually, some jerk might take advantage of the situation. Nick was broke from the asbestos setback, he needed a reliable truck, and he was sweet. He understood the charm of Audrey's childish enthusiasm and of the world she built around herself. He had kissed her and confessed to it, as if that were the end of it. But it could be the beginning.

She went to her closet where vintage t-shirts rebelled and elbowed their way back into the footlights, insisting on release, demanding to be worn. She knelt down, dug for the gin box, and extracted the shoebox buried under the blouse and vest she'd held back. She had not been prepared for the strength of that bond between herself and her baby girl, the intimacy they shared, the protective closeness motherhood had awakened in Eve.

The selflessness.

If her own mother had felt some fraction of this force, she had not responded to it. Daphne, the artist who did not understand the art of nurturing another human being.

Like a crowd at the foot of the stage, the concert t-shirts surrounded her, swayed on their hangers as she rose with the box in hand and brushed against them. That period of her life when she was at the helm, harnessing the wind and moving herself in a direction she chose came rushing back. Her rock arena adventures offered a way out of loneliness, that same isolation that seemed to trap Audrey in those dreams that made her weep. An introduction to sexuality could help her let go of childhood obsessions, those unicorns with their sticky-sweet beauty and sharp horns.

Eve tried to think through the possibilities once more, the worst-case scenario, the down side. But her focus kept drifting back to Audrey's safe passage. The kind of desire Nick had stirred in her might be the only force strong enough to pull Audrey from the enchantment cast by a world of unicorns.

Downstairs, shoebox tucked under her arm, she passed the open front door where she could see Fred and Isaac in the shade of the olive tree on the front lawn. Nick was alone in the kitchen, measuring and marking the walls.

"Just who I want to see," he said, tilting his head a bit and smiling like he was waiting for her.

"Me, too," she said.

"I have questions about the island. I'm running electrical for two sets of outlets, but it might be good to have a third on the backside."

"There's another modification I'd like to discuss," Eve said, setting the box on his worktable.

Her heart raced. She had not propositioned a young man in so long. Her skin felt electric under the Chili Peppers t-shirt.

"The asbestos has set you back. Quite a bit," she started.

"That's not your problem. Your husband made that clear."

"And you don't have a reliable truck, which is critical in your line of work."

"Again, not your problem."

"No, it isn't my problem. But I do have one I think you can solve, and it may help you with your own circumstances."

She lifted the lid off the shoebox, revealing stacks of bills. Hundreds, twenties, everything.

"I'd like to hire you," she said.

"You already did," he laughed, those blues eyes not seeing what was coming.

He was California stunning. He was honest. She wanted to trace his jawbone, run her hand through his hair. She inhaled the breath that would form the next words she spoke.

"I'd like to hire you to be with Audrey."

He smiled and let the tape measure snap back inside itself. "To babysit?"

"To date her," she said. "Not just to date her. To be intimate. To introduce her into the world of sexuality."

His smile faded.

"Don't decide yet. Let me finish. She's only ever been a child in this world, needing me to show her everything. You've seen her. She's so far from other girls her age. She needs an experience that makes her want to live in the real world and not the world of unicorns and rainbows. I'm her mother. I know her better than anyone. She needs someone to show her how to be a woman. How to experience a part of herself she's neglected. She's naïve and vulnerable. You've seen this. You know what I'm talking about."

"Whoa, Mrs. Tilden. If I take that cash and accept your offer, it makes me—"

"A tutor. A teacher. A guide. Not unlike hiring someone to help her with math. You would be doing me—us—a huge service." Eve blushed at her words, at what that "service" suggested, but she kept going. "Knowing that she was with someone trustworthy and careful is invaluable. I know in some way you care for her. And," she paused and tapped the shoebox, "this will keep you from going broke on this job. You'd be doing this because you care about what happens to her, and because you could keep your head above water on this remodel."

A lovely affair, a safe way for Audrey to find her own sexuality, a bridge from here to womanhood.

"She's underage. It's a felony. What about your husband?"

Carl wouldn't understand that this was just like hiring a math tutor. But she was fairly certain he would accept Audrey's interest in someone as handsome and kind as Nick, who had become part of her home life.

"He doesn't know. I want to keep it that way. Wait. Don't leave. Hear me out. I need this for her. I've tried everything else I can think of to help. I refuse to medicate her, to send her to specialists. I won't do that. Audrey is trapped in herself. Watch her. She's tortured sometimes by her own fears. I'm asking you to help me, to help her. I'm taking a risk, too. My daughter, my marriage. That should be enough insurance for you that no one is pressing charges against anyone."

Eve moved away from the money and stood by the large window frame that had no glass. One more step would drop her six feet into to the backyard.

"How many weeks do you have left on this kitchen?" she asked.

"No more than three."

"How about if you give it some thought," she said. "Get a little bit closer to her. See if it makes sense for you, and for her. Maybe show her a little of what she's missing. See how she responds."

"And let's suppose she and I, you know. After that then, what?"

"After that, the kitchen should be finished. You can go your way."

Nick ran his fingers through his hair, clenched and unclenched his jaw.

The doorbell rang, and she went to answer so she didn't see if he picked up the shoebox. Let him think about the job, let him be with the cash on the worktable.

Cheryl Moncrief stepped through the open doorway, a whirl of energy and color and salutation.

"Goodwill," she said, bright and friendly.

Eve didn't understand until Cheryl indicated the bag of unwanted clothes piled by the door.

"Oh, sort of. I've found a thrift store."

"Look at this," Cheryl said, stooping to pinch a sleeve and to dig a bit deeper. "Valentino. Is that Paloma Picasso? I can't wait to see what you've traded up to."

Eve looked down at her Chili Peppers t-shirt.

"What a great idea," Cheryl added. "I have a few bags that have been sitting in my closet forever. I was going to put them on the porch and call the army."

"Why don't I take yours when I take mine? I was going to go right now. I'll follow you home and get them," Eve said, stepping toward the door to bring Cheryl's visit to a close.

"That would be fantastic," Cheryl said. "What a generous offer, and I suppose if you're going, then okay." But as she spoke, Cheryl walked further into the house. "But come by tomorrow, I'll leave them on the porch. Oh, look. Let's see your remodel. I love looking at the underside of a remodel. And I'm so sorry for not calling first, but I took a chance. I was spontaneous and – well, hello. You must be Eve's contractor."

Eve hurried after Cheryl to the kitchen where Nick knelt over the beams that cantilevered above the slope of the yard. The shoebox on the worktable was gone. He stood, wiped a hand on his jeans and extended it to Cheryl.

"My god," she said. "This is visionary."

Cheryl winked at Eve. Uncertainty rippled through the air between the triangle the three of them formed; Eve searching to understand Cheryl's innuendo, Nick shifting as if he might turn and simply run, and Cheryl correcting her lipstick with her little finger.

"Nick, this is Cheryl."

"I hope the pleasure isn't all mine, but I'll bet it is," Cheryl murmured, not letting go of Nick's hand. "I'm so glad I stopped by."

"I guess you're here about the photos," Eve said. "Come this way. They're in Carl's office." She motioned Cheryl to follow, and glanced again at the vacant surface of the saw table. Nick stepped away, stared at his boots, and then turned to consult the blueprint.

"I'm going to have to think twice about the qualifications of my next contractor," Cheryl said, trailing after Eve to Carl's study.

"Oh. Ha, ha," Eve said.

"Listen, Madison has been telling me of Audrey's interest in a boy."

"Madison?"

"Girls talk. Oh, they talk. It's cute. I think Madison feels like she's doing some good helping Audrey find her way in that department."

Eve looked back at Nick, who moved through the kitchen with pieces of lumber.

"What did Audrey tell her?"

"There's a boy at school. Madison says he's interested in Audrey. Has she not mentioned anything?"

"Nothing. What's his name?"

"I don't remember. He's new. Madison doesn't know much about him. I think it's just a crush. But you never know where it could go."

"You never do," Eve said.

Her proposal to Nick had better timing than she realized. Eve led Cheryl into Carl's office, into the midst of Daphne's photographs. He had made more visits, acquired more photos that "needed to be cleaned." Black-and-white landscapes with variations of fences running through them leaned against wall and desk. The only thing missing was the old woman lying in her chrome-railed bed.

"My god. This is fantastic," Cheryl said. "Don't you just want to hang them all over your house? The room just hums with her brilliance. Can't you feel it?"

The only humming Eve heard came from the kitchen.

"I'm ready," Cheryl said. "Show me the Daphne Delfin no one has ever seen."

Cheryl closed her eyes and waited like a child.

"These?" Eve asked.

The triptych of a stone fence had been stacked on Carl's desk. She spread them out.

"You should be using gloves," Cheryl admonished. "The oils from your hands leave a stain. Oh my. Oh, these are something."

For a long time, Cheryl stood in silence, raising her hands to cover her mouth, lowering them, inhaling and exhaling, her reverence for the huge stone fence that ran from one photo to the next overpowering her chatty self. Then she nodded, agreeing with some internal dialogue. It was hard to imagine Audrey with a crush on a boy from school, or a boy with a crush on her. Her behavior around Nick contradicted this.

"She hasn't said a thing," Eve said quietly.

"Who?"

"I mean Daphne. She hasn't positively identified the location."

"So we'll ask."

"It isn't that simple. She's not herself anymore."

"This is definitely Daphne Delfin. It has her sensibility all over it. The way the fence defines borders and breaches them, from one photo to the next. Brilliant. And a triptych, even though it's a new direction for her, the work comments on its own form and content."

"Or she couldn't fit the whole fence into the viewfinder," Eve said.

"Think of it. These are the only existing prints. We need the negatives. That would be proof. Can you find out? Can you look through her files? This will be the crown jewel in the exhibit. We can unveil her undiscovered work. The press will come. Buyers will come. And they'll bid. I need those negatives, proof these are hers, which I don't doubt. The triptych will have its own separate wall. And how many others should we hang?"

She looked around and poked the air with her index finger as she counted each photograph in the office.

"If I had a tape measure, I could solve a few problems," Cheryl said. "And I know just where I can find one. Yoo hoo," she called and headed to the kitchen.

An electric current crossed Eve's arms and throat, making her legs move in a hurry after Cheryl, not wanting her to be anywhere near Nick, not wanting her to flirt with him in any way, even if it were just to borrow a tape measure. Eve cut her off before the doorway, grabbed the tape measure from the top of the gray toolbox and ushered Cheryl out of the kitchen. Nick had stopped the table saw and was about to lift his safety goggles when Eve waved her hand not to bother.

Cheryl looked astonished by the way Eve had sprung to life but followed her back to the office. After Cheryl had measured several photographs, she slid the metal tape back in its orange housing.

"You know," she said, dragging out the 'o'. "If I could take a photograph with me, I could get a better sense of how the show will hang."

"Absolutely. Take two," Eve said, blindly choosing two prints, handing her the heavy frames, shoving them into her arms.

"Let Daphne know that I promise to be careful. And let me know if you turn up the negative. I'm thrilled to have her attend the show in person. Let her know that. It will guarantee press."

"Oh, Jesus. That's really. Fantastic. Carl will be thrilled."

The saw resumed as if it knew they had both run out of anything else to say. Eve practically pulled Cheryl out the front door and helped her load the framed photos into the back seat of her white BMW. After Cheryl drove away, Eve made her way to the kitchen where Nick stood over the long yellow strip of tape measure.

"Look, I can't make this work," he said, his shoulders dropping with resignation.

Her offer was being rejected. She had been foolish. He was right. None of this made sense. The herd of unicorns pronounced victory over Audrey's capture.

"I understand," she said, her voice coming out with calculated calm.

"The cabinetmaker must have measured the counters wrong. There's no way to put in the Thermador you want. If we bring the carpenter back, you'll be looking at an additional delay of a month," he said. "But if we can find a range with closer specs, we can create a molding made out of the same cabinet material to cover any gaps."

We.

The word lingered in the air with the smell of raw wood and ozone from the drill. He was discussing a kitchen range. He was not declining the deal. He was not reaching into his pocket to give her back the money.

"It should accommodate a standard range," he said.

"You accept my offer?" Eve asked.

He set down the drill and went about changing out the bit.

"I get what you're doing. There were so many times when I wished someone could have explained to me how to give a girl an orgasm. I used to think it was because I was the only one who didn't know what I was doing. So I get it. And, yeah, there are some things that really do rock your world at her age."

Once he had the new bit tightened down, he squeezed the drill and made it spin.

"There are pros and cons for her if the remodel gets delayed," Eve said.

"Find me that range," Nick said. "We'll make it work."

"Thank you." She nodded.

He went back to the frame of the cabinets, a wooden sketch of drawers and cupboards, a gap where a refrigerator and range would live. Drill and two-by-four argued with each other, preventing further conversation. The phone rang, and she moved away from the noise in the kitchen.

"This is the absence line. Your student has been marked absent for one or more periods."

The robotic message went on with instructions about what Eve should do to excuse her student, but she didn't listen, returned the receiver to the phone. This was a mistake, a misdialed number, a computer error. Audrey wasn't absent. Eve had dropped her off at school that morning. Some teacher must have overlooked her quiet, invisible daughter and marked her absent. Audrey would be home in an hour and she'd ask her about it then. But on the way to her room, she stopped at Audrey's door. It was closed, which was unusual. Audrey insisted it be left open so the herd on the shelf could be free to wander.

She opened the door. The unicorns were lined up at the edge of the shelf, as if they had wandered over as far as they could. They faced Audrey's bed, staring at someone lying there, curled up asleep.

It took Eve a moment to recognize her daughter, hair clumped and clinging to her pale face.

"Audrey?"

She didn't respond. Her breathing was shallow. Eve took a step toward the bed and stubbed her toe on Audrey's English book. She sat down carefully and placed the back of her hand on Audrey's forehead. Damp, clammy, no fever. To be sure, she leaned over and touched her lips against the same spot, the way she'd learned to measure a fever when Audrey was an infant. Audrey did not pull away as she might whenever someone kissed her forehead.

Audrey slept deeply, without any indication that she knew Eve was present.

"Hey," Eve whispered.

No response.

She lifted Audrey's wrist to check her pulse. Audrey pulled her arm away, turned from Eve in a leave-me-alone gesture. When had she come home? It was as if Audrey had materialized in her room, transported from the lunchtime warfare at school. There were no answers here, only questions.

"Audrey," Eve said more firmly.

Audrey stirred, gathered the smoothness of her face in pain and raised her arms to hold her head.

"When did you get home? What happened?"

"My head. Please make this stop."

The construction downstairs whined and screamed and banged up through the floor. Two tears slipped from Audrey's eyes, diamonds of pain. She clutched her head in agony.

"Oh, sweetness. Let me get you something. Some pain reliever."

"I'm going to throw up."

"I'll be right back."

She had seen a headache induce nausea in Audrey, overwhelm her as if her body sought any way possible to expel the discomfort. A rush of sympathetic misery flooded Eve.

In the kitchen, the howl of the drill made it impossible to speak. Eve waved her arms to get Nick's attention.

"Stop," she pleaded. Fred and Isaac stood over a band saw and shut it off. "I need you to stop, please."

Nick lifted the safety goggles onto his head.

"Did you see Audrey come in earlier? Did she stop and talk to you?"

"I didn't know she was home."

"She must have gone straight upstairs to bed. She's not well. I need you to finish for the day."

Nick dropped his arms in exasperation but turned to Fred and Isaac. "Es necessario a tener silencio por una hora."

Eve hurried back to Audrey with a glass of water and two tablets. Audrey flinched at the sight of them.

"Pain reliever. Take it."

Audrey seemed to finally comprehend, and almost drank the entire glass of water until Eve pulled it away. "Slowly, or your stomach will reject everything. Take it easy."

She lay back down, her gaze fixed on Eve.

"Audrey, did you have a headache at school?"

Audrey nodded.

"And you just left?"

Audrey nodded again. Eve was vaguely aware that she was supplying answers by way of her questions.

"Did anything else happen?"

Audrey closed her eyes, looked as if she might be asleep again.

"You can't just leave. You need to go to the nurse's office. Use your cell phone for emergencies. I don't care about school rules. I will always come and get you. I sent Nick home for the rest of the day so you could have quiet."

She wailed and collapsed back onto her pillow, her feelings for him so transparent even when she didn't feel well.

"He'll be back tomorrow." A hopeful look on Audrey's face inspired Eve to keep going. "Daddy and I have to look at ovens tonight and I don't want to leave you alone. If you go with us, you can stay home tomorrow if you don't feel well."

Audrey wiped her tears with the edge of the pink sheet and whispered "ok" to the wall.

She and Carl walked with Audrey between them from the parking lot to the massive warehouse. Audrey's careful steps made the three of them walk slowly, her head still fragile. They made their way through a maze of ready-made kitchens, as if a customer could walk in, point to one, and take it home. The first offered a game of chess, with its black-and-white tile and black-and-white cabinets daring you to live in full color. Carl went right to it. If he could, Eve thought, he would hop the fence and live in her mother's photographs, where everything was black-and-white. Audrey sat down at the table and put her face in her hands.

"She should have stayed home," he said.

"I can't leave her home alone when she's sick, and we have to take care of this."

Eve walked into the next kitchen, country French overrun with roosters. Carl followed. The rafters and air ducts above them were a million miles away, no attempt to hide their industrial function except distance.

"Look at her," Carl said. "She doesn't feel good."

Audrey remained at the table, her head pillowed by her forearms.

"I'm aware of that. You make it sound like I have no clue. I know everything about her. And I also know she can manage to go with us if we don't drag this errand into something that takes longer than it should. And if we don't take care of this, there will be a three-week delay, and that will make a bigger mess."

Carl opened an oven door. "Let's get this one and be done with it."

"That's the one that doesn't fit."

"Did you bring the new measurements?"

Eve searched her purse, but the slip of paper Nick had written out sat on the dining table at home. If she'd left Audrey there, she could have phoned her and had her read the numbers.

"You're kidding, right?" Carl said, and slammed the oven door.

"Oh, like you never forget anything."

"Not really."

"How about those concert tickets?"

"That's different, not important."

"It's important to me."

"I'll get them."

"Carl, I try to take care of everything. Everything."

"What do you think I do all day? You think I don't contribute?"

"I never said that."

Strangers glanced in their direction. She felt like part of a floor model, a kitchen complete with domestic argument. There should have been a window at the sink with a sublime view of a garden. But there was only another kitchen.

Carl followed her into it, held up his phone. "Cheryl sent a text. You didn't tell me she dropped by."

"You two text?"

"She says the press will come. She wants to be sure Daphne will be there," Carl read.

All the model kitchens collided. The combination of Daphne and the press had to be a formula for disaster.

"And," he continued, "She wants the negatives for that triptych."

"I'm going to hand that chore to you, Carl."

The chair in the black-and-white kitchen where Audrey had been sitting was empty.

"Where's Audrey?" Eve asked.

They both looked around, checked the nearby kitchens.

"I'll take this half of the store," Carl said.

Eve raced through her half of the maze, calling Audrey's name as if she'd lost a five-year-old.

"Can I help you?" a security guard asked at an intersection of lamps and trash containers.

"I've lost my daughter."

"Not a problem," he said, raising his two-way radio. "What's she wearing? Where'd you last see her?"

"A pink top with flowers on it. We were in the checkerboard kitchen."

He relayed this into his radio.

"How old is she?"

Eve hesitated. "Seventeen."

His eyes widened, and it took a moment for him to formulate his next question. "Is she, you know, special? Like special ed?"

Audrey 11

People passed through the fake living room as if I wasn't curled up on the couch, holding my head with my arms. The fist inside my skull clenched tight and punched at the back of my eyes. My mother and father didn't notice that I had to leave the black and white kitchen while they argued over ranges and ovens. I needed to lie down, even though this wasn't home and the couch I chose smelled like plastic. I closed my eyes to erase the people who came and went, but the dark warehouse with its tangled images blossomed on the underside of my eyelids. My arms and legs remembered lying on the mattress raft. I wanted to open the doorway Nick and I made when we kissed. But Lucas had left a kiss on my forehead where no one was allowed. The pressure under my eyes drummed louder, trapped me wherever I was. A hand on me felt gentle and cool, quieting the ache in my head. I opened my eyes to see my mother kneeling next to me. Behind her, a guard in a uniform stood with his arms folded.

"That's exactly what I'd do if I didn't feel good," he said. "Lie down on the couch."

He laughed but his squawking radio cut him off. He spoke to it, told it that they'd found the missing girl. Me. My mother thanked him, helped me get up and walk to the front of the store. We had to pass through four living rooms and five bedrooms that had no house.

"You take her to the car," my mother said when we found my father. "I'll go buy the stove."

Lit by the white-blue light in the front seat, Daddy stared into his phone. He clicked the keypad to answer messages that made him shake or nod his glowing face.

"When did you first kiss Mom?" I asked.

He looked at me, and then looked far away through the windshield, as if he could see a long time ago.

"We were at a concert. Wow. I don't remember which one."

"Did you love her when you first kissed her?"

"I did, but I didn't know it yet. Why?"

"I don't know who I love yet."

He laughed. "There's no hurry," he said.

Then the buzzing glow from my father's palm pulled him back into that world and he didn't say anything more. I moved into the middle of the back seat, making room for someone on each side of me.

In the morning, my mother came in to get me out of bed.

"Are you better?" she asked, touching my forehead with her lips. "Do you want to stay home? I think maybe you should."

My heart leapt over the railing that school days made around me, but I was careful not to get out of bed and run.

"Go back to sleep, my love," she said.

I lay there for a long time, only getting up to bring Blue under the covers with me. Stiff legs and sharp hooves poked me, so I put him down on the floor to balance on his rear legs. He wanted back up, but I left him on the floor. My cell phone rang and displayed Mitzi's number. My empty seat in English class must have made her worry for me, and her worry colored my room yellow like the sun coming out from behind a cloud.

I had friends, just like my mother wanted.

"Are you a rat?" Mitzi demanded.

"A rat? I'm a—"

"Did you tell anyone about your adventure yesterday? Did you tell your mother about your trip?"

"No. But I thought you were going to give me a make-over."

"Didn't Lucas give you the make-over? Don't you feel like a different person?"

I looked at my arms and legs, closed my eyes and listened to my heart.

"No."

"But now your boyfriend is real."

I shrugged, felt stupid because I didn't know what she meant. I needed to go downstairs and see Nick, see if anything had changed. I got out of bed and reached under the mattress for one of the lost items – the hammer – and went to the kitchen. Pieces of wood had risen out of the floor and become outlines of counters and cabinets. The walls were still naked plywood, waiting to be covered, but I liked the wood all around me. Fred and Isaac lifted a huge glass window toward the rectangular hole in the wall. Nick called to them which way to go, how to place it. When it was in and secured, the room was finally sealed off from the breeze and the cool air and the nighttime that snuck in. The house had closed up. The outside would no longer be part of our furniture, our meals. I felt safe, protected from harm. I followed Nick to the backyard to see how it looked from the other side. On the grass, I let go of the weight of the hammer in my hand, and it landed on my toe, making me wail in pain.

"What happened?" Nick asked, and raced over to me. Then he saw the hammer near my bare foot.

"I stubbed my toe," I said.

He picked up the hammer and studied it, but did not throw his arms around me like before.

"Is this some kind of game?" he asked.

I nodded.

He sat down on the bottom step of the deck, his knees making right angles to the grass. I wanted my legs to be close to his legs, so I sat next to him and made my legs bend the same way. He let out all the air in his lungs so I secretly inhaled some of his breath.

"This game, Audrey," he said. "I don't really know the rules."

I shrugged.

"Aren't you home because you're sick?" he asked.

I nodded. Then I shook my head and let out the breath I was holding.

"Faking?" he smiled. "I used to do that."

I wanted to move closer to him, but he stood up.

"Back to work," he said, and squeezed my toe with his warm hand.

My heart flew up to the sun until I made it sit still inside me as he walked away. I ran upstairs and slid out of my nightgown. Instead of rushing to put clothes on, I walked naked to the unicorns and the window and back to the dresser. Jeans and a flowery shirt, then back downstairs. Once in a while, he passed through the kitchen doorway, carrying planks of wood, dragging a ladder or an electric cord. I sat at the dining table, spread my fingers out on the wood then cupped them into hooves, then spread them out again. I couldn't see the other two workers, but their radio played music made of bright colors, and an announcer rattled out Spanish words like they were spicy. After a while, Nick stopped and looked at me. I stared back at his messy hair and tan arms.

"You want to go down to the beach with me at lunchtime?" he asked from the kitchen.

I nodded and stood and pranced in place. Then I made myself stand still. He undid his tool belt, dropped it next to the floor and ran his hand through his hair. He said something to the two men over their radio, and I followed him to the curb. Instead of his old beat up truck, a new one was parked at the curb. It was shiny and nice, but it was like every other new truck that didn't have many dents. It smelled like carpet cleaner and plastic. The dashboard had no cups or slips of paper. A pale blue surfboard wrapped in a towel lay in the truck bed. I climbed into the cab and pulled the door closed. Nick did the same on his side and twisted the key to make the engine purr.

"I'm still not used to it starting the first time."

"What happened to your old truck?"

"Probably became scrap metal and sailed to China."

We wound down the streets that took us to the ocean. I put my hand on the seat between us in case Nick wanted to hold it. But he kept his hands on the steering wheel. I looked all the way to the horizon, but the canvas of the ocean was only decorated with a single sailboat.

"I don't see your old truck floating to China," I said.

Nick laughed, put his hand on mine and squeezed my fingers. I held very still so he would keep his hand there. But he didn't. He let go to grab the steering wheel hard, making a U-turn across the highway so the ocean was on my side. Then he pulled over and parked above the beach.

"Little peelers, but they're doable," he said. "Mind if a catch a few?"

I shrugged, not sure how anyone caught peelers or what they were. He got out and yanked a black skin made of rubber from the truck bed. Then he took off his shirt and then his jeans. Madison would probably tell me that if he was going to stand naked next to the highway in nothing but his underwear, then I was invited to watch. But he had swim shorts on under his jeans. After he zipped up the black skin, he unwrapped the surfboard, tucked it under his arm and walked around to my window.

"Do you want to come down to the beach?"

I followed him as he balanced his board and made his way down a dirt path to the sand. The waves turned from blue to white, rushed toward the shore and pulled away, only to be chased back to the sand again.

Nick turned back to me. "Here's the key, if you want to go back to the truck."

I didn't want to go back to the truck. I dug my feet into the warm sand and sat down. Nick walked into the waves, then he lay on his board and glided across the water. When a wall of white came at him, he dove under and the ocean swallowed him. But he reappeared on the other side. He was like a sea otter, a fish, a dolphin. I waved to him, but he didn't see me, and I tried not to blink so I wouldn't lose sight of him. But he became just another surfer among the small black shapes that bobbed beyond the waves. Once or twice I thought I saw his blue board, but I was never sure. The key dug into my hand as surfers slid down waves, peelers, and raced ahead of the foam. Further out, the sun danced on the water. Before me, the sand whispered to take off my shoes. The wet sand felt cool, and it was harder than the dry dunes where I had been sitting. The slope of the beach spread away from me, inviting me to play a game where I ran toward the water and ran away before it could get me. My feet grew numb as I raced down and back. Then I just ran alongside the water, looking far ahead at how long the shore stretched out before me. When I turned around to see how far I'd gone, the surfers were gone. The truck was no longer parked by the road because the road had become a row of tall houses. I'd run too far.

I raced back the way I'd come until I saw the truck, and found Nick standing next to it, pulling off his sealskin.

"Where did you go?" he asked.

I pointed. "The sand told me to run so I did."

"Whatever. Can I have the key?"

I held up my shoes, one in each hand, but there was no key.

"You're kidding. Right? You're playing a joke? Check your pockets," he said, frowning. My pockets didn't have anything either. "Shit. Fuck. Hell." He looked down at the beach, the miles of sand that might be hiding his key, the water that might have taken it away.

"I'm sorry," I whispered.

"You're just a child. This is— I can't— Wait here for me. Oh, fuck," he said. "Don't cry."

I wanted to tell him that I wasn't a child, but I followed him down to the beach like I was.

"Maybe where I was sitting," I offered.

We looked down at the beach, but there was no sign of where I'd been sitting. I traced the steps I'd taken down to the water, walking slowly and carefully, examining every footprint and dune for my own path, but they all looked the same. Every stick and half-buried piece of trash became valuable for a quick moment.

"It's like we're on a treasure hunt," I said, hoping he would smile.

"We're fucked if we don't find the key."

Near the water, I searched for where I'd sat down to take off my shoes but the water had erased everything.

Then I stepped on something sharp.

"Ow," I said, and dug his key out of the sand under my foot.

"Hell yeah," he said, grabbed the key then put his arms around me and squeezed me hard. His skin and t-shirt were damp and cold.

"You smell like the ocean," I said.

"Sorry for yelling."

"I'm not a child."

"I know. That was a stupid thing to say. I hated it when my mom used to say that to me."

"Listen. Can you hear the sand whisper?" I asked.

He listened. "It says you can run fast. But I can run faster."

I took off running. I was faster and he howled that he was going to get me, which made my legs move harder. I turned so he couldn't get me but the soft sand was hard to run in, and I sank. Then he reached out, caught my arm and pulled me back to him. We both stumbled and fell, and slowly his kiss met my kiss.

Nick became Mitzi and Madison hovering over me, Mitzi's mouth on mine the way Nick's was now. Then just as Nick had become Mitzi, she became Lucas floating next to me on the raft of his mattress in the dark warehouse. There were too many people in this kiss. Nick's lips pressed against mine and then his tongue slipped between my lips. I opened my eyes and pulled away but Nick put his hand on the back of my head.

"Try this," he whispered.

My tongue was shy and when it touched his, I tried to break our kiss apart, but again he held me until his tongue found mine, and the dance between our mouths drew me down into a world beneath the sand where heat and darkness erased our separate forms and shapes. He moaned from somewhere deep in his chest, a sound that vibrated against me until I also moaned. Nick's hands roamed across my pink flowered top, and I held his wrist but I didn't pull his hand away. After a long time, he sat up and looked at me.

"Hey," he said. "Do I know you?"

"I don't believe so."

"I don't either," he said, as he looked at the horizon and flicked some sand on my leg. "What are we doing here?" he asked, suddenly serious.

"We were looking for your key."

"Oh, shit," he said, frantically raking through the sand where he sat.

"You're kidding. Check your pockets," I said, exactly the way he had done at the truck.

He stopped and looked at me, and then at the shape of something in the pocket of his jeans. My hand went to it, but there was another shape near by. I put my hand on it.

"You're a beautiful girl, Audrey," he said. "Not like anyone I know."

He moved my hand away, kissed my fingers and then my lips. I kept my eyes open this time, memorizing the curve of his eyelashes, the smell of the wind that had to bend itself around of the two us, the feel of his hand on the back of my head.

"Is that your boner?" I asked. "Can I see it?"

When I tried to touch that mysterious shape again, he moved back.

"You are way ahead of me, Audrey."

"That's because you're slow," I said, getting to my feet. "To the truck. Ready? Go."

I got a head start, but he passed me. But I wanted him to be ahead of me so I could watch his arms and legs move as he raced across the sand.

Eve 12

There were no bags of clothes on Cheryl's porch. Eve felt foolish for having volunteered to be an errand girl but now she could skip this. If Cheryl asked, she could tell her she had tried, and it would be Cheryl's fault for having forgotten to leave anything for her. But a small opening between door and frame drew her toward it. She pressed the solid oak with her palm and it gave way.

"Hello," she called, and rang the doorbell.

No answer. She walked in.

"Cheryl? You home?"

The house absorbed her voice.

"Cheryl?" she called again, her voice louder with alarm. "Everything okay?"

The house was huge, twice the size of Eve's. She headed toward the kitchen out of habit. Eying and evaluating counters and tile and layout for the last year had become an automatic response to kitchens everywhere. This one had chrome surfaces like a professional kitchen but the Italian tile and mahogany countertops gave it intimacy, too. The impracticality of expensive wood, the constant worry over ruining its surface with every snack or drink or meal placed there weighed itself against the sophistication of its texture and color.

"My god," Eve said to the wood-burning pizza oven she hadn't seen at first.

Brick built into the stucco wall. A wine collection and a set of wine glasses hung nearby for those evenings when the family made pizza together. Eve had never considered a pizza oven.

Where would it go?

In her house, they would have to pick up a phone if they wanted pizza. She started back to the foyer where three bags of clothing sat beneath the curving staircase. Had Cheryl meant for her to come in? Something upstairs thudded against the floor. Her heart responded, beating recklessly in alarm. There might be an intruder. Cheryl might be unable to answer the doorbell. Eve fished out her cell phone and held it ready to call for help.

"Cheryl?" she called for a third time.

With a few steps, Eve ascended the stairs and moved through the hallway. The guestroom was untouched. The master bedroom was immaculate, accented with matching vase and throw pillows. Like a ghost, Eve moved down the hallway, passing bathroom and home office. Madison's room, the last doorway on the right, was filled with signs of a struggle. The back of Eve's neck went cold and prickly. Clothes, shoes, books, belts all strewn across every horizontal surface. Was that a body sticking out from the bed? No, only sheets and blankets half twisted off. A chair contained a pile of sweaters. The dresser was cluttered with hair accessories and lotions. Pairs of shoes divorced from one another had fled across the carpet. Eve started to close the door to Madison's room, seal off its chaos from the rest of the flawless house when a large orange cat leapt from sweaters on the chair and darted past her.

"Jesus," she said, putting a hand to her racing heart.

The front door closed downstairs, making her heart accelerate. The bedroom mirror reflected a panicked woman in a U2 t-shirt with car keys in hand. She hurried away from the mess.

"Cheryl?" she called, racing the way she'd come.

Cheryl looked up at her from the bottom of the stairs. "You scared the life out of me," she said. "What on earth are you doing up there?"

"The door was open. Then I heard what I guess was the cat. I called out, but you didn't answer, so I thought something might be wrong."

"There's nothing wrong. I had to run an errand, and left the door open for you to get the bags. Which are right here. Never mind that. I just came from the gallery. We're going to need to build out some walls. But it won't be too difficult. Will your mother be up for coming in to talk about placement? I want her to be happy."

Eve came the rest of the way down to the landing to Cheryl, who just wanted her mother to be happy.

"It's going to be amazing," Cheryl bubbled. "I can't wait to surround the gallery with her work. Have you found the negatives?"

Eve's heart slowed to the pulse of concrete. She picked up two of the plastic bags of clothes.

"I haven't had time to see her. With the kitchen remodel and all. In fact, I need to get back," she said. "Audrey stayed home sick."

Cheryl followed her with the second bag of her cast-off clothing. "Madison says she's been spending time with her. Isn't that cute? Which reminds me, some of Madison's clothes are in the bags in case Audrey is interested in updating her look. Or just having something new. Well, I mean, new to her."

"I'll let her know," Eve said.

More than likely Audrey would sniff the fabric, and its strange scent would make her run in circles. Eve carried the two bags back to her car, relieved to have extracted herself from the house. She had essentially walked into Cheryl Moncrief's house during broad daylight and snooped around. At her car, she opened one of Cheryl's garbage bags and pulled out a top. Burn-out black velvet, sheer, risqué. One of Madison's discards. A blouse that could make a girl look like a woman. She sniffed it herself, dropped it back into the bag, and was seized with regret about this deal with Nick. He might not understand Audrey well enough. No one did, except Eve. She needed to get home, to see her baby girl. Delivering Cheryl's clothes to the thrift shop could wait.

When she returned, her house was also empty. For a moment, she stood in the doorway and observed the silence, a thief intruding again, a stranger eavesdropping on signs of someone else's life. Audrey must have gone out with Nick. Carl was at work. With burn-out velvet blouse in hand, she wandered through rooms and peered through empty doorways, an observer of the artifacts of an early-century suburban dwelling. Audrey's room was immaculate, every article in place. She opened a dresser drawer with pink and purple cotton t-shirts folded and exact. The black velvet top with its low neckline did not belong, but she folded it and placed it there, a surprise, an offering, an accessory for some future occasion. The unicorns observed this without comment, frozen in their poses on the shelf.

"Boo," she said to them, but they did not scare.

A truck pulled up to the house and she closed the drawer. From the window, she could see Audrey get out and wait so she could walk next to Nick. Strands of their laughter wove together as they entered the front door. A surge of confidence filled Eve as a sense of Audrey's well-being and safety became her own. This was the right choice. He knew what he was doing. Eve had almost ruined everything, would have if she'd responded selfishly to Nick's subtle advances. It would have been fun. But she could still close her eyes with Carl and imagine. Eve headed for the stairs to greet them, but just before she descended, the music of their voices stopped her. Their chatter about tracking sand into the house floated into a curious quiet, a stillness that could only surround the intimacy of a kiss.

Eve waited. Then she cleared her throat and called out.

"Hey there. Where have you two been? Feeling better?"

Then she waited another moment before she walked down and went into the dining room. Audrey hid a smile by turning away and facing the window, unaware that her infectious mood brightened the entire house.

"The ocean always makes me feel better," Nick said. "I took her down to the beach."

Audrey spun suddenly, her face dark. "That was a secret," she pouted, folding her arms across her.

Nick put his hands in his pockets to search for his keys, then dangled them before her.

"I almost lost these," he said, which made Audrey laugh. The sound of her happiness brought out the sun again. Something passed between Nick and Audrey that they might have thought was invisible, except Eve saw it.

Audrey 12

I hurtled down the street in the passenger seat, my mother a statue behind the wheel, my own voice silent as I held it inside. The velocity of the car carried me, tearing an invisible rift behind us that ripped the air apart between me and the man whose kiss my mouth kept remembering. That deep rumble stirred in me again, this time leaving my body and surrounding the car, until I realized a city bus had pulled up next to us and exhaled on our car. I thought about the field trip with Madison and Mitzi. I thought about Lucas on the mattress raft. That day seemed like years ago, miles from where Nick and I had kissed on the beach. As the bus pulled away, I held my breath, tried to recreate the way both kisses had made me stop breathing. Lucas might be at school today, but I wanted to go back the way we came and spend the morning near Nick.

"We should go back home," I said, as the large windows of the school stared back at me, their blinds lowered like eyelids that wanted to sleep, to dream.

"What happened here?" my mother said as we turned the corner.

Two police cars blocked the front of the school, their lights flashing in the sun. Behind them, yellow tape separated a part of the building where graffiti covered the stucco. Someone had tattooed the wall with spray paint in blue and black and white designs.

"Who would have done this?" my mother asked.

At first it was hard to tell where the blue paint stopped and the black started, but then I could see they created shading, making a three-dimensional image on a three-dimensional building. Officers stood with their arms folded, interviewing two students who held their cell phones out at the end of their arms snapping pictures. The painting was on more than the building now. It was traveling through the airwaves like water rippling away from where a stone fell.

I laughed because it was wonderful.

"This is vandalism," my mother said, so I stopped laughing. But everyone saw the wall differently now. Teachers lined the walkway, urging students to move into the building and to get to class, as if there was nothing to see.

"Is this a gang sign? Can you read it?" my mother asked. "Maybe I should come into the office."

"No."

I got out and walked past the police, past the paint that made us all see something beautiful where there used to be something ugly. In the hall, I navigated slamming lockers and the exchange of fake punches, trying to remember that not far from here, the beach dazzled the sky with sparkling sand. Waves of white foam surged and retreated like a first kiss, and then a second. I found my way to class and took my seat while Nick moved through my house, tracking footsteps across the floors, balancing wooden beams in his hands.

Madison and Mitzi grinned.

"You look sick," Madison said.

"Love sick," Mitzi added.

"Did I see a love note on the school building for you?" Madison asked.

Then more questions attacked me.

"Why haven't you been at school?"

"Why don't you answer your fucking phone?"

"What exactly happened in the warehouse?"

"You're not telling us everything."

"You can't just leave us out."

"Did Lucas Bixby vandalize you?"

"I don't vandalize," Lucas said, dropping into the empty seat next to me. He turned his desk toward mine, rested his chin on his folded arms and stared. Mr. Ross stepped between us.

"Mr. Bixby, you're wanted in the principal's office."

"But I need to be here," Lucas said, and stared at me. "There's stuff I need to know."

"I can call them to come for you, if that's what you prefer."

"That's not who I prefer to come for me," he said, still staring at me.

Mitzi and Madison laughed, but I could hear a sadness, a loneliness in his voice. Mr. Ross picked up the phone to call from his desk and spoke to the class at the same time.

"Everyone take out your anthology and let's get started."

"I don't have my book," Lucas said, scooting his desk close, sliding the side of his torn sneaker next to mine.

I studied the blond wood of my desk, trying to quiet the urge in my arms and legs to get up and run back to the man in my house who could make doorways to somewhere else.

"You okay?" Lucas asked.

A wad of paper hit him in the side of the head and without looking back, he held up his middle finger to Mitzi and Madison behind us. He opened my book, turned the pages and his hands trembled. I reached for his wrist to hold them still. His fingers were stained with black and blue paint.

"It was you," I said. "Everyone took pictures. Your art has gone up to the satellites and back down. Maybe all over the world by now," I said.

He smiled, leaned in, but held his breath like too much would spill out if he spoke.

"Do the two of you have something you'd like to share with the class?" Mr. Ross asked. "I'll wait."

Lucas turned a page, acted like he was reading. Mitzi and Madison opened their books.

"We were wondering," I said, "if the Trojan war was worth it."

Lucas raised his hand and spoke without waiting to be called on. "I say yes. Fighting for a woman who's been abducted by a man named after a French city. What choice does a guy really have?"

He took the pen from my hand and drew in the margin of my book. Four legs, a strong neck, a wisp of hair that wound itself around a thin horn. Mitzi got up out of her desk, pulled me by the arm, excused the two of us saying that I was going to be sick, that she would escort me to the girls' bathroom. Mr. Ross rushed over and yanked my pen from Lucas's hands.

"Come back here," he shouted, pointing my pen at me. "Both of you."

But Mitzi pulled me through the door, down the hall and into the girls' bathroom. The stalls were empty, the tiled floor pale and ugly. Madison burst in moments behind us.

"Do you remember anything?" Mitzi asked.

"Did he take off your clothes?" Madison wanted to know.

"Mr. Ross has my pen."

The door opened and Lucas strolled in.

"Ladies," he said. "I was feeling left out." He walked into a stall, looked around and walked back out.

"Is he good?" Mitzi asked, looking Lucas up and down. "Oh, how would she know? Never mind."

"She knows there are some things you can see more clearly in the dark," Lucas said.

Then he cupped my face in his paint-splattered hands. Our eyes were so close we couldn't see anything but each other.

"Mr. Ross has my pen," I said again, which made him smile.

The door burst open again. Two police officers rushed in, grabbed Lucas, and held his arms behind him.

"Lucas Bixby, we need you to come with us."

Lucas twisted toward me but the officers forced him into the hallway and the door closed behind them. Then the bathroom was cold tile and metal like before, with no proof that Lucas had just been here.

"What the hell just happened?" I asked.

"You said hell!" Mitzi laughed until her eyes watered, then she and Madison high-fived each other. They both hugged me.

"And your boyfriend got busted," Madison added.

"Your cool factor just skyrocketed," Mitzi said. "Make-over accomplished."

Eve 13

A teenager spinning in the bathroom mirror made Eve stop in the hall. As a little girl, Audrey used to twirl like that in her room, fall to the floor, then laugh at being dizzy. Now she looked older as she stopped to study her reflection, adjust a hair clip and examine a bottle of perfume she'd taken from Eve's bathroom. The young woman in the mirror tossed her hair back then raised her eyebrows like a quick question, which she answered with a warm smile. That radiant smile, which used to be reserved only for Eve, was meant for Nick.

Eve stepped back so Audrey would not catch her spying, and went downstairs. The possibilities Nick could invoke had taken hold. She wasn't sure he understood what Eve knew, that he'd started to replace more than old cabinets and walls. She should be delighted. But her heart was shadowy, maybe from the unexpected vacancy left there when the possibilities she'd imagined for herself were no longer hers. Audrey's radiance had turned in a new direction, shining elsewhere.

Eve stepped into the kitchen where naked plywood surrounded her. The walls still needed a solution. Neither paint nor paper made sense. Neither belonged with the house. This kitchen needed something contemporary. Something urban.

"What about concrete?" she asked the plywood surfaces just as Nick walked in.

"Concrete," he repeated, balancing a length of wood on his shoulder.

"Can these walls be finished in concrete?"

He leaned the wood against the table saw, stepped back and studied the room.

"I like it," he said.

He ran his fingers through his hair. He had no idea about the power of his charm. Eve steadied herself with one hand on the table saw.

"Polished?" she asked.

"I think rough is better," he said. She turned away. "But a warm color," he went on. "These two walls facing each other will have the most exposure. That one, of course, will have cabinets on it. It would be cool. Totally urban."

"Can it be done?"

"I've worked with concrete, but never on a vertical surface."

Nick put both hands on the plywood.

"Damn," he said. "That's exactly what this kitchen wants. I'll do some research."

A dangerous thrill sped through her limbs. He was close enough to touch. This must be what Audrey felt. She grinned at the plywood surrounding them, followed him as he guessed he would have to cover every surface with woven wire to hold a thin coat. He talked through the process with excitement, to himself as much as to her, debated the tricky phases of applying and drying, and how each phase depended on timing and temperature.

Through the oversized picture window, blue sky made it hard to imagine a damp day lay ahead that might make the concrete set too slowly. A pale figure lay on the deck and it took Eve a moment to recognize Audrey, sunning her sensitive skin in shorts with her t-shirt pulled up so her stomach was exposed.

"Damn," Nick said again, looking out the window, too.

Audrey's eyes were closed and her head turned to the side. She was oblivious to the damage the sun could do. Eve started to hurry toward her, trying to think where she'd last put the sunscreen, until she saw Nick staring in the same direction. She was displaying herself for him. He wiped his hands on a dirty rag.

"So, she asked me to take her surfing," Nick said. "I'm giving her that first lesson this evening."

Eve froze at the kitchen doorway. "Oh. But."

"That's still what you want?"

"Yes. But. Yes," Eve hesitated. She had not seen this coming. "She'll need protection."

"I have protection," he said, putting a hand on his back pocket.

The sexual tension she'd felt near him was absurd. His attention was elsewhere.

She backed away, retreated to her room overwhelmed, not ready. She felt foolish being in the house while the two of them made their plans. Didn't want to be there when they left together. Didn't want to think about Audrey crushed by the surf or the seduction of his arms. She would make plans of her own. She would go do something she hadn't done in a long time. Empty business suits confronted her with their dark cloth and straight lines. Carl had never gotten her tickets. But that wouldn't stop her. Never had. She searched with her smartphone till she found what she wanted, then found the original t-shirt from the band's first tour in the '70s.

Music and lights and theatrics would let her get lost for the evening. And she would know how to find her way back.

Audrey 13

Nick held up the lifeless black skin, shapeless without limbs to fill it.

"Put this on," he said. "It's a wetsuit. It will keep you warm."

It gave off a toxic scent.

"Take it."

I pinched its thickness between my thumb and forefingers and sniffed.

"Just put it on."

I removed the cotton dress that covered me and stood there in only my swimsuit, which was like wearing nothing at all. His eyes went all over me, and I wanted to cover up. But I also wanted him to look. He held up the wetsuit and I held onto his shoulder as I stepped each of my feet into a leg. Then he pulled hard to move the neoprene up my legs so I could put my arms in. I was covered in black, hardly able to bend my elbows and knees.

"It could be tighter, but it will do," Nick said. "You do know how to swim, right?"

I nodded, but I could hardly breathe. The rubber consumed me, and when he zipped up the back, I was trapped inside.

"I don't like this," I said.

"I'll be right next to you. C'mon. Nothing will happen."

He placed his surfboard on the sand and told me to lie on top. I lowered myself onto where he would be when he surfed. With my ear next to the board, I listened but there was only thick silence. The horizon tilted and I wanted to get up, but the wetsuit held me inside the shape of Nick's body, which made me feel safe and protected. Waves came toward me but couldn't reach me on the sand. So I pretended to paddle out to them.

"Perfect," he said. "You're an alligator. Now jump into a crouch like this. You're a tiger. Put your toes toward the side of the board and stand up. But keep your knees bent. You're a hunter."

The rubber around my arms and legs made it hard to move.

Alligator. Tiger. Hunter.

"Again," he said, and made me repeat the moves over and over.

"Okay, let's get wet."

He smiled, tucked the board under his arm and kissed me quick. I thought we might keep kissing but he pulled me to the water. When my feet touched the cold, I yanked away. That icy feeling was going to swallow me.

"Wait," I said. "I can't do this."

"You'll only get warm if you get wet."

Then he splashed water at me, but the sealskin protected me and kept me dry, like armor. I ran into the waves, jumping over the tiny ones. My feet were cold but the rest of me was safe. He put the board down on the water and it floated alongside me, then he patted it.

"Come on," he said.

I climbed on and lay flat across it as Nick pushed me over the small waves, but we moved toward bigger whitewater and its churning crash. My heart went into my throat.

"We're going under the next one," he said. "Hold on. Hold your breath."

White water rushed over me and then I was underneath it where the world was calm but the suit filled with cold. I wanted out, I wanted to be warm. I came up on the other side of the wave next to Nick, sputtering and choking. He was still with me. Salt water stung my eyes, but I saw him. My teeth chattered and I shook my head and looked back at the sand.

"Count to ten," he said.

I did and then I wasn't cold any more. The water inside the sealskin became warm against me, like he was hugging me with his body.

"We're going to turn you around," he said. "Just alligator. Don't stand yet."

The next wave crashed behind me and raced toward the bottoms of my feet at the back of the board. Then it lifted me up, I floated and then I sped across the water. Faster, lighter. White water bright and beautiful all around me. Like snow.

I screamed with delight but the wave shrank and lost its power. The surfboard slowed but kept moving toward the beach until it wedged itself onto the sand. I stood up and laughed. Nick raced across the waves to me, his arms and legs flying sideways as he hurried.

"Again! I want to go again," I said, and lifted the board under my arm to carry it back to the ocean.

This time when the wave picked me up I surprised Nick and became the alligator, the tiger, and then the hunter. But I leaned forward too far and lost my balance. I fell into the water, and the board threatened to slam into me. I went under and when I came up for air, a second wave shoved me back down into the turmoil and ground me into the sand. The sharp fin on the bottom of the board lurked, waiting to slice me. I needed air. Once more, I came up just as the board flipped, and a wave slammed it into my shins.

Knocked over, I was as powerless as a piece of seaweed, tossing in the churn. I didn't belong here and the ocean punished me for intruding. I surrendered just as Nick grabbed me, pulled me up and held onto the board so it couldn't hit me again. Salt water had rushed into my nose and mouth, and I coughed and sputtered to get air. My eyes stung and my throat and ears ached. Nick led me out of the water and sat me down, but I couldn't rub my eyes. My hands were covered in sand, which invaded my hair and got into the wetsuit. He ripped the leash away so I was no longer attached to the board, and laid the board on the sand. I was not an alligator or a tiger or a hunter. Unicorns didn't surf, and they didn't belong at the beach. I had been stupid to try.

I wanted the wetsuit off me, but I couldn't begin to find my way out. I rolled over and struggled to get it off as more sand attacked. Nick pinned me down, held me still as he unzipped the back, but I struggled to get away from him, to pull it off by myself.

"Hold still. I'm helping you."

The weight of him on me, the force and insistence made my heart slam into my ribs. The black rubber stuck to me, would not let go. But neither would he. I started to scream, but he put a hand over my mouth.

"First one arm," he said.

He peeled one sleeve off and then the other. With my upper body free, I could breathe better, but I still kicked to get my legs free. Then he lay on top of me and I couldn't move. I was covered in sand, and I lay there like the wetsuit, crumpled and defeated. I scrunched my eyes against everything.

"Hey, it's okay," he said.

"The sand is all over me."

"The sand is clean. The waves wash over the sand every day, every night. Sifting and rinsing."

I rubbed my fingertips together.

The sand did feel clean. I stopped struggling, let myself be on the beach with him pressing down on me, let the sand be rough on my skin, but let it be pure too.

Nick moved to my side but kept one leg across me, didn't let me up.

"Open your eyes."

"I can't. There's still sand."

He brushed my eyes with his fingertips and blew on them so gently I had to laugh. When I opened my eyes, his forehead was close to mine, to where my silver spire was. But I wanted him to stay close. I touched his arm then his thigh. My fingers left sand on him, dust from the ocean.

Something stirred, not hooves, but a low tremor insisting on his nearness.

"You okay?" he asked."

"No. I want you to take me home," I said.

"Sure."

"But not my home."

"Audrey," he said, sitting up. "You make this too easy."

He pulled a piece of dried seaweed from the sand and threw it away from him. Down the beach, two pelicans glided across the water. I stood up.

"Hunter, tiger, alligator," I said, moving through each pose in reverse, pushing him to the sand and kissing him the way he taught me, the way that made heat rise up between us. Even when he convinced me to go back into the water one last time, to rinse our bodies clean, the heat persisted.

We drove to the end of a row of cottages near the pier, each little house made different by flowers in pots or wind chimes or a rusty bicycle. Nick's house was decorated with two halves of a broken surfboard and a pile of red bricks. He unlocked the door, and I stepped inside. A huge bed built on a tall wooden platform took up most of the room, its blankets and sheets messy from where he'd left them when he'd gotten up.

"Have a seat," he said.

There was nowhere to sit except the edge of the bed. Nick leaned against the doorframe, the sun behind him stretching his shadow across the floor, across his empty work boots and notebooks and laundry. Tucked in the corner, a small kitchen could barely contain all the dishes and glasses waiting to be washed. On the bookshelf, two melted candles stood on each side of a box of Rice Krispies and an empty serving bowl.

Part of me felt trapped. There was nowhere to look that wasn't covered in clothes or dishes or books. Nick stepped in, closed the door and the room became dark. The blinds had been pulled down on the only small window there was. Next to the bed, pennies and nickels and dimes covered the nightstand. The empty bowl had nothing to hold, so I scooped them up and put them in. Nick sat down next to me.

"Don't clean up the money," he said, took the handful of coins from the bowl and scattered them across the room. "Let's leave money out of this."

He took my hand, kissed my fingers where they wove between his.

"Let's shower," he said.

He took off his clothes in front of me as if he'd done this a thousand times. So I took off my clothes too, dropping my swimsuit next to his. But I covered up, folding my arms across myself and turning away. When he was completely naked, I saw what hung from a patch of curly brown hair. It was wrinkled and helpless looking, and I laughed.

"Oh, thanks," he said.

Nick stepped toward me, and I shrieked and jumped up on the bed.

"Doesn't it get in your way?"

"I hope so," he said, taking my hand and pulling me down from the bed.

He led me to the bathroom. When the water was hot, he motioned for me to step in. The shower was so tiny but he followed me in. That part of him touched the back of my leg. I tried to move away but there was no room. He put both hands on my shoulders, turned me around and ran his soapy hands across every part of me. I wanted to scream and laugh and run at the same time. But I held my breath and let him touch me. Everywhere.

"Wash me," he said, and gave me the bar of soap.

I did, taking care, moving my hands across all the curves of him that I always wanted to touch but never knew. Except I stayed away from his private part, which kept pointing at me. He held my hand, showed me how to bathe him there, how to make him sigh. The sand and salt and soap washed away. The water ran clear on our skin until he shut off the tap. Droplets clung to us, gems on our skin. The newness of having no clothes shaped itself to me. Nick picked up a towel from the bathroom floor. I tried not to think about its earthy smell, and watched him collect the tiny jewels of water droplets from my arms and legs as he dried me.

Orange sunlight tried to crawl in under the door but the room was dark. He led me to his bed and handed me a book of matches.

"I don't know how to do this," I said.

"I'm about to show you. A lot of things. But if you want me to stop, you just say so."

He pulled off a match, pinched it between the cover and pulled it sharply. A flame blossomed on the end of it, but he did not hold it to the wick. He blew it out and handed me the book. My hands shook, my body shivered. I did what he did, but my match did not blossom.

"Pinch then pull quick," he said.

When an orange flower exploded at the end of my second match, I yelped and dropped it. He threw a shoe on it, laughed, and put his hand on my wrist. The second time we both held the flame to the wick. Then we got under the blankets, his closeness warming me. The sheets did not smell like my sheets. I shivered and thought of the coins flying everywhere. This wreck and mess could be its own perfect. I would trust him, and I held that trust behind my eyes as I closed them. His kisses traveled from my mouth to my neck to my stomach. But when he kept going, my face became hot. I put my hand on his damp hair to pull him away.

"Find your pleasure, Audrey," he said, and continued to move further down my body, bending my knees so his mouth could be between my legs. Searching, and finding. Pleasure.

Red orange light under the doorframe disappeared. The candle danced bravely in the dark. Completely naked with my head on his pillow, I became aware of a mysterious creature that emerged from the shadows. She stepped closer, didn't mind the dripping candle wax or the dust or the discarded coins. The more I let myself be exposed on his bed, the closer this animal came to me. I knew her. We met once on the grass under the stars. I struggled to separate myself, move away from her, from this bed, from this man, but he made my heart beat with her willfulness.

Only when I gave in and joined her to chase total abandon did this creature finally let go, release me back into myself. Only then, did Nick lie next to me, his hand on my heart while I floated over gentle waves that lifted and fell and brought me back to shore.

"Hello," he said.

"Who was that?"

"That was you."

His face moved close to mine.

"We're not done," he said, putting my hand on his penis, making me stroke him.

Unafraid of his silkiness and fur, I explored his shape, his strange parts. He moved himself over me, and I let him find his way in between, touch me with the tip, then pull away.

"What?" I asked.

"Condom," he said, reaching for something in the drawer, tearing it open, sliding the thing over himself.

"Always," he said. "Promise?"

I nodded, wrinkling my nose at its medical scent.

Slowly, gently, he divided me in two, destroyed me with kiss and caress and pain. Then he held still, waited for me to dissolve around him. I could no longer tell where he ended and I began. He waited for me to move, so I did. My hands traced the shape of him, my arms made a circle around the two of us. I didn't know I could be this close with anyone. I didn't know we could merge together and float on a shifting tide. His own creature unleashed its power over him, but I held on until it finally let him go.

When the waters calmed, when our breathing slowed, he slipped out.

"I meant to wait for you," he said.

"But I'm right here."

He kissed me on my forehead, and my silver self was no longer there.

"Nick," I said.

"Don't talk."

He turned away, blew out the candle. Smoke lifted into the room like the tail of a creature as it turned and left. We listened to our breath, to the closeness between us. He curled his knees against the back of mine. When he fell into sleep, I turned my face into the pillow.

"I love you," I whispered, and smiled at the coins and dirty towel and melted candle, at what I could see in the dark.

Eve 14

Black marks punctuated the hall where equipment cases had skidded against paint and across linoleum when amps and racks and dollies had been recklessly rolled through this passageway en route to the arena. Every surface was yellow with age, or maybe it was just bad lighting. Eve turned right, then left, heading in directions she thought she remembered. The artists' entrance was somewhere in this labyrinth, which could be taking her out, not in. A cluster of people in loud clothes stood like a beacon up ahead. Leopard print under a military coat mocked camouflage. Burnout velvet pants revealed all if one stared. Halter-top and porkpie hat drew attention to a bare back. She was headed in the right direction. These were the privileged, tagged with the same backstage pass she had acquired from a scalper.

She had found her way backstage once more. That part of her she'd left packed in a box had come back to life, just as an undiscovered part of Audrey must be coming to life somewhere in her lover's gray-and-white bungalow along the coast. Audrey would step into Nick's arms and be safe, taken care of.

Which meant Eve could let go.

Conversations did not falter or pause as she approached the eclectic group. No one backstage took note of her or her authentic t-shirt. A lost toddler in pajamas wandered toward the crowd, a small child who didn't belong here. No one seemed to notice her except Eve. The little girl laughed and wove through the forest of adult legs just as a young woman full of purpose came out of the green room and called to her. Had to be the nanny, because the mother wasn't far behind. Early thirties, clad in bracelets and strands of silver, she skulked after nanny and child in her skinny white jeans, losing sight of them as the crowd pulled her focus and she stopped to take inventory of who was there. A similar woman came out of the green room, drink in hand, followed by another nanny who herded two more toddlers, sippy cups in hand.

These must be second or third wives. They weren't going to let motherhood interfere with their good time backstage. And the men. Once wiry with youth and possibility, now tented in Hawaiian and Cuban shirts concealing middle-age thickness. Silver hair shaved close or the lack of it razored off. Grooved crow's feet. Whitened teeth. Glad-handing each other as they came to pay homage to the band or to their past.

Eve leaned against the wall absorbing this cathedral of posturing, overwhelmed by how old everyone had become. She was no different. A bodyguard stationed by the door to the dressing room took brief note of Eve standing apart but determined she was no threat to anyone. A woman across the hall tossed her long black hair. The petite singer-actress, almost unrecognizable without a spotlight, stood in front of a Hollywood actor who might have just won an Oscar or started a production company or slugged a photographer.

A hush swept through the hall. Everyone turned toward the bodyguard at a door. The crowd parted on cue. All five band members emerged, dark shirts, fingers clad in heavy rings, expensive athletic shoes giving them the support they needed to prance and strut and work an audience into a frenzy. They became ageless as they passed by close enough for Eve to touch. Which she did. Just briefly, in a way they wouldn't notice. Their translucent skin extended their vitality beyond what time had etched into their faces. She couldn't help smiling as if she recognized an old friend. All five glanced briefly at her as they passed, a posse of legends who charged the air they moved through.

What the hell was the bass player's name?

It would come to her.

As quickly as they'd entered the hallway, they disappeared, ushered by their mafia-looking manager who led them through the stage door. He threw a look into the hallway that dared anyone to try following. Beyond them, the stage was visible for a brief second, a pathway lit by stagehands with flashlights aimed at the floor. Drums on their platform, instruments tuned, mic stands waiting. The arena, filled to capacity, reveled in the dark. A roar went up as these rock gods plugged in, hit their mark, and split the crowd wide open as the first chord penetrated.

That first time, the one that writes itself in indelible ink on a young girl's life, would be an encounter with the pleasure of womanhood for Audrey.

Why was losing your virginity a loss? Why did women lose?

Audrey was gaining her sexuality, a fuller scope of womanhood. Tonight would banish the mythic creature that kept her a prisoner of childhood.

Eve was sure of this. But at the same time, the gravitational pull of motherhood made her want to reel Audrey back to her through the distance between this abandoned hall and Nick's bed.

Eve hesitated, reluctant to follow everyone who had an all-access pass. They pushed through a second doorway that led to the foot of the stage. She fingered the laminated card on its lanyard, took a few steps toward the green room. In its dim light, she could see unfinished glasses of wine and beer left behind, a basket of tortilla chips and a bowl of salsa abandoned on a low table.

The stage door opened and closed, releasing a blast of sound from the arena. She'd come this far, she might as well go in. A familiar phrase of music reached out and pulled her toward the arena. She flashed her pass to security, a young man who offered no expression, no nod, just an open door. Echo and reverb assaulted her as the amps magnified music inside the arena's concrete casing. The privileged who got this close to the stage stood packed together in a mosh pit. Eve laughed, understood the band's joke that dared and invited their older fans to behave like they were still young.

The crush of fans pushed forward.

Eve wove her way into the heat and sweat, turning sideways, twisting against bodies that swayed and bounced with ecstasy. Tresses glowed orange and red, an inferno dancing on the screen behind the musicians as they pouted or shoved a fist into the air. Their shadows pranced larger than life, celebrating triumph over time. The refusal to abandon rock was a variation on rebellion.

Or a groove into which the needle had got stuck.

So what, the lead singer seemed to say with his strut and pose.

Better to burn out than fade away.

But better if you kept on keepin' on.

Drums and bass vibrated through Eve's body, altering her heartbeat, making it pound to the same pulse. A guitar solo sliced across the arena, responding to the nimble fingers that danced on the strings, teasing out licks weighted with overdrive and crunch. Vocal harmonies soared, blending then separating. The band offered it up the way everyone liked it, just as it had for the last thirty years.

No.

Forty years.

Men and women mesmerized by this performance stared and grinned and sang the words as if they'd been transported back into the past. Bodies surged toward the bridge, anticipated the chorus, held onto each beat. Packed in a sea of middle-age, Eve tried to embrace the performance. Touching, breathing, perspiring against one another, the fans surrounded her with intimacy. Vocalizing and falling silent, finding the same rhythm. Seeking a musical sustain that emanated from center stage and radiated to the edges of the arena.

Down on the floor, there was no room to move.

No air to breathe.

No way out.

Someone fell against her, a huge man with no control of himself, and she collided with the woman wearing the porkpie hat who shoved back. A stiletto heel stabbed Eve's foot and pain radiated up her leg, made it hard to stand. Something was damaged, maybe broken. She would not be devoured. She raised her fists, used her elbows and launched herself toward the exit, forcing the bacchanal to separate, to release her back into the scuffed and yellowed hall.

It was ten o'clock when the front door opened and closed quietly. Soft footfalls on the staircase drew Eve from her bedroom. She turned on the hall light and Audrey grinned, her hair a wild tangle, her shoes in one hand. She said nothing, went into her room, and the empty hall felt as if a ghost had passed through and left.

It had been done.

Eve followed. Audrey did not go directly to the unicorns, did not immediately consult with them or check on them. Instead, she went to the mirror of her dresser and stared at herself. After a long minute, she touched her hair, tried to comb it out with her fingers.

"Do you want help with your hair?" Eve asked.

"No."

Audrey touched her hair again, examining strands of it woven together in tangles. Then she brushed past Eve on her way to the bathroom, shut the door and locked it.

After a long shower, Audrey's bedroom door closed. A few minutes later, Eve heard her yelp. Knocking softly, Eve waited for an invitation to come in. Nothing.

"Audrey, sweetheart? You okay?"

Eve pushed the door open and found her daughter facing the mirror with a wild head of seaweed, a comb dangling in the middle, wrapped in a snarl of hair.

"Oh, my sweet baby. Let me help you."

Audrey pouted, followed her to the bed and sat obediently while Eve gently tried to untangle the mess.

"Ow."

"Sorry."

"You're hurting me."

"I'm trying to get these tangles to let go of each other."

Audrey went rigid, her hair refusing to release the comb.

"Did you have a good time?" Eve asked.

At that moment, the front door opened and closed. Carl came upstairs, stood in the doorway and looked at the two of them.

"You and I need to talk," he said.

 Eve's skin turned to ice.

"Ow," Audrey said again and moved away, taking her mess of hair and comb from Eve.

Seconds passed like minutes.

"There's no way that gallery will be ready in time," Carl said. "I stopped over there after I finished at the office. Cheryl's people have made a mess of it. She took a chance on some new carpenters."

"So postpone the opening," Eve said, holding relief in check.

"I want to hire Nick," Carl said. "He could use the money. Don't you think?"

She laughed, couldn't help it. Stopped herself. Then laughed again.

"Absolutely."

Carl walked away but then doubled back.

"Have you found the negatives?" he asked.

"I thought you were handling that."

"And where have you been?" Carl asked turning to Audrey.

Audrey froze.

"I went to that concert," Eve said. "You never got me tickets, so I scalped one."

"How was it?"

Eve hesitated, couldn't find the right words.

"I tried to tell you," Carl said smugly, and headed down the hall.

Eve went back to combing out the tangles. Audrey tensed her shoulders in anticipation of the pull and tug, so Eve was gentle and patient.

"I can do this myself," Audrey said and took the comb from her. She rose and stood by the door to dismiss her.

Audrey 14

The unicorns were quiet and watchful all morning. They didn't request anything. The handful of flowers my t-shirt offered brought them no joy, so I left them and went downstairs when Nick arrived. The kitchen had become larger, with its huge window that let in sky and clouds and trees. I went to the corner and watched him.

"You okay?" he asked, coming over to me with a warm, lingering hug.

"I am."

"I hope you had fun yesterday."

"More than fun," I said.

"Hey," he whispered. "You're not a virgin anymore."

We smiled at each other. I felt alive inside his arms in a way I'd never felt anywhere else. I didn't want him to let go. But he did, to get a measuring tape.

"I could help," I offered.

"Ever used one of these?"

He pulled the long metal tongue from its bright orange box, laid it along the floor by the base of the counter, then snapped it back into place. The flat snake hissed and bit, warning me that it could hurt. Nick held it out to me, showed me how to push the lock to keep it from coiling too fast. I measured, called out feet and inches and he wrote down what I said. Sometimes I stood close, trying to find a way back into his arms. But he mostly gave his attention to lengths and widths.

"Can we go to the beach again?" I asked.

He moved to the other side of the island. "I really have to finish."

He loved the beach. It was his special place. I wanted to show him a special place, but it couldn't be the unicorns. My special place would be the thrift shop. I held one end of the tape measure and he marked pieces of wood with a pencil. This thin metal ribbon connected us until all its inches and feet wound back up inside and we were close again. He took the tape measure and walked away, didn't see me lean against the plywood wall and close my eyes. I could sense where Nick was in the room by listening to him move around, by following the sound of him.

"Hey," he called. "I need to run some power tools. You might want go upstairs."

"I'm not afraid," I said.

But when he made the blade scream, I retreated to the dining table, and covered my ears. He laughed and I knew it was safe but I hated the screaming.

"I love you," I said softly. Then I said it louder when he fed a piece of wood to the table saw and the blade's pitch rose higher.

Then he laid the cut pieces on the floor along the counter and stepped back. "What the fuck?" he said. "They're too short."

He re-measured. "Everything is off by five inches," he said.

He placed the tape measure at the end of a wood strip then had to pull it out further to get to the end of the counter.

"You took the tape measure and not the tape to the end. Shit."

He kicked the rest of the wood near his feet. This was my fault. I had made a mistake. It was bad. This upset him and his face frowned at me. I put my head down, hid in the darkness of my arms. I had gotten in his way and messed up his work when all I wanted was for him to hold me, to be with me like we were yesterday. I didn't mean to cry, but a sob escaped. After a few moments, Nick sat down next to me, put his hand on my arm.

"Forget it. It's no big deal. I should have explained," he said.

He held my hand, laced his fingers in mine. Then he kissed me, made me forget everything except what it felt like to be connected. He could make me feel better and I smiled.

"I like kissing you," I said. "Can we just do that the rest of the day?"

He laughed. "You want to go to the hardware store with me?" he asked.

"Yes, but can I take you somewhere first?" I asked.

"Not to bed," he said, which made us both laugh.

Each step toward Nick's truck felt like it would be the last one before I took flight, lifted into the air, sailed away on the delight of being alone with him. I climbed into the passenger seat and we pulled our doors closed at the exact same time, sealed ourselves together.

"Where exactly are we going?" Nick asked.

He leaned back against the seat, checked his cell phone, breathed out slowly like he was trying to hold onto those moments right before a surprise becomes something you know. His thumb tapped against the steering wheel, excitement wiggling like it did in me.

"I'm taking you on a treasure hunt," I answered.

The key turned, the engine started. My tummy hummed the same pitch. Nick drove down the street and I knew the way. I looked ahead, remembered the streets, the donut shop, the tiny park with no one in it. When I told him to pull over, he stopped the truck at the curb and looked out the window.

"A thrift shop? Audrey, I don't have time."

"It's full of treasure, and it even has a rainbow," I said, jumping out.

The bells tinkled as we walked in. He lingered by the door, probably because there were so many treasures in the shop. I went back for him, took his hand, led him to the middle where he stood for a long time. He folded his arms, looked at me for help.

"I need to get back to work."

"Do you see a rainbow?"

"What rainbow?"

I showed him the circular rack of clothes sorted by color in the middle of everything. A few colors hanging in the wrong group needed to be moved, which I did, and then the rainbow was perfect. Lydia came out of the back room and I introduced her to Nick. When she turned, I pointed out her long braid and Nick nodded.

"Nick, is it?" she said, looking over the rim of her glasses at him. "Well, Audrey has an eye for what is special, so I guess that makes you special. Audrey, if I'd known you were coming I would have prepared tea."

"But you did," I said, and went to a small wooden table set with tea for two.

On the table, mismatched plates and saucers waited for us. I moved a cup of yellow roses to a saucer of yellow leaves. Then I switched the blue flower cup so it was paired with the blue hummingbird plate, and arranged tiny spoons near each cup and saucer. In the middle, a fat china teapot dotted with wild flowers waited for someone to pour.

Nick stayed by the rainbow of clothes, shifting from one foot to the other, checking his phone.

"Audrey has invited you to tea. If you're a gentleman, you sit," Lydia said.

He sat down. I lifted the pot and poured.

"There are raspberries or scones," Lydia said, offering us a plate painted with cherry branches.

"Raspberries," I said and put some pretend fruit onto my plate. If I scooted forward, I could make my knees touch Nick's under the table, which made him look up at me.

"Would you care for one?" Lydia asked, holding the plate to Nick.

He hesitated, didn't know what to choose.

"Raspberries or scones," Lydia said again. She tilted her head and he finally made up his mind. He chose raspberries.

"May you never be too old to live in your imagination," she said, and she chose a scone.

"We could play Argue about a Refrigerator. That's what my parents do. I'll vote for chrome. You vote for white. But that game always ends badly."

"Does it?" Nick asked.

I nodded. He reached for my knee under the table, squeezed it, left his hand there. Something electrical raced up my leg and made the middle of me turn to liquid desire. I wanted to be in his bed, naked with him, doing all those things that were so new to me.

"I have a game we can play," Lydia said. "I think Audrey will be very good at this. Pick any object in the shop and Audrey, you tell us a story about it."

"Okay," I said, trying to bring myself out of his bed and back to this shop full of treasures.

"That ceramic bowl," he said, taking his hand from my knee, pointing to a dish with pale green glaze on the rim and dark brown glaze at the base.

"That's not just an ordinary bowl," I told him. "That's a trough for unicorns. They used to drink the dew that collected in it each night in the forest. They would gather around its edges and sip and talk."

"They talk?" he asked.

"Not like people. To us it looks like listening, without words. Sometimes they nod or shake their heads, or use their horns to point when it is someone's turn to be heard."

"What do they talk about?" Lydia asked.

"How they are disappearing. But when they are around that bowl, it feels like they are many, like they might live forever. Being near each other reminds them of who they are, the way a mirror can remind you of yourself even though it isn't you."

"How did the bowl end up here?" Nick asked.

"A careless traveler passed by, thought it belonged on a shelf, took it without looking closely. If he had, he would have seen tiny hoof prints, a long strand of white tail hair, silver eye lashes on the grass. Things that whisper about the magic of unicorns when you listen with your eyes."

They both stared at the bowl because now they could finally see the ghosts of unicorns gathered there. I lifted a delicate teacup and its painted hummingbird flew toward my lips.

"The traveler took it with him to use for horrible casseroles and smelly stews. Then it was forgotten, put it in a box and brought here."

The story I told enchanted Lydia, I could tell. My words wove strands around her. But Nick's small smile made me realize my story belonged to the world of a child. He was not inside the story. He looked at his watch and I looked at his jawline, wanted to put my hands on it. He caught me looking.

Winked. And I melted again.

"Hey, I need to get to the hardware store," he said.

"Audrey, why don't you stay?" Lydia asked. "I'd like to offer you a job helping me out around the shop. I'll pay you. You can rearrange all these treasures."

"That's a great idea," Nick said. "It would be good for you."

He stood up, rattling the cups and saucers. "I can pick you up later."

A job arranging treasure sounded important, but I wanted to be with Nick. And maybe not everything was really treasure. Lydia reached for my shoulder, and kept talking to me.

"I still have some of those bags your mother brought the other day, and two boxes of shoes I don't know how to arrange. Won't you stay?"

"We have to go," I said. But I felt bad for all those shoes stuffed in their boxes.

"Any time you want to come in, Audrey. I'm here."

When I reached the door, Lydia was still standing by the tea service but the plates were empty. There never had been tea or raspberries or scones. Just mismatched saucers and cups.

The hardware store echoed with voices over an intercom that demanded assistance and forklifts that beeped danger as they backed up. High walls and ceilings surrounded tall shelves that towered over everyone wandering through the maze of aisles. I tried to follow Nick but he walked fast and I kept stopping to look. A shelf full of shelves made me laugh. When I turned to follow him again, he was gone. Men pushing metal carts ahead of me made it impossible to run in his direction. Clerks in their bright yellow vests did not look like they wanted me to ask them for help.

I needed to find where the long strips of wood were kept, replacements for the ones I had measured wrong. A wave of regret flashed across me. It was my fault Nick had to make this trip and do extra work. A display of sharp saw blades made me shiver. Their jagged edges and metal teeth wanted to leap from the display and slice something. Further down that aisle, a shaggy haired boy with a plaid shirt stopped at a display of paint. I knew his shape, his outline, the texture of his hair and flannel.

"Lucas?" I called, but he was too far to hear.

I hurried after him. I knew him, even with his backed turned to me. I knew him here in the middle of a giant warehouse full of home parts.

"Just three," he said to a man who examined paintbrushes. "Green, gray, and black."

Before the customer could answer, a clerk with a tie and bushy eyebrows stepped in front of me.

"Sir," he said to the customer looking at paintbrushes. "Is he bothering you? Trying to get you to buy something?"

The clerk's plastic tag spelled out Randall under the word "Manager." He wore a white shirt like my father's.

"He wants spray paint."

"You're that graffiti punk," Randall said, his voice surrounding everyone with anger.

Lucas froze in that trap until he saw me.

"Audrey! Jesus. I thought I lost you. There you are," Lucas said, grabbing my arm and hurrying me to the next aisle.

I ran with him, though I didn't know why we had to run. He kept looking over his shoulder and finally stopped when he saw that the eyebrow man with the tie had not followed. We were surrounded by toilets, rows of them on each side of us.

"We keep meeting in bathrooms," I said.

"Which is kind of a shitty place," he said, closing the lids of two toilets, gesturing for me to sit on one while he sat on the other. "I'll be king and you be queen."

I liked his words. I wanted to play king and queen with him so I sat down.

"These are our thrones," he added, and I laughed because a toilet could be a throne.

"Does that make this our kingdom?" I asked.

It was Lucas' turn to laugh.

"Your majesty," I said.

"Yes, my queen?"

"We are out of toilet paper."

"This is the underworld," he said. "They never have toilet paper. But that's okay because they don't have shit here."

We laughed again and he put his painted fingers on my hand. I lifted them to look closely at the different colors of gray, blue, black and green. He pulled his hand away, looked down the aisle away from me.

"I'm a mess," he said. "God. Maybe my dad was right. 'You're a mess,' is all he ever told me. 'You'll never amount to anything.' Audrey, I'm not coming back to school."

"Come back to school," I said.

"I can't. I'll never make it out of there."

His face looked like pain was flashing sharp edges inside him, leaving invisible cuts. I didn't know what would happen if you didn't make it out of high school. I didn't understand why he wouldn't make it out. I wished I could look again at the wall he'd painted inside that cavernous warehouse. Maybe its big chunks of color and shape could tell me more about him.

"Lucas," I said. "Painting is messy, but it's just paint."

He looked at his fingers, smiled, didn't speak for a long time.

"Audrey, there you are!" someone yelled at the end of the aisle. Nick hurried toward us holding thin pieces of wood in his hands like spears. He frowned at Lucas but spoke to me.

"You okay?" he asked. "I thought I lost you, Audrey. Jesus."

Lucas stood up, looked from him to me. "Seriously?" Lucas said.

"C'mon Audrey. Let's go."

"Who is he?" Lucas asked.

They both waited for me to answer.

"I'm her surf instructor," Nick said.

"You surf?" Lucas said.

"Who are you?" Nick asked.

"We're classmates," Lucas said. "In high school."

Lucas stepped toward Nick faster than he meant to and knocked into the wood strips. They clattered to the floor making a loud, terrible sound. People stopped to look.

"Is he bothering you? Trying to get you to buy something?" an angry voice asked behind us.

The manager with his angry eyebrows appeared out of nowhere.

"He needs to keep his hands to himself," Nick said, and bent down to pick up the wood.

The manager grabbed Lucas by the arm and walked him away. "You've bothered enough customers."

The man's face went red as he kept lecturing Lucas and walking him toward a wide door that led out into the sunlight. Lucas turned back to me just before the security guard took him. Nick took my hand, led me to the register, and paid for the wooden rods. In the parking lot, there was no sign of Lucas. I was quiet as Nick drove away, looking down side streets for a boy with a skateboard. Nick reached out and put his hand on my knee then my thigh, making that wave of liquid heat race from my knees to every part of me and then back.

Eve 15

Home again after the fruitless search, Eve went straight to the kitchen, a habit
she'd adopted since demolition began. For the first time, when she walked in,
she did not fall in love all over again as she usually did with the open space
and the light that flooded through the huge window. Surrounded by walls
of chicken wire, she turned slowly to imagine how it would look when it
was finished. This was risky but texture and color could tie the whole house
together if she chose correctly.

Eve had visited four countertop suppliers over the course of two days,
only to conclude that every color and composite of granite was wrong for
her kitchen. Traditional materials like tile and Corian wouldn't work with an
urban look. After Nick had anchored chicken wire across the plywood, the
kitchen became confused as if it were trapped in a cage. Maybe the concrete
walls were wrong.

Unfinished cabinets gaped and yawned without drawers and doors, waiting
for dishes and cups. This kitchen hardly seemed like a place where her family
could eat and laugh and live. She spotted the newest addition: the sink and
faucet had been installed. She lifted the chrome sink handle, but nothing came
out of the faucet.

Something caught her eye outside through the oversized picture window.
Nick stood with Audrey in front of a pomegranate bush. Globes of red fruit
hung like ornaments among the yellow leaves. He really did care about her. He
was spending time with her. Eve folded her arms and watched. Her attraction
to him seemed foolish. Calculating which of her t-shirts might elicit a response
from him was really about her own response. He laughed at something Audrey
said, and she moved in for a long kiss, held onto him to steady herself. He
pulled back, twisted a pomegranate from its branch, scored it with the X-Acto
blade from his belt and cracked it open. Then he offered her the deep red
seeds that he exposed. She pinched off several with her fingers and ate them,
red juice staining her lips, then his.

As if he could feel her gaze, Nick glanced at the window.

Eve jumped back, crouched down below the sink where she could see the
plumbing was not connected. From where she kneeled, she spotted a bowl on

the dining table, not something from her kitchen. She got up, moved closer. The pale green glaze along the top was the color of new shoots of grass growing out of a deep soil color. She picked it up, surprised by its lightness.

"That's a gift," Nick said, walking in alone with a bucket of what smelled like varnish or glue.

"Thank you. That's thoughtful."

"I mean it's for—"

"Will you stay for dinner tonight? I'll serve our meal in it."

"I don't think dinner is a good idea," he said.

Eve put the bowl in the middle of the table. "It's Carl's idea. He'd like to ask you about an additional project."

Nick raised his eyebrows but before he could speak, Audrey came in with several pomegranates in her hand.

"They're ripe," she said. "We ate one!"

"I invited Nick to stay for dinner," Eve said.

"You're staying," Audrey announced, her smile brighter than the sun.

Eve poured couscous from the take-out container into the pale green bowl, and spooned roasted vegetables over everything. Audrey and Nick sat across from Carl, sharing a look, a giggle, something that excluded everyone else. She started to correct Audrey's lack of social skills. But hadn't she bought and paid for this conspiracy? She couldn't really resent their smiles and whispers. Steam rose in curls from the take-out food. She offered the serving spoon to Nick. He transferred a scoop onto his plate, and passed the spoon to Audrey. Instead of spooning food to her plate, Audrey lifted the bowl as if she were going to sip from it.

"Audrey," Eve said.

Nick smiled at some secret message in her gesture. Audrey served herself in an overly serious manner and passed the bowl to Eve.

"So," Carl said, stabbing at the silence that had settled. "Did we decide on the refrigerator? Chrome or white?"

"Chrome or white?" Audrey asked Nick.

"Carl, we agreed not to discuss the kitchen."

Eve sensed that someone knocked someone else's foot under the table. Audrey grinned, kept stealing glances, following Nick for cues. She sipped water when he did, wiped her mouth a moment after he did. Laughed when he laughed at Carl's story about the neighbor who was irritated with their driveway debris but kept taking scraps of wood from it.

"It won't be much longer. Two weeks?" Carl said, looking from Nick to

Audrey and back.

Nick nodded. "Maybe less. I need to coat the walls, and appliances have to be installed. Then there are just details like drawer pulls and switch plates."

A dark cloud passed over Audrey's face. She put her fork down, put her hands in her lap. Nick glanced at Eve.

"I'm looking forward to everything being finished," Carl said, turning his attention to a roasted carrot while his daughter retreated into gloom. "But I'd like to discuss an opportunity that might mean a delay in the kitchen."

He explained about Cheryl's gallery, the deadline, the poor workmanship that needed to be fixed.

"It's a day of work. She can pay you five hundred for your services. If it takes more time, it will be five hundred for each day. I thought you could use the money, help make up for the asbestos expense. What do you think?"

Nick stopped eating.

"Maybe you want to think it over," Eve said.

"Cheryl is someone to know. She may have work for you remodeling something in her house. And you can probably charge her double for your services," Carl went on. "Do we have a deal?"

Nick remained motionless for a long moment then placed his napkin on the table. Audrey did the same. "We have a deal," Nick said. "Thank you for dinner. I need to head out to take care of some errands."

He rose.

Audrey rose.

Despite Carl's protest or Eve's offer of more food, Nick thanked them again and walked away. Audrey followed him to the door. While Carl raised his fork to his mouth, Eve stared at the bowl in the middle of the table, listening for the front door to close, for Audrey's return.

"I think her schoolgirl crush on him is good for her," Carl said, and winked at Eve.

She had to look away.

A day's work at the gallery turned into three. The kitchen froze in its state of undress. Cabinets waited for countertops. Carpentry waited for hinges and hardware. Chicken wire waited for concrete. Eve was anxious to see how it would look, eager for the starkness of cement that would make the kitchen simultaneously inviting and daring, domestic and metropolitan. The 1960s aquarium had almost been eradicated. Audrey roamed around, touching the unassembled cabinets, staring out the wall-sized window into the yard. Moping.

"Why don't you go pick pomegranates?" Eve asked. "They're all going to be eaten by the birds."

Obediently, Audrey went out and twisted the fruit from their stems, filled the green-brown bowl with five more red spheres, left them on the table and went to her room. When Eve passed by later, Audrey lay on her bed facing the wall, arms embracing her pillow. For three days she hardly spoke, complied when it was time to get ready for school, moved like an empty paper cup the breeze could easily blow around. She went back to doing her homework in the kitchen, curled in a corner of wood and wire.

Come watch a movie with me. Let's paint our toenails. How about ice cream? She tried to think of invitations that would entice Audrey out of her solitude, hoping she might share something about being with Nick. In one last desperate move, she asked if Audrey wanted to invite Mitzi and Madison over.

"God, no," Audrey said.

Almost as a slight to her, Audrey brought the unicorns down, one by one, and placed them on the floor of the kitchen. Eve's stomach jumped and turned each time. Her throat went tight at the sight of her daughter reverting to the company of the fairytale creatures that had been her closest companions until Nick's attention changed all that.

"Hey," Eve said on Sunday. "How would you like to go see Nick?"

Audrey squealed, jumped up, leapt over the porcelain beasts, over her books and papers. Instead of racing out of the house, she hurried to the bathroom, came out with her hair brushed, and was that mascara on her eyelashes? A honeysuckle scent rose from her skin. A smile lit her eyes.

Walls of pure white divided Cheryl's gallery into dozens of surfaces that waited for Daphne's work. Eve had wall envy. She wanted her walls finished, but the gallery had preempted the kitchen. Audrey went through the gallery, straight to Nick in the far corner where he examined broken ceramic tiles along the base of the wall.

"I'm seeing a ghost," Cheryl Moncrief said, stepping out from a partition and making Eve jump. "I was starting to think you'd never come down here. Not even for the opening. Is Daphne ready for Saturday night? Only six days. Is she excited? I can't wait to meet her."

Nick stirred something in a plastic container with a metal putty knife, handed it to Audrey, and showed her how to smear the paste and then press a broken tile into place to repair the baseboard. Cheryl followed Eve's gaze to the two of them in the corner.

"They've become friends while he's been at the house," Eve said.

"I'd like to take him home myself." Cheryl's serious expression finally exploded into laughter. "Have you found the negatives? I can't tell you how much they'll help with verification and establishing value."

"I'm heading over there to look."

"When?"

"Now."

"Perfect. Everything is perfect! Tell me about Daphne."

"She's not completely sure–"

"Well, reassure her for me. I'll make this show perfect."

"Cheryl, she isn't always—She isn't who she used to be."

"Oh, who is? I don't expect her to be. But she's still an inspiration to so many. We're fortunate to have her, and her presence will be an honor on Saturday."

"Looks like you're almost finished," Eve said to Nick, stepping away from Cheryl.

"Almost," he said. "I was going to stop by the house and work there for the rest of the afternoon, getting the walls ready for tomorrow."

"That would be perfect," Eve said.

He stopped moving, waited while Audrey examined his paint-flecked skin.

"After I visit my mother, I need to check out a chrome countertop in Torrance. It could be a few hours. Do you think you could take Audrey back to the house with you?"

He moved the container out of his way and stood. "A few hours?"

"At least," she said, their eyes finishing the conversation, glancing at Audrey.

"Sure. I understand," he said, and sealed a lid onto the container of mastic paste.

"You're speckled," Audrey said, touching the back of his hand.

Eve backed away, left the gallery and sat in her car where she could see Audrey follow Nick from one side of the gallery to the other. Smiling. Gesturing with her hands, buoyant, elated. She had once felt that way when possibilities lured the young woman in her forward. Audrey's expressions and movements revived a glimpse of who Eve had been before so many years separated her from her former self. It was working. Eve had predicted this, and Audrey had started to change. It must be the thought of visiting her mother that made her heart darken.

The empty reception desk and vacant hallway filled with ghosts. They stepped from doorways and closets in search of families, and the past, and the present. The green bench where the old and lonely usually waited was empty. Had they all passed away? Everyone must be in the dining hall or some other part of the building. Eve called out but no one replied. Daphne hardly ever ate in the dining hall. She hurried toward her room, reassured by the sound of a muffled television behind a door. Her mother sat in a chair by the bed, an old woman, almost unrecognizable. Staring out the window. Dreaming perhaps of her past.

"Hello," Eve said, forcing herself to add the word 'mother.' Hello Mother.

"Who is that?" Daphne answered.

Eve hesitated, wasn't sure how to answer. Me. Eve. Your daughter.

"It's Eve," she said, settling on the safe distance of third person.

"Dear Eve," Daphne said with unexpected tenderness.

These were two words Eve had never heard combined out loud.

"I was just thinking of you," Daphne went on.

"Me? Where is everyone today? The place feels empty," Eve said.

"I feel empty," Daphne mumbled, and her weak voice stirred an unexpected flurry of care in Eve.

Her mother was losing the war with age as Eve surely would at some point. Weak, helpless, her mind returned to an infant state, kept alive by a body that was so much less desirable to hold and help.

"Oh, Mom," Eve whispered, to herself more than to her mother.

Daphne opened her eyes, stared at her.

"Why have you come?" she asked.

"That gallery is going to exhibit your work. Remember Carl talked about this? Those three new photos, the triptych. I need to find the negatives."

Daphne closed her eyes, sank into the chair.

"For Carl. The negatives are for Carl," Eve said.

Daphne came to life again, pointed at a cabinet on the far wall. Eve opened the doors and found herself face to face with binders filled with negatives. She pulled one out and opened it. Sections were separated by old postcards with dates and locations on them, like the ones she received from Daphne when she traveled.

"Italy in the summer was different, when sunlight was its own gold. The fields of Tuscany were rich with that sunlight. You can't see that kind of light anymore."

"You remember," Eve said. "This is good. There was a stone fence."

Italy. Tuscany. The sides of the binders had locations written on them. Negatives filed by location. She would have to methodically look through everything in the Italy binder.

"You took pictures. Photographs. Of a stone fence. Was that in Italy?" Eve asked.

"Hand me that orange binder," Daphne said.

Daphne opened it and lifted a postcard from inside. "Dear Eve," Daphne read.

Her mother's term of endearment startled her. Daphne handed the postcard to Eve. It contained a faded picture of a grassy field with the same stone fence that was in the triptych. On the backside, a typed caption contained the word Tuscany, and a note in loopy cursive began *Dear Eve*.

Her heart thudded again at those two words. The rest of the note, a total of two sentences, was an apology for having intruded on her and her lover in their apartment the night Daphne had come home unexpectedly and then left without coming back. She'd gone to Tuscany, and had taken photos of the stone fence, then hidden them away.

That's when Daphne must have written this postcard.

But she never sent it.

"I know I'm not there for you," it read. "It's probably better for us both."

This was as close as Daphne had ever come to the acknowledgment, understanding or even apology which Eve had sought her entire life. Here it was scrawled onto the small surface of a postcard that had no stamp.

"That triptych is a fraud. I found the fence on a postcard. Then I found the fence. Someone else's work, not mine."

"Mother, why didn't you send it?"

Daphne stared out the window.

"It must have been difficult, your childhood. I never expected you to understand. You resented me for not being there."

"But you resented me for being there. What about abortion or adoption?"

"It wasn't so easy then. Either choice. It never will be, I suppose. When you create beauty, like my photography, you have to protect the life that lets you do that," Daphne said. "Do you understand?"

"Maybe I do," Eve said. "Audrey is the beauty I have created."

Daphne looked at Eve with new understanding and clear eyes. That lucidity made it seem absurd she was even in this facility. With tenderness, she reached over and stroked Eve's arm. This was a dream that was going to end at any moment. Eve would find herself impaled on her mother's cold heart at the side of this medical bed next to a shriveled woman who despised her. Eve waited, but her mother continued to hold her hand, to caress her forearm. The touch, the contact, the warmth of apology reduced Eve to a child who needed her mother. Tears welled and spilled.

"Eve, you have a beautiful daughter," Daphne whispered.

"Oh, Mother, you remember. Audrey. She's seventeen."

The same age Eve would have been that night her mother intruded into the apartment and abandoned her again.

"Have you made sacrifices for her?"

"Many," Eve said.

"Those sacrifices subtract from your own life, and then after a while you won't have one anymore."

"Taking care of her doesn't subtract from my life. It makes my life rich, like the sunlight in Italy."

Daphne touched the postcard. "It wasn't like that for me. I'm glad it is for you. I hope the teen years are not difficult."

Eve hesitated.

This was the moment to have a mother daughter talk, a heart to heart exchange with honesty and understanding. Eve wanted to share, to unburden herself of what she had told no one. And Daphne would never remember.

"Can I tell you something?" Eve asked. "Audrey is seventeen. She's barely been interested in anything but unicorns. Which was fine when she was five, or even twelve."

"There will be boys," Daphne smiled.

"That's very delayed. So I found someone to be with her."

"Be with her?"

Her mother's eyes shifted to something far away, beyond the window. Daphne was starting to drift. She would not remember this conversation.

"He's a sort of tutor or guide. I hired him to teach her about intimacy."

"Is he a stranger?" Daphne asked, looking at her without judgment.

"Not really. He's my kitchen contractor. He's practically been living with us."

They sat together, and Eve shared everything while the window of understanding was open. Daphne listened to the story about Nick as Eve let it rush forth. Telling Daphne everything felt good, like a release from so much isolation and resentment. Then Daphne finally spoke.

"I'd like to meet your daughter," she said.

"But you have."

Daphne smiled. "Am I that bad? I'm sorry."

"It's okay. It's good to be with you."

Their hands reached for each other's. Daphne smiled.

"Is your daughter very young?"

"She's seventeen."

"Is she interested in boys?"

Daphne held the question in her expression. Eve exhaled. Daphne would remember nothing. She let go of Daphne's hand, and closed the binder of negatives.

"I'm afraid I've stayed too long and exhausted you," Eve said.

"How old is your daughter?" Daphne repeated.

"She's seventeen."

"I'd like to meet her."

Eve lifted the postcard to study her mother's handwriting, the date and the empty corner where a stamp belonged. On the wall across from her, Daphne's photograph offered a prison wall with razor wire on top, ready to wound anyone who attempted escape.

"Daphne, I don't know if you remember, but an art gallery downtown is celebrating you and your work. May I take these negatives for a day or two, to help them verify some of your prints?"

"No one can take those."

"They'll be safe with me. They'll be returned. You'll come to the gallery and see all your work in one place."

"My work sets me free," she said. "It's the only thing that ever has. You can't take these."

"But you'll get them back. It's for a little while, just for the show."

"They're all I have."

There was no way to win this argument. She should have talked about the pictures first, when her mother was lucid and fresh, but the postcard had lured her to the past. Carl would have to deal with this. It was time to go. Daphne dropped her head for a long time and fell asleep. Or passed away. Either was equally possible. Eve could just quietly take the binder of negatives. When Daphne woke she wouldn't remember or know they had disappeared. But the postcard in her hand made her hesitate. Eve moved closer to the photo of a prison wall.

Daphne jolted awake, looked up at her with an angry frown.

"What are you doing in my room? Who are you? Get out."

"Daphne. Mother. Please."

"I'm not your mother."

Daphne reached for the call button, shouted for help. Eve gripped the binder, and the postcard in her hand slipped to the floor. She backed out of the door and watched from the hallway as an aid spoke to Daphne, stroked her arm, calmed her.

"Stop her. She's a thief. Who are you?" Daphne shouted, pointing at her.

"I'm Eve," Eve said to herself.

Audrey 15

Nick brought me home but I didn't want to get out of his truck. "Let's go down to the beach. The sun will set soon. Let's go to your bungalow," I pleaded at the curb.

But he brought me into the house because he needed to finish working.

I leaned against the kitchen wall and looked at the fence in our backyard, how it ran through the middle of the view framed by the window, just like in one of my grandmother's photographs. I wanted to tell my mother about the fence and how the window created a photo, but she wasn't home.

"Don't you have homework?" Nick said.

"You sound like my mother," I told him. He shrugged, went back to his work.

I spread out my books and papers at the table where I could see him when he crossed the kitchen. Sections of wire, pieces of wood; whatever he carried and touched, I wanted to become. His head bent toward drill and tool. I wanted to be what he concentrated on. Every muscle and limb recalled his touch, the way we moved, the combinations of how we fit together. I could not stay at the table and do homework.

He turned off the kitchen light as if he could not stand being apart either.

"I'll be back tomorrow to coat these walls," Nick said. "Pretty soon I'll be done. Do you understand that?"

When his back was turned, I threaded my arms through his and held tight.

"I'm never letting go."

"Come on, Audrey. Let go and I'll give you a kiss."

He turned around but it was me who gave him a kiss, one that plunged us both downward, into the realm of helpless desire.

"No," he said. "Not here. Let's go down to the beach."

He made himself pull away. I raced out of the house ahead of him, doubled back and put my arm through his.

We watched the sunset, facing west with everyone who came to see the horizon tilt us toward the night. Color slid from the sky as it did from his small bungalow when I turned out the light, found a book of matches on the nightstand and lit the candle. This time, I made an orange flower blossom with the very first match.

"You've been practicing," Nick said.

I touched the flame to the wick, making light flicker across his face and I could see his eyes close when he kissed me because I kept mine open.

The vines of our selves became tangled in each other. Our separateness dissolved. This man against me, touching me, encircled by my arms made my whole self give in and complete our closeness. For the second time, he showed me how to move, how to curve and twist and bend with him.

"Nick," I whispered. "You are my love."

"No, Audrey. I'm your lover," he said, and he kissed me with so much tenderness and desire that I could barely move until I was seized with hunger for him, eager to explore every part of him, to discover every sensation I could provoke in him because his pleasure was my own.

When he collapsed beside me, I moved against him again, sparking a new flame. He laughed, rolled away and told me we had to wait. Then he held me, quiet and soft as the flicker of the orange flame straightened out and burned steady.

I had a lover.

I was someone's love.

But the next morning, I had to be a high school student.

It didn't make sense.

It didn't feel right.

Something was missing, the way Lucas was missing from class for too many days. Mr. Ross' words stumbled and lurched as he tried to get the class to talk like before when we talked about hope. But no one was interested. Twice, I had seen Lucas taken away. His empty seat held the memory of his shape, his shaggy hair, his fingers covered in paint. I didn't want to be here, either. I got up and moved to his plastic chair in case it could tell me where the boy might be who used to sit there. But it said nothing.

Mitzi sat down in my seat and Madison took the seat behind her but I didn't turn around.

"I heard Bixby went to juvie," someone said to them.

"I heard he was busted for dealing."

"Did you know he was homeless?"

"He dropped out of school."

"And started a meth lab."

"Hook me up!"

"Is there a problem over there?" Mr. Ross asked.

"No problem," Mitzi said.

I concentrated on the slice of blue sky in the window that promised freedom, and I waited for school to end so I could walk home and imagine that every white truck was Nick coming for me because he couldn't wait to see me. When I got home, I went to him, eager for that secret moment when he would manage to kiss me quickly, secretly.

His hands were busy with buckets of heavy gray paste and his workers mixed and carried buckets of their own. They worked alongside each other where I wanted to be, covering the walls with a wet coat of concrete. Nick scraped the gray goop onto a metal spreader, then smoothed it out across the chicken wire the way my mother frosted a cake. The kitchen smelled like some place deep in the earth, and soon the wood and wire that held the concrete in place turned the walls into sidewalk. Nick said everything was drying quickly but I touched a wall and it felt cool and damp. If I pressed hard enough, I could leave a handprint.

But I didn't.

I had ruined his work once. I did not want that feeling again.

Nick paid his workers and drove them away for the last time. I was glad for them leaving until I understood that it meant all the work would soon be done.

The next afternoon when I tried to be with Nick, the doorbell rang and deliverymen brought chrome monsters that fit into the vacant geometry of wooden cabinets and became dishwasher refrigerator oven hood. The kitchen filled in with things that said "wash, cook, eat." But that wasn't what I wanted to do each time I walked in and found Nick.

By the afternoon, he had packed up his tools and moved them all to the corner, then started to load them into his truck making separate trips. My heart fluttered inside, trying to get out and fly. I did not help him. I wanted to hide all of his tools under my bed but I knew that would not change anything. Dark wooden cabinets against concrete walls held nothing in them, empty the way the kitchen would be after Nick left. My mother walked in and put her arms around me but I pushed her away.

"Why so sad?"

"The cabinets are empty."

I opened the doors and their empty shelves gaped at us.

"They need new dishes," my mother said.

"This could be a home for all of Lydia's unwanted and unmatched dishes. They could live here and be together," I said as Nick walked back in for more tools.

My mother and Nick looked at me.

"That might work," my mother said with too much happiness. "Why don't we go to her shop and find some?"

"Why don't you go?" I said.

I didn't want to leave. I wanted to be alone with Nick.

"Is it three already?" my mother asked.

"Not yet," Nick said.

"Yes it is," I said. "It's four o'clock."

"In that case, Audrey you stay here," she said. "I'm going out. Carl won't be home till seven and neither will I. Will that make it three?" she asked.

Nick nodded but would not look at me. After she left, I ran to him and tried to hold him. He put his face in his hands and leaned against the island in the kitchen.

"Are you sad?" I asked.

He didn't answer, kept his face in his hands.

"Hey," I said, touching the soft hair on his arms with the flat of my hand. "I know how to make you happy."

My finger traced the length of elbow to his hands, pried one finger gently away from his face, then another and another.

"Everything is almost finished," he said, with an endless emptiness in his voice.

I put my arms around him, searched for his lips with mine but he pushed me away. I fought against the hidden tide that made an ocean well in my eyes.

"I miss you," I whispered.

"I'm right here."

"But you're not."

Then he grabbed me, kissed me in that way that took us both to the rim of the chasm, the place where we both stopped breathing and the feeling of want purified us, where shape and touch erased our separateness and redefined everything.

"I love you," I said, when we pulled apart.

He kissed me again, silencing my words. I unbuckled his tool belt, let it fall hard to the floor, and took his hand to lead him upstairs. He stopped in my room and the way he studied my unicorns made them freeze, made them a collection of porcelain that needed to be dusted. He surveyed my bed, lowered the blind, and turned off the light but daylight intruded. After a long moment, he sat next to me.

"I'm too old for you, Audrey," he said. "You should be with someone your own age."

"I want to be with you, with nothing between us."

I took off my clothes, let him see everything about me. Then I reached for his shirt, his pants. Finally we held each other on the tiny raft of my bed, where we floated on an ocean of touch. My hands found his face, found his eyebrows furrowed together just before he dropped his head against my shoulder and dropped into me. He held still but let out a moan that sounded like pain.

"Am I hurting you?" I asked, the way he had asked me so many times.

"Audrey, I'm sorry," he said. "If I hurt you," he whispered, his tender voice traveling my ears to my toes.

"You're not."

Our coupling collapsed into wordless contentment, our hearts beating the same dance. We lay close to each other on my small bed until Nick stood, dressed in the dark, opened the door quietly and stepped into the hall. Then he walked back into my room. I pretended to be asleep when he leaned over me for a long time, then kissed my forehead. I smiled in the dark at this small kiss, proof that his feelings for me would not let him walk away from me. He felt the same as I did.

"Good bye, Audrey," he whispered.

Eve 16

Bells hanging from the door rang brightly, announcing Eve's arrival with hope and levity. But she walked into an empty shop. She called out. Still, no one answered. She moved past clothes, shelves of books, tables crowded with picture frames until she found Lydia in the back room, unpacking boxes and sorting through more cast-offs and discards.

"Sometimes," Lydia said, without looking up, "something is a treasure not because it is rare, but because its value is found." She talked as if she and Eve had been in the middle of a conversation. "Wouldn't you agree?" she asked, turning with a warm smile.

"I hadn't thought of it that way," Eve answered.

Lydia stopped what she was doing. "Eve," she said. "How are you?"

This unlikely woman, with her honest eyes and shapeless wardrobe, had asked this simple question that inquired more deeply than a thin layer of small talk. The confession she'd given her mother about Audrey had been misplaced. She could see that now. Daphne would not remember the important parts.

"I'm on an errand by myself. Audrey stayed home. She has so much schoolwork. But her grades are fine. Except math. That's always been a problem."

"I asked how you were." Lydia winked.

"Me? Fine. I'm fine," Eve repeated.

She wanted to say more, to force herself to talk about herself. But she could not think what to say. "My husband has been swamped with a photography show that opens in a few days. My mother's photography." Eve could talk about everyone but herself. "How are you, Lydia?"

"I'm doing well, largely because of your clothes. Thank you for insisting I sell them. Do you have more treasures?"

"Actually, I came in search of treasure. Cups and saucers. I'm starting a new set."

"I hardly have sets."

"That's exactly what I want. A set of mismatched."

"That I can do," Lydia said. She led Eve to shelves of dishes. "Audrey would be good at this, you know."

"She would turn each cup upside down and pretend they were hooves."

Eve took two cups and demonstrated how Audrey tapped out a trot on the table.

"They do sound like hooves," Lydia said. "That's marvelous."

"It was charming when she was younger, but she's too old for all that now."

Lydia took the cups from Eve. "May that never be true. I don't know if I should tell you, but a few days ago, she was here with a young man. He was a bit older than her, and he didn't understand how to have a pretend tea party. Mismatched is exactly the word."

Eve's skin went cold.

"May she always find a way back to those childhood impulses most of us give up on," Lydia said, and tapped the cups on the table.

Audrey had not pretended with cups since her birthday party. She no longer galloped around the house or stampeded when she was upset. Her attention had turned toward Nick, and away from such childishness. Having a lover drew her away from those obsessions she used to cling to, and she had become a young woman. Eve knew her daughter well enough to know that Nick's attention would cause this change. But a sudden ache made Eve sit down at the table set for tea. She ran her finger around the rim of a cup, over the chip of an otherwise perfect piece of porcelain. Audrey was in love. She could see that when Audrey stared out the window at Nick, or wandered the kitchen when he wasn't there. And Nick was fond of Audrey, too. He stopped what he was doing to say hello to her, found excuses to go outside so she could follow and they could steal a moment together. But Audrey had never shared her feelings with Eve. She kept her experiences and discoveries to herself. Eve had no to right to be part of this, but still she had hoped Audrey would share and confide some small piece of her experiences.

Eve assembled saucer and cup, pairing and re-pairing them, then lifted the thin porcelain to the light and admired the botanical pattern of apples and berries that suggested abundance and beauty. She placed the teacup on a saucer with a strawberry pattern. Leaves went with leaves, flowers with flowers. Colors didn't matter, because something charming began to emerge among them.

"Look at you," Lydia said, joining her, matching pairs. "Playing with teacups the way your daughter might."

Eve quickly matched eight sets, but it was too soon to go home. She would be interrupting or interfering with whatever transpired between Nick and Audrey. An involuntary tear escaped, a surprise rush of longing for her delicate baby girl. She turned away from Lydia and pretended to be interested in an old crystal doorknob that had no door.

"Are you okay?" Lydia said.

Eve waived away the invisible, ineffable confusion that rushed at her. "She's been confined by her imagination for so long, that maybe it has confined me, too. But she's finding her way out, I think. It's hard to explain."

Lydia placed a hand on her shoulder. "I think she'll like all of these, and she may find ways to pair them that you don't see."

Then she moved away to wrap each cup and saucer in newsprint, black ink smudging the porcelain. Eve would wash each one when she got home. Maybe Audrey would help her, and enjoy pairing them differently. Maybe they could have their own little tea party. The thought made her brighten.

When Eve returned, Nick's truck was gone. Her bright mood dropped again. She walked into the house, went to the kitchen, and stopped in the doorway.

It was finished.

The tools were gone, the counters and floors were immaculate.

Elegant.

Beautiful.

Empty.

Cold.

Urban textures hummed with simple lines and surfaces. She stood by the island, palms pressed against the chrome counter, inhaling the chalky scent of cement. Behind her, a professional range waited for her to sauté green beans or maybe fry an egg. When she opened the refrigerator, clean light spilled out from the shelves that waited to be stocked. She turned a full circle and took in the brilliance, modern but timeless, held together by warm gray walls. They would have a baptismal meal after she stocked the refrigerator and replenished the cupboards.

Just the three of them.

The corner where Nick had placed his tools was swept clean. Carl walked in, stopped a moment and put his arms around her.

"It's really something."

Eve smiled, nodded.

Carl let go. "I was thinking we could hang some of your mother's work here after the show. These walls are so empty."

"I want to leave them empty. For a while."

Carl shrugged, placed a checkbook on the counter and wrote out a check. "What time is Nick picking up the final payment?"

"Tomorrow morning."

"Does Audrey know?"

"She'll be at school."

Carl started to say something. The moment became heavy with everything that had transformed beyond these walls, everything about his daughter he could not explain, but Eve understood.

"I wonder," he finally managed, "if Daphne needs something new to wear to the opening. I don't suppose you could take her shopping?"

Eve turned away, ran water from the faucet and watched it swirl down the drain.

"Never mind. I'll handle it. Here's the check. Thank Nick for everything. I'm going to change and head over to the gallery for one last walkthrough before the opening tomorrow. Want to go?"

Eve shook her head as Carl ripped the check from the book and placed it on the chrome counter.

Audrey ran into the kitchen, pulling the black burnout velvet blouse down over her stomach. "Is Nick still here?"

"You're home! I thought you were gone," Eve said. "No, sweetheart. Nick is gone."

"The kitchen is finished. Beautiful, isn't it honey?" Carl said. "Look at you. You're beautiful too."

Dressed in black, her pale skin looked translucent, her hair fell in silky waves that begged to be stroked. She stood in the empty corner where Nick's tools had last been. Eve understood that her head slowly lowered under the weight of separation from her lover.

Carl sang out a goodbye, turned and hurried out the door.

In the morning, sunshine streamed in through the kitchen window, but the same weight continued to hold Audrey's head low. Eve drove her to school, pretending not to know what troubled her beautiful girl. Longing for a lover's company was more than Eve could stand to watch. Audrey remained silent during the car ride. In front of the school, painters coated the exterior with a mismatched shade of beige. Audrey got out and walked away, wordlessly.

"Audrey," Eve called, then hesitated, hating herself for the words she could not hold back. "I could invite Nick to the gallery opening. He did build the walls."

"Would you? Will he come?" Audrey asked, the brilliance of her face illuminating all that had been bleak, her smile full of dazzling hope.

"He might."

Eve knew she should not have offered this.

A clean break sooner rather than later was better than prolonging the inevitable. Audrey's young heart would heal, but not if it kept racing after a lover she would never catch. She blew Eve a kiss, skipped toward the school. Eve drove home, angry at every red light that caught and held her in the stupidity of her impulse. When she pulled into the driveway, her heart thudded like a schoolgirl at the sight of Nick's truck parked outside.

"Nick?" she called, hurtling toward the kitchen as her daughter had minutes ago. Her heart shook when she saw him, hands in pockets, muscular form beneath his worn t-shirt and jeans. "Hey. It's so great to see you. We miss you. Audrey misses you. She wants to know—"

"Hey," he said, cutting her off. "I took a chance you were home."

An older woman stepped out of the kitchen behind him.

"I'd like you to meet my mother," he said.

She was Eve's age, dressed in a coordinated skirt and jacket, her hair done up and sprayed into place. Everything said she was on her way to the office for real estate or accounting or paralegal work. She extended a hand, which Eve grasped weakly. She'd come to Eve's kitchen to admire her son's work. Of course he had a mother, a woman who'd held him, fed him, consoled him and encouraged him. She stood next to the chrome countertop, turned circles in Eve's concrete temple of domestic brilliance.

"I keep telling him how talented he is," his mother said. "Just look what he made. Look what he can do with his hands. It's marvelous. I don't understand why you're not proud of this one."

His mother pulled him to her, made him bend so she could kiss his forehead. Nick twisted away like a little boy, and moved away from both of them. The words it would take to extend an invitation to the gallery opening hovered in Eve's throat, in her mouth, on her lips. She turned away from the kitchen, from the boy and his mother. His mother must have sensed that the final transaction needed to occur without her.

"I'll be in the truck," his mother said, and walked out the front door.

They were alone. His eyes would not meet hers. Not proud.

"I found the check on the counter," Nick said, his voice abrupt.

"Nick, thank you for everything you've done. All of it."

He shrugged.

"It would be nice if you came to the gallery opening, I mean, after all, you did work on those walls as well."

"I won't be there," he said flatly.

She thought about offering him cash, but his expression told her not to. Before she could extend her hand for one last handshake, a friendly gesture of goodwill and completion, he hurried to his truck where his mother smiled when she saw him.

Audrey 16

One moment Nick made my heart race, the next he was a memory making
me listen for the past. One moment I stepped into the afternoon to bring him
a glass of water in the backyard, the next these concrete walls buried him. I
stood alone in the kitchen at midnight.

I stood there again at midday.

No nails, no sawdust, no sharp tools.

Every shadow empty.

Every muscle in collapse.

I wanted unfinished surfaces and blank walls. I wanted to erase cupboard
and appliance. Doorknob, hinge, and running water made no sense. Cupboard
and counter demanded plate and apple instead of saw and hammer. I could
tear the doors off, pull the drawers away, create reasons he would need to
return and make repairs. But I would have to damage what Nick had worked
to create. And the love I had for him was part of that creation.

The day faded again. Night began to gather.

I sank down in the corner and dialed his number but he didn't answer. I
called again, held the blue glow of the phone to my ear and listened to his
outgoing message over and over. Color drained out of the sky framed by the
kitchen window. My mother walked in with her arms full of groceries, which
she placed on the counter. Then she turned and opened the refrigerator, spilling
light onto the floor and onto my bare feet.

"Jesus. What are you doing down there? Why are you sitting in the dark?"
She flipped on the warm glow of the overhead lights that hid in the ceiling.

"I don't want the kitchen to be over," I said.

She reached out her hand to pull me up, but I did not take it.

"Because of Nick? He was special. But there will be other special people
in your life. Come on, help me put away our new dishes and make this our
kitchen. Hey, maybe we can have tea."

I did not want tea. I did not want her hand. I remained on the floor and
looked nowhere because I did not want anyone else to be special. I did not
want Nick to be part of a collection. Tears pooled, though my face remained
like stone; part of me wept, part of me watched. She filled the shelves with

boxes and cans, emptied pears into the green-brown bowl and placed the bowl here, then there, then here again. Until it was perfect.

But it wasn't.

"Audrey, come on. It's time to get ready for your grandmother's show."

"Will he be there?"

"I have no idea."

Upstairs, I moved past the museum of a little girl with her clay ponies and their pointed horns. I used to live here, I thought. She used to be me. I crawled in bed and tried to hold onto some trace of Nick. Tried to recreate us together. Willed him to want me wherever he was now, whatever he was doing.

"We leave in thirty minutes. Get up and get ready," my mother said, invading my room, standing over me. "No more drama."

I waited for her to leave, then undressed. The herd stared out from their lifeless eyes. I stood on two legs, my arms empty, my breasts uncovered, the soft curls exposed at the top of my thighs. I placed a finger in the dimple that once attached me to my mother before I knew how to remember. I turned away from the shelf of unicorns and dropped a peach-colored dress over my head. As it draped down to my legs, I became sunrise and hope.

No underwear.

I was pure animal under this dress. If Nick came to the gallery, I would place his hand where he would know what I wanted, and we would share that secret in the middle of a crowded room.

Those unicorns stared, accused me of neglect.

He had to miss me, had to feel that same hollowness when we were apart.

"What?" I said, as I brushed my hair. "You have each other."

They spent their days and nights together, even if I didn't take them off the shelf much anymore. They missed me, but I missed Nick.

I chose one. Just one. Sapphire Jones would go. I walked downstairs, careful not to step on the hem of the sunrise I wore. I could not go to my mother in the kitchen. Could not look through the doorway that once begged me to step through it and find him. Finally, she came out.

"Look at you!" she said. "Beautiful. Turn around."

As I turned, I shifted the delicate unicorn from one arm to the other.

"Oh, Audrey. Why?" my mother asked.

I looked down at the unicorn's awkward shape where I cradled her in my arm, where Nick's arms should have been threaded but weren't.

My mother shook her head, sighed and pinched her eyes closed for a long time. "I thought you were done with all that. Let's go," she said.

A room full of people who'd come to see my grandmother's photos stared briefly at me when I walked in. They stared at my dress, at my unicorn. Then they went back to looking at fences. Her photos covered the room with fences, surrounding the crowd; dividing, capturing, claiming. I was the only one who came to see the walls and not the photographs hung on them. Nick had built them. He'd put his hands here and here. I smelled the paint.

I shifted the unicorn to my other arm and wished I had not brought her. It. This was childish. If Nick came into the room, I would not be able to put both arms around him. But Nick wasn't here, wasn't coming. I could sense the truth now. Pictures of fences and the walls they were hung on held me apart from the person I wanted to be with. I wanted to give this porcelain creature to my grandmother, return her to where she'd come from so I would be ready. I wandered along the walls Nick had repaired and painted, touching their smooth surfaces. The unicorn grew stiff and made my arm ache.

Nick was not coming to see the photos.

He was not coming to see me.

More people entered the gallery, filling its maze of photos. Bodies moved from fence to fence, talking, glancing, staring at me. I felt foolish for hoping and leaned against the wall between two photographs. A small plastic tub tucked in a corner across the room called to me; the tub of glue Nick had used to fix broken tile on the floor. He must have left it when he finished, didn't see it when he cleaned up. I wove through people and caterers with trays of tiny things to eat to retrieve it. Prying the lid off, I inhaled the toxic scent of something that binds one thing to another. My lover rushed at me from the container of gray paste. My nakedness waited for him under the thin fabric of my dress.

Mitzi and Madison entered the gallery wearing nighttime colors as if they had descended from the sky to wander among these mortals and their fences. I was the sunrise; the pink and orange promise that starts each morning. They lifted three champagne flutes from a tray as a server passed by and laughed because no one said they couldn't have a drink. Mitzi pointed at me and started to walk. Madison held her back, but finally let go and followed.

"Is that your special friend? Your date?" Mitzi smirked at the unicorn in my hand.

"Mitzi, let it go," Madison said and handed me a thin glass, but I could not take it because I held the tub of glue in my other hand.

"Nick left this," I said, lifting the tub of glue.

"That's proof of something?"

Mitzi touched the rim of her glass to Madison's and took a big sip.

"To make-believe and imaginary lovers," Mitzi said.

"He's not imaginary."

"What's it like?" Mitzi asked, draining her champagne. "To be high all the fucking time?"

"I'm not high," I said. "He was here. He left this."

"Whoa, down girl. Sorry. Whatever."

"Mitzi, let it go. Just ignore her, Audrey," Madison said.

"Ignore who?" Mitzi said, turning on Madison.

I backed away from them toward the center of the room where my grandmother drew the crowd to her like a sun pulling planets into its orbit.

Eve 17

The crowd parted with Daphne Delphin's arrival, making room for Carl to wheel her into the gallery. When he stopped, she rose, shoved the wheelchair away, took his arm to help her balance and let him escort her into the center of her solo show. With a handsome man at her side, Daphne gave the impression that she was lucid and in control. Overhead lighting illuminated her pale skin, etching her face with fine lines that made her look beautiful with wisdom. The gallery's sharp contrast of dark floors and light walls suggested that the place itself was a black-and-white photograph. Daphne and Carl stood next to the veiled triptych, tugged gently on the light cloth that covered it so it fell to the floor and revealed the three photographs that, together, made a single stone fence. The crowd murmured, surged forward. An entourage of men closed in. They, too, were lined with age and experience, and as they shuffled toward her, they stood straighter, adjusted their shoulders and clothing. Eve struggled to remember their names. Charles Patrick. Reynaldo Fey. The dashing Clint Baker still wearing his Panama hat. Daphne's colleagues—all male—had come out of their comfortable retirement to pay homage to the woman who once stood shoulder to shoulder with them, her vision equal to and as precise as theirs. Maybe they'd come to see if her revival might rub off. Daphne's lips, weighted with deep red lipstick, barely moved as she spoke.

"Thank you. You're all so kind. Thank you so much," she said to the compliments issued her.

Her white hair contrasted with the deep aqua gown Carl had purchased. He'd found the time to shop, to please her. She smiled and accepted everyone's hands in her bony fingers as they adored her and paid their respects. Carl grinned and nodded, steadied her as they moved through a gallery that hummed with her vision. Photographs surrounded everyone with fences from all over the world. Barbed wire, stone walls, hedgerows, wooden rails, plastic caution tape. A cluster of guests crowded in front of the triptych, jockeying for a closer look, tilting their heads to speak to each other in hushed tones. Daphne's work corralled everyone, and everyone encircled her. They drew close to admire the way she saw the world.

"Her work is iconic."

"She looks great."

"We're in the midst of authentic talent."

"Daphne Delphin is a national treasure."

"Someone should call MOMA or LACMA."

Eve needed air. She stared at her shoes to still the pulse that quickened. This admiration for Daphne made her feel invisible. Again.

"Excuse me," someone said. "Are there more of those stuffed mushroom thingies?"

"I'm not the catering staff," she said.

For the first time in weeks, Eve had worn something from her old wardrobe, a black-and-white combination of the crisp white blouse and black vest she tossed into the gin box to cover the get-away cash that was now spent. "I'm Daphne Delfin's daughter."

"She has a daughter?" someone else said.

She felt unable to move.

But Daphne beamed, as if she stood in the center of the universe. The walls were filled with her fences; human constructs that determined what belonged and what didn't, what was protected and what was left out. It was time for Eve to congratulate her mother. Perhaps she was still the kind woman she'd spent a few minutes with at the nursing facility. Or perhaps she was the dehydrated woman who wouldn't recognize her. Then Eve could slip away, retreat into the shadows, wait for this circus to be over. Carl left Daphne's side to find something for Daphne to drink. Eve worked her way in her mother's direction, elbows bent, hands becoming fists, moving sideways as if she were working her way toward the foot of a stage.

"Look at you. My beautiful daughter," Daphne said.

Eve opened her arms to hug her, but Daphne reached past Eve. Perhaps if she had gotten there sooner, the old woman might not have had Audrey in her grip. With one hand, Daphne clasped Audrey's elbow, and with the other she smoothed her white hair. Audrey clung to her unicorn, and something else. A plastic tub of mastic.

"Oh mother, she's not your daughter," Eve said, smiling apologetically to the crowd.

"Of course she is."

"You're confused. She isn't your daughter. It's okay. We understand."

"I should know my own daughter," Daphne said, her words like sharp steel. "Isn't she lovely?" Daphne said to Mitzi and Madison, who had followed Audrey.

Mitzi and Madison exchanged a look. Eve stepped closer, placed a hand on Audrey's other arm.

"Audrey, come with me. Let's get your friends some lemonade."

"Excuse me," a young man said, waving a narrow notebook. He identified himself from some photography website. "Huge admirer. A thrill to see this collection in one place. Your work has given you an amazing life," he said.

"Thank you," Daphne said.

"The triptych," he said. "Everyone wants to know where that was taken."

Daphne smiled, a twinkle in her eye, gratitude for his compliments helping her stall because memory could not name a place for her work. Eve waited.

"Everyone wants to know," Daphne said. "Why is that?"

"So, what you're saying is that place is a matter of where we are, not where we were?"

"You're a quick one," Daphne said, fluttering her eyelashes.

"If you had it to do again, would you do anything differently?" he asked.

"Not a thing," she told him. She squeezed Audrey's arm, held onto it, and looked at Eve. He wrote as Daphne talked. "My life has been perfect, a gift. I have made a living out of what I love most."

Daphne beamed at Audrey. Eve read the agitation in Audrey's face. The crowd had made her uncomfortable and Daphne was gripping her too hard. Eve knew how to read that expression that said she needed to escape. Every instinct told Eve to free Audrey who was trapped, like the unicorn pressed against her rib cage.

"Please let go of my daughter," Eve whispered in Daphne's ear.

"Proof it has been perfect," Daphne said, holding up Audrey's arm and the container of mastic.

The crowd of glad-handing art patrons became a fence of chatter enclosing Eve and her mother and her beautiful Audrey.

"But she's not your daughter," Eve said.

"Of course she is."

"Then who am I?" Eve said.

Confusion filled Daphne's face.

"Who am I?" she said louder.

Nothing. No response, no answer, no idea.

"I'm your daughter," Eve said.

Madison and Mitzi moved closer. The crowd shifted toward them.

"You're not," Daphne said. "You're too old. This is my daughter," she said loudly, gripping Audrey's arm harder. "This lovely young girl."

Audrey glanced at Eve with a face full of fear.

"Let go of her," Eve said. "You're hurting her. I'm your daughter. She's your granddaughter."

"That's impossible," Daphne laughed.

"Sweetheart, she's losing her mind," Eve tried to explain to Audrey.

"Runs in the family," Mitzi said.

Madison shoved her.

"Me losing my mind?" Daphne said. "I don't think so. This is my daughter and that photograph was taken in the fields of Tuscany, alongside a small olive oil estate."

"She isn't your daughter. She's mine. I raised her and cared for her. I love her."

"You? You paid your kitchen contractor to have sex with her. What mother would do that?" Daphne boomed.

Her words bounced off the faces of the crowd, off the glass-covered photographs of every fence.

"Does she mean Nick?" Audrey asked.

Time slowed.

"No," Eve said.

Audrey's face contorted as Daphne's words sank in. Eve pressed her fingers to her own lips as if that could hold back the twisted sound Audrey made.

"Audrey, she's not thinking clearly."

"Did you?" Audrey asked.

"Let me explain."

"Did you, Eve?" Audrey asked again. "No. Don't talk. Don't answer."

"Wait," Eve said, as she reached to pull Audrey out of Daphne's grip.

"This is so sick," Mitzi said. "Does that make her lover real or not real?"

Mitzi's unrestrained laughter was silenced by a sudden slap from Madison.

"Enough," Madison said. "Leave her alone."

"Fuck you, bitch," Mitzi said.

"You're the bitch."

When Mitzi drew her arm to strike back, Madison lunged, and the two of them went down to the floor in a blur of hair and heels.

"Audrey," Eve called over their tussle. "I want to explain."

Carl returned with a plate full of stuffed mushrooms, a flute of champagne, and a grin that faded when he took in the chaos. Audrey squirmed and twisted free from Daphne and now from Eve, exploding the plate and champagne into the air. Stuffed mushrooms tumbled and rolled. Glass shattered on the floor. The crowd stopped talking.

Audrey howled, and became a flash of sunrise that disappeared through the crowd, out the door, into the night.

"Audrey!" Eve shouted.

Daphne faltered, reached for help and latched onto Eve.

They both fell to the floor.

"My leg. My hip," she cried.

Her eyes creased with pain as fragile limbs struggled to get up, and she collapsed again. Eve held Daphne, kept her head from hitting the floor, but she kept her eyes on the doorway Audrey had gone through.

"Don't move. Someone call a paramedic," Carl said, kneeling on Daphne's other side. "Don't move. I'll take care of you."

Daphne closed her eyes and rested her head against Carl's shoulder.

"Go. Just go," Carl said.

Eve was on her feet as soon as Carl had Daphne in his arms. She raced away from him and her mother, from the reporter and the wide-eyed girls in their dark dresses and ragged hair and Cheryl Moncrief whose confusion fastened onto her until she was out the door.

Audrey 17

I ran.

Swift.

Breathless.

Lengthening the distance from too many lies.

I could run forever.

Faster than electricity shooting through the powerlines above my head.

I was no one's lover. I was no one's daughter. I was not tied to anyone.

The staring streetlamps followed me as I raced over sidewalk, over shadow, over asphalt rivers. My guardians. White and yellow paint on the street meant nothing. Headlights illuminated the way, then surrendered me to the dark. Fences and faces and words shrank behind me until I could not find my way. Until I was surrounded by bars on windows, streets full of shadows, a collage of dark buildings. Until there was no way back and not enough air to breathe. No buses came to the bench where I rested. A car slowed, throbbed with a bass beat. Did I want a ride, hey baby, I'll give you a ride, come on sweet thing. I roared back a whinny that became a scream. Teeth flashing, fury shooting from my eyes. I raised the unicorn and bucket of paste, ready to launch them at the monsters that came for me.

The car accelerated into darkness.

I won. I scared them away.

Pink-black sky hovered above the Cyclops of street lamps searching the sidewalk, following her as she walked further into nowhere. She dove inside herself, under the crush of love that was never love. Waited for the whitewater to stop. Waited until she had to breathe again, still alive, still walking away from empty caress false touch prepaid insistence a wave of desire rose and fell refused the facts spread across thigh and stomach an ache that demanded and destroyed someone who became somebody anybody that ran from fences and faces and traffic lights ministering permissions and restrictions to no one on every corner where invisible footprints made silent steps across asphalt and left no trace of a creature who lived right here in these concrete canyons in this chaparral of metal warehouses in this city with its hidden pipes and wires and passages.

Somewhere at the dark base of a jagged skyline, the last unicorn turned into an alley. She ran from what had vanished, and became what never existed.

Eve 18

The sidewalk offered nothing. No indication, no clue. Audrey was gone. She had taken off. Eve didn't know if she should turn left or right. She chose, forced hurried steps halfway down the block and stopped. Concrete ran empty in both directions. The street was still. Nothing moved, nothing made a sound. She could cover more distance if she drove. She doubled back for the car.

First her headlights crawled over expensive cars parked near the gallery, then over empty streets with their spiked fences and ugly metal walls. Ominous structures rose out of the asphalt. She slowed as she neared a human figure. Her heart rose in her throat and she rolled down the window to call Audrey's name. But the figure wasn't her daughter. She drove on, and passed a sleeping heap of someone in an alcove. A wave of vulnerability washed over her, certain she sensed what Audrey felt at that same moment, somewhere else. Alone. Frightened. On the next corner, two people stood together smoking. Eve's skin pulsed as she lowered the window again.

"Have you seen a girl?" she asked, describing Audrey's long hair, the color of her dress, the white unicorn she held.

They had not seen any girl and stared blankly back at Eve.

The strength it took to keep breathing, to hold it together and thank them and drive away, depleted her. She pulled over along a stretch of curb, dialed Audrey's cell phone and listened to her young voice, shy and halting, telling her to leave a message, words Eve had coached her to say when she had given her that phone, insisted that she have one so she could be more like every other teenager. She drove on, alarmed by the bars on the windows, barbed wire on the fences, metal doors pulled shut. Doubting every turn, she became furious when she found herself in front of the gallery again. There had to be a method, a way to round the blocks and expand the radius of her search street by street.

She dialed Audrey again.

"Hello?" a man's voice answered.

"Who is this?" Eve said.

"It's Carl. Did you find her?"

"How do you have her phone?'

"She left her purse. I heard it ringing."

"Shit."

"Your mother refused the ambulance but she needs medical attention. I'm going to take her home."

"Carl, our daughter has run away. Please help me."

"She can't have gone far. I have to take your mother back. She needs a doctor."

"Carl, I need you. I'm outside."

Every shadow warned of danger that stalked Audrey on one of these streets. Every streetlamp refused to help. Every second made it worse.

"Give her space."

"How can you say that?" she screamed. "She's run off into the streets."

"She'll come back, Eve. She won't know where else to go."

Buildings crowded together, full of emptiness and lunatics. Audrey did not need space. She needed protection. Eve ended the call and drove on alone, street after street, through the industrial side of the city. Every block offered a pinhole of hope, which vanished as she drove past empty warehouses with ominous shapes. She pulled over, got out to look down an alley, then returned to the curb and sat in defeat. Let the criminals come, let them beat her, steal from her, take her keys, her purse, anything, but please give her back her daughter. Blocks away, sirens flared in response to her emergency, then faded toward someone else's.

Her cell rang, making her heart race. Her limbs jolted to life with the sole purpose of answering the call, which had to be Audrey. But it was Carl calling back. Daphne was sedated, nothing broken. He was going home to see if Audrey had found her way there. Then he hung up without waiting for a reply.

The thought that after all this time, Audrey was safe in her room gave her hope. Surely Audrey had found her way back. This needed to be true. Audrey had an innate sense of direction. It could be possible. Eve would wait to be sure.

When Carl called again, it was to tell her no one was home.

"Tell me where you are," he said, exhaustion in his voice. "I'll come to you."

"Stay there," Eve said. "In case she shows up."

She drove the streets for hours, never sure when the darkness became gray, and then morning sky that lightened toward the east. The expression on Audrey's face at the gallery, when she realized her lover did not actually love her, played over and over in Eve's mind. A city bus came toward her and passed. Inside its window, Eve saw Audrey with her face pressed against the pane. She pulled away from the curb and followed the bus west. Had it been Audrey? The face had passed so quickly.

At the next stop, three people got off. The end of the line brought Eve to the beach and the bus pulled over to wait for its scheduled departure. She hurried to it, held up a hand to signal that she wanted to speak to the driver and he opened the door. A rush of warm air spilled over her.

"I'm looking for my daughter," Eve told the driver, who listened to her description then shook his head.

She looked toward the city skyline, dark against the dawn behind it. She had left Audrey there roaming helplessly in a cold canyon of warehouses. Air from the ocean made Eve shiver. She turned to the west where waves crashed against the dark sand. As each wave drew back, it sang a song of loss. Eve tried to understand, to think, to feel what Audrey might so she could find her. She had to be devastated, angry with her, and with good reason.

Further down on the beach, a single surfer in a wetsuit cradled his board in one arm and walked out across the sand.

"She went to Nick's," Eve said to the anguish that plagued her.

He'd told her where he lived when she'd asked if he was homeless, and she knew exactly which gray-and-white bungalows he'd described. They were just up the coast. She drove there, found the bungalow with two surfboards, knocked on the door and twisted the knob. It turned.

"Nick," she called. "Audrey? Are you here?"

It took a few moments to adjust to the dark room, to understand that a man had jumped from the bed where her daughter lay covered with just a sheet. She rushed toward Audrey, relieved, and embraced her.

"I'm so sorry. I meant to protect you, never to hurt you."

"What the fuck?" the girl in her arms said, pushing her back.

"Let me explain," Eve pleaded.

"That isn't Audrey," Nick told her, and made no effort to put on clothes.

Relief turned to horror. She got off the bed, moved away from this mistake, from the blindness of her desperation to end the search.

"Jesus," Nick said.

"What the hell?" the woman said.

"Have you seen Audrey? She knows the truth. She ran off. I thought she might have come here to see if you love her."

"Love who?" the woman in bed said, sitting up, unconcerned that the sheet no longer covered her.

"She hasn't been here. God. How long ago?"

"I don't know. Nine o'clock, ten o'clock last night."

"She didn't go home?"

"Love who?" the girl in the bed repeated.

Nick pulled on his jeans, walked Eve outside.

"I never told her I loved her."

Eve nodded, accepted what he had left of his integrity, which was far more than what she had.

"If I see her, I'll call."

"Please. Thank you. I'll pay you."

"Mrs. Tilden, we have no more business to transact."

Eve sat in her car for a moment, her arms hanging heavily from the steering wheel. She was a horrible person. She was trapped by the very love that had made her protect her daughter. This is what her mother had run from, fearing the grip of such power. Muscle memory in Eve's arms recalled the joy of holding Audrey, the exact weight of her. Then that recall became repulsion for having embraced the naked stranger in Nick's bed. Finally, she drove home, exhausted, desperate for some indication about what to do next. For the first time in months, she did not head directly for the kitchen when she entered the house. Bolting up the stairs two at a time, her thighs tensed and released, defying the force of gravity that tried to keep her from Audrey's room. She stepped through the doorway and turned on the light.

Clothes on the chair.

An unmade bed.

"Carl!"

Her scream sent him running from their bedroom.

Every unicorn was gone.

Audrey had been here and left, and had taken all of them with her.

"You didn't notice when you got home?" she asked.

Carl shook his head. "I just saw the empty bed, the room was dark. I didn't go in."

A box of trash bags lay on the carpet, one protruding from the box after another had been pulled out. Audrey had walked out with her unicorns in a plastic bag where they must have knocked into each other, chipping and breaking.

She had come for them, careless in her haste to get away from Eve. These mythical creatures gave her what reality couldn't. How could it? The affections of a lover were as imaginary as a horse with an elegant horn. Eve fell to the floor, held her head in her arms and wept, unable to undo.

Carl sat down on Audrey's bed.

"Eve, I need to understand what happened and why."

Eve could barely nod, curled up on the floor, everything draining out of her. Lifeless.

"I hired Nick to date her, to be with her."

"To pretend to love her?"

"To tutor her. So she wouldn't want to live in a world of unicorns anymore. She needed something else to occupy her imagination, her interest."

"You can't even say it. You hired the contractor to have sex with our daughter."

"It isn't exactly like that."

"It is. Christ, Eve. It's not like hiring a fucking math tutor. This is statutory rape, god damn it."

"No, it isn't, because I hired him."

"Which is child endangerment."

"Don't you dare. You saw Audrey change. You saw her blossom. She stopped playing with those toys and running hysterically through the house. Tell me you didn't see a young woman in her that you'd never seen before. She was never in danger."

"She is now, for Christ's sake."

She wanted this, sought his harsh words. At least she could feel something in this vivid agony. If he shouted at her loudly enough, words of accusation would slap her and make her blood pulse and surge.

"She's fine, you said," he yelled. "She's fine. You convinced yourself, and I let you convince me. We should have had her diagnosed. We should have been diagnosed. Jesus, Eve. She wasn't fine," Carl fired at her. "She has never been fine, and you never believed in her."

His words struck, made her bleed with memories of loneliness, flooded her until she let go of the struggle to make everything right, to make Audrey a young woman, to make up for what had been missing.

"I've always been everything she needed."

She sobbed, could not breathe, could not speak. Carl did not go to her, did not offer comfort. Not this time.

"I don't know how you could do this," he said.

He shook his head, walked away, walked back as if he knew the answer to everything.

"I'll bet she's gone to Nick's," he said.

Eve inhaled, held her breath, let it out slowly. "I've been there. He hasn't seen her." She shivered at having held and rejected Nick's lover.

"What about those two girls?"

"Mitzi and Madison? They were at the gallery."

"She might have gone to them after she came here."

Eve sat up.

"I'll bet that's it," Carl said. "She found her way there. They had a sleep-over. Ate ice cream, you know, had her girlfriends console her."

Eve wanted to believe in Carl's scenario, wanted him to be right and could almost see the empty carton of ice cream, the three girls upstairs in that messy room, each with their own spoon. She dialed Cheryl, talked to her, struggled to explain that Audrey had not come home the whole night. Cheryl's footsteps echoed as she hurried away to check, then grew louder when she returned. Audrey had not been at her house.

"There's a boy," Cheryl said. "Madison says he has a thing for Audrey. A new boy, a skater. He lives downtown. She thinks he might know where Audrey is, thinks she might have gone to him. But it isn't pretty. He was kicked out of school for vandalism. He may be homeless or a drug dealer. Or both."

Eve went into her flawless kitchen, leaned against the chrome refrigerator and stared at the empty counters. Carl followed, waiting for her to repeat Cheryl's words as they fell out of the phone. Urban concrete walls surrounded her, blank and silent.

"Madison may know where she is," she told Carl after she hung up. "She's agreed to take us to a downtown warehouse."

Eve 19

The sun approached the top of the sky, reminding Eve of all the hours that had passed since Audrey disappeared. The four of them made an odd search party in the middle of the day. She and Carl, Cheryl, and Madison converged in this desolate warehouse district, huddling in front of the gray sheet-metal building they were about to enter. This place wasn't far from the gallery, maybe eight blocks, and a shiver claimed Eve to think that Audrey had been somewhere this near while she searched downtown for her. Cheryl and Madison stood behind Eve, who waited for Carl to pull open the unlocked door. He swung the metal away and sunlight invaded the cavernous warehouse. They filed into the darkness. After they'd walked several feet, the door fell shut.

"Classic," said Madison.

Their eyes adjusted to the thin light that seeped through the ceiling vents.

"Hey, Bixby," Madison yelled, startling everyone. Her voice rang out and diminished.

"This is not how I pictured a meth lab," Cheryl said in a harsh whisper.

"It isn't," Carl said.

"Then what is it? What's that smell?" Madison asked.

"Paint," Eve said.

Their voices bounced around, suggesting that whatever this place was, no one was here. Carl moved forward, his foot knocking into something metal that rolled away. He reached in his pocket and brought out his cell phone. Its flashlight app revealed spray paint cans littering the floor.

"Get out your phones, too," he said.

The combined light from their screens cast a blue glow over dozens of cans. Eve moved toward an old mattress, then followed everyone to the large wall. The flashlights in their phones revealed painted shapes and buildings that cascaded into an underworld beneath the ocean on the wall-sized mural.

"Whoa, shit," Madison said.

"Vandalism," Carl pointed out.

"Graffiti," Eve corrected.

"Street art," Cheryl said. "Who did this?"

"Lucas Bixby," Madison said.

Carl made sure every corner was empty. Eve stood beneath the massive wall and angled her head up, trying to decipher the ceiling-high graphics. There was a city skyline, but it could also be the underground pipes and drains that weave beneath a city.

"This is a shit-show," Madison said.

"It's quite good," Cheryl murmured.

The grungy mattress made Eve shiver and fold her arms around herself. No one was here. No trace of Audrey. After absorbing the emptiness, they turned to leave and navigated through the paint cans back to the door. Outside, sunlight punished them with its yellow cheer.

"Why did you think she would have come here?" Eve asked.

Madison sat down on the curb, placed her feet in the gutter and held her head against her knees. A sudden sob escaped her.

"Mitzi and I tried to make her be someone she isn't. Mitzi wanted her to lose her virginity with the boy who lived here. It was wrong. I knew it. But Mitzi took over. I didn't understand Audrey. I'm really sorry."

"My god," Carl said. "Was everyone in on this? Was it a contest?"

Eve sat down next to Madison and put an arm around her.

"I understand," Eve said. "It was your way of trying to help. Mine, too."

"It was lame," Madison sobbed again.

The skyline ran jagged with warehouse rooftops tied together by telephone wire. What Eve could not understand was the porcelain unicorn that stood at the base of a lamppost. It looked so real.

"She was here," Eve said, and moved to the creature.

This was the figurine Audrey had brought to the gallery, glued in place.

"Let me," Carl said.

He pulled and twisted but could not detach it.

"Don't break it. She put it here for a reason, maybe."

"She had that tub of glue at the gallery," Madison said. "She's with Lucas Bixby."

"It makes you question reality, doesn't it?" Cheryl said.

The four of them scanned the street for another clue to tell them which way to go. But there was nothing. Warehouses and asphalt and traffic were no place for this delicate creature. Eve wanted to take it home. It would not last here. It would break. Someone would destroy its gentle attempt to exist in the world. But there was no way to separate it from the sidewalk.

The unicorn stood resolute but abandoned. Like those shelves of vases and paperweights and dishes.

"The thrift shop," Eve said, rising to her feet and turning to Carl. "We have to go there."

Eve's hopes lifted as the bells on the door announced their arrival. Lydia came out from the back room, her arms wrapped around a box that she sat on the counter.

"Eve," she said, a smile lighting up her face. It was as if she didn't see Carl, Cheryl, and Madison follow Eve into the shop. "I've just learned something you'll want to know."

"It is about Audrey?" Eve asked, her throat unclenching for the first time in twenty-four hours.

The search party stood still.

"I found out that a herd of unicorns is called a blessing," Lydia said, looking up at the collection of people in her store. "Isn't that wonderful?"

Everything toppled, all control fled. Eve's face clouded with pain as her eyes filled. She could see her own expression mirrored on Lydia's face, along with confusion.

"Audrey has run away," Carl said.

"Please Lydia, have you seen her?" Eve asked.

"She was here this morning, when I opened. I thought you sent her."

"Thank god. Was she okay?" Carl asked. "Did she say where she was going? Was she alone?"

Lydia pushed a box of t-shirts toward Eve. "She told me you sent her here to sell your t-shirts. She seemed to expect the cash right away. I gave her fifty dollars for them and told her I'd give her the rest after they sold. That seemed to make her happy. Is she okay?" Lydia asked.

Eve wanted to explain the situation, why the four of them had come to this sanctuary where Audrey had created rainbows out of clothes. But Lydia's expression made her unable to speak. Carl quickly filled in the story, stumbling over some details, using great care to leave out the part about a hired lover.

"She fell for our kitchen contractor," Carl said. "Then the job ended."

"Ah," Lydia said. "The young man she brought for tea last week. Or was it the week before? He didn't understand her very well."

Everyone looked at the place settings on a table by the window.

"But that's not who she was with this morning. He was younger and had a skateboard," Lydia said.

"Bixby," Madison said.

Eve backed away, found herself next to the rainbow of clothes on the circular rack. She looked into the center as if she might find her little girl hiding inside.

Lydia went on. "I offered her a job, and told her she was welcome here anytime."

Carl put his face in his hands. "Did she say anything about where she was going?"

"I'm so sorry," Lydia said. "Do you want the t-shirts back?"

Eve looked at the box of shirts, her past shoved in there, her lifeline to who she thought she was. She reached in her purse and pulled out all the cash she had.

"No, I don't. But give Audrey money if she comes back. I can bring you more. Thank you, Lydia."

She needed air. She needed to be alone. Everyone followed her outside and stood with her in defeat. Then they saw the same thing all at once. Next to a rain gutter's downspout, a mother unicorn looked down protectively at the colt curled next to her.

Glued in place.

Eve shook her head. "I don't understand."

"It could be a message," Lydia said. "To let you know she is cared for."

Eve sat down and leaned against the wall. She wanted to call her daughter back to her, to reverse time, to explain, to wail. She reached out and stroked the unicorns as if they could feel her touch.

Eve 20

When they returned to the house, Eve raced upstairs to her closet, to the empty hangers on her side of the closet. She must have taken them when she came for the unicorns last night. The only t-shirt left was the one Eve had been wearing for the last twenty-four hours, Quadrophenia with its bomb-shelter symbol of yellow triangles on black fabric.

Carl called the police, summoning a young officer who looked like he was barely old enough to shave. He stood next to the island, across from the picture window that opened up the modern kitchen and filled it with light. Carl sat nearby and completed a report on a standard form. This was never what Eve had imagined occurring in her kitchen. This was not supposed to be happening here. She stood at the opposite end of the island, sick with despair, arms folded as Carl described to the officer the kind of student Audrey was, and explained about the gallery, where it was located, how she had run out.

"Can you say what might have triggered this?" the young man asked.

Eve could not say.

"The man she thought loved her, doesn't," Carl offered.

"A man? How old?" The officer looked at Eve, questions in his eyes.

Eve and Carl shared a long, silent exchange.

"A boy," Carl said.

"She isn't right," he finally told the officer. "She's like a child." Carl's voice cracked. "It may be autism."

"We don't know that," Eve said. "We never had her tested."

The officer took notes, finished his business, and couldn't offer anything hopeful. Angry teens ran away. She had not been abducted. It had not been 48 hours. This changed how department resources were allocated to her search. A bulletin would be issued. Patrolling officers who cruised the usual teen hangouts would be made aware.

After he was gone, Eve could hear Carl upstairs moving across the floor, stopping where her rack of t-shirts had hung. Then moving on. He should abandon her, pack, leave, get away. She understood that much.

Still in her clothes, Eve woke on her bed late in the night. All the lights were on. She must have fallen asleep but Carl had never come to bed. Black windows reminded her of the dark places where Audrey might be. The urge to wail and weep for the fear of Audrey's well-being made it impossible to lie there any longer. Eve got up, went downstairs. Carl was asleep on the couch where Nick had once slept. Carl had not packed and left, but he did not want to share a room or a bed with Eve. She would give him space, would not insist on anything. She had no right. She walked past the couch and went into the city in search of her lost girl.

She drove all night, stalking every person on the streets around the warehouses, pulling over and questioning them. No one had seen anyone like Audrey. She drove back to the unicorn that stood under a streetlamp and parked. From her car, she watched and waited. The air became cold and she worried for Audrey, wished her warm and safe wherever she was. Some time past 2 a.m., she got out, took a flashlight with her and went into the warehouse. There were noises, sounds of scuffling, and she rushed past the heavy door, only to find two rats running for the corners. She scanned the wall with her flashlight, lit up the painted city that offered no clue about Audrey. Outside, she curled up along the warehouse wall, laid near the unicorn, put her head on the concrete as if she might hear her daughter's subterranean footsteps approach from far away. The sidewalk was icy. Above the city, night sky turned pink with artificial light. Below the roads and sidewalks, miles of plumbing ran in all directions. The graffiti inside the warehouse seemed to show what everything was made of, what was underneath or inside. Making the invisible visible.

The ground and air grew colder. Eve shivered uncontrollably. No one was meant to sleep here. But people did. Maybe Audrey had.

Eve returned home at sunrise, but Carl had left already. She called him twice during the day, but he didn't answer. Didn't reply to her texts. She avoided the kitchen, could not eat, did not want food. Carl came home late to avoid her and slept on the couch.

Again, that night, she went out searching for Audrey. This time she parked under a bridge and studied the graffiti, tried to decipher the writing, tried to comprehend the graphics with their large, twisted shapes. Maybe someone would come and paint. Someone who might know the boy from the warehouse. But no one came. She drove home through the downtown streets as the sun rose.

Again, Carl was gone before she got home in the morning. A ghost in the house that left the couch an empty mess. From the kitchen doorway, she studied the still life of pomegranates in the green-brown bowl, the fruit she'd asked her daughter to pick to distract her from being heartsick over Nick. The skins were like leather, shriveling around the seeds hidden inside. She went out, picked fresh fruit and replaced the dried ones in the bowl. Then she went upstairs to change, but there was nothing to change into. None of Carl's lifeless suits offered help.

In Audrey's room, she opened the chest of drawers. The black burnout velvet shirt that once belonged to Madison lay where Audrey had placed it after the only time she'd worn it in hope of seeing her lover. Beneath it, pink and purple shirts waited to give the world their handfuls of flowers. She knelt before the drawer, gave in to the gravity of grief, and inhaled deeply as she lifted a floral shirt from the top. Then she pulled it over her head. It barely fit. The childish bouquet offered simplicity, a gift Eve had never fully accepted. Audrey had offered her these bouquets of flowers for seventeen years and Eve had refused them. Loneliness clutched at her throat. She would force herself through another day of searching, but today she would not do it alone.

Light from Daphne's window bathed half of her face and hid the other half. She clutched the aqua gown from the gallery opening as she sat up in her bed.

"Is that you?" Daphne whispered.

Did her mother recognize her? Or was the "you" someone else?

A bowl of cold oatmeal sat on a tray. Empty slippers waited on the floor.

"Would you like to get out of here?" Eve asked.

"Do you mean that?" Daphne asked, half rising from the bed.

Eve reached for the Nikon on the nightstand. "Let's take your camera with us," she said.

Daphne took it from her as if she'd never seen it before, but then she looked through the viewfinder and pointed the camera at Eve.

"Most people think that a rectangle confines what you see. But it focuses you." She adjusted the settings and fired off several shots. "How quickly you've grown up. I feel like I've missed it all. You're a beautiful woman, Audrey."

"But I'm not–" Eve looked down at the cheerful t-shirt she wore with its handful of flowers. "Thank you," she said.

She could be whoever Daphne needed her to be if it would help ease the divide, if it would remove the fences between them, the absurd constructs that attempted to split nature; to define separation. Eve drove Daphne through the industrial streets where Audrey had first run off, where a unicorn still stood as the only proof of Audrey's existence. She expected to find it destroyed or removed, but it was still there. People had left it unharmed, let it stand under the streetlamp where a small weed grew and kept it company.

"I used to think unicorns didn't exist," Eve said. "But look."

They got out of the car and, without Eve having to ask, Daphne took pictures of the figurine, changing angles, changing settings, capturing the impossible creature that lived on the city streets.

A week passed. Six days, to be exact. Nausea turned to numbness. Despair turned into resignation. Carl avoided being home when she was there. He screened her calls. She could not blame him. She could only give him room. She continued her search every day while Carl ran through every administrator at the school for information on the boy, then hired a private detective who could never come up with anything.

Daphne never tired of the repetition, never realized they'd made the same trip the day before. They looked through the city for unicorns, for signs of a lost girl. Dressed in Audrey's t-shirts, Eve who had once been a wild child at the edge of the stage drove obediently through the warehouse district, past the gallery where Daphne didn't recognize her own show in the window, and always past the first unicorn that still stood alone beneath a lamppost. Daphne often dozed but sometimes she raised the camera to her eye and pointed it at something. Sometimes she would request that Eve pull over so she could roll down the window to shoot, but then she would change her mind, lower her camera, and tell Eve she had been mistaken. Mostly they didn't speak, but they also didn't argue. She wasn't sure her mother knew who she was. But there was refuge in being the kind stranger who took her out for a drive.

One morning without warning, Eve pulled over abruptly and parked the car at a red curb. Hand to mouth, Eve got out and approached an electrical box painted with a city skyline of heavy black outlines that defined green and purple buildings. A city turned inside out with its plumbing and electrical exposed. On top of the box, a unicorn stared down at the asphalt then at Eve when she moved into his line of vision. This stallion had a chipped ear, a horn broken and glued back with the same mastic that held its feet to the metal. Audrey's collection had been jostled together in the garbage bag she used to carry them through the streets. Daphne got out with her camera and without Eve asking, took photographs, documenting what wasn't real, helping Eve capture another unicorn before it vanished. Eve called Carl, but again, he didn't answer. She took a picture with her phone and sent it to him. Her phone rang back.

"Where are you?" he asked.

Her heart flooded with his words. For a moment, she could pretend it was her he wanted to find. He met her by the electrical box, surprised to see

Daphne nearby clinging to her camera like a child.

Neither of them could speak.

"This is the work of a street artist," Daphne said. "It's innovative. Usually they only paint. But this is creative. A statement about what's possible, not what is real."

Carl started to say something but stopped himself.

"She's out there," Eve said, leaning against the metal box. "She's asking everyone – asking me to believe in her world."

Every bridge, every ledge, every retaining wall suddenly offered hope that Audrey was somewhere, leaving unicorns for those who were careful enough to notice. A street artist. But the paint had been done by someone else, by the boy. She had a companion. It didn't matter who he was. She was not alone.

"I'm tired," Daphne said. "Forgive me. I'd like to go home. But I don't know where that is." She put her wrinkled hand to her face to cover her sorrow and confusion.

Despite her aging face, she looked like a lost girl, tired and frightened and helpless.

"I don't know either," Carl said.

Eve looked at the two of them, at the invisible triangle that connected them through the weave of their history.

"I know where home is," Eve said.

When they arrived at the house they could see the front door was open. They got out of the car and approached, adrenaline relief alarm swirling as they hurried, unable to explain to Daphne. On the porch, an overturned planter exposed the spot where a spare key should have been. Eve moved past Carl, into the house, calling out for her daughter. They were both met by the sharp smell of paint.

Signs of a struggle, evidence of vandalism drew them to the kitchen. Smooth concrete was covered over with spray paint. Cabinets had been ransacked. Cereal and cracker boxes were taken. The green-brown bowl had been emptied of its pomegranates. The warm gray of walls was now graffiti from floor to ceiling, the paint still wet.

Eve's kitchen had been ruined. And it hadn't. The fresh paint defined a cityscape of jagged buildings rising from an underworld of pipes and sewers. This rebellious, intrusive message showed her the garish city where her daughter had disappeared. It was frightening with uninvited beauty. And concrete walls were made for it.

She stepped back, held her hand to her mouth, speechless, beginning to understand. Audrey had not stayed. But she had come home. There on the top of one of the buildings, lording over the whole cityscape, was a blue glass unicorn broken in half, its torso glued in place so it protruded from the wall like it was springing forth into the world.

Like it was coming to life.

With gratitude

To my mountain biking posse who listened to complaints about the ride and the writing, and to Marilyn Schram who made it clear on the steepest part that I had to write the novel. To Tina Demerdjian for spending countless lunch hours with me remembering who we really are. To the Pasadena Writer's Group led by Bernadette Murphy who helped this novel emerge. To my earliest readers: Andrea Grossman, Seana Graham, Rebecca Wilkinson, Amelia Munson, Molly Johnson, and Crystal Craft, and to my latest readers, Clyde Derrick and Kirsten Jasna; all of you made me a better writer because you were paying careful attention. To Carolyn O'Keefe for helping me step out of my comfort zone and filling my living room with more readers who taught me to listen: Judith Pettigrew, Bobbi Koonse, Andrea Bradshaw, Louise Leef, Valerie Tuna, Paddy Lock, Rebecca Fitzsimmons, and Debra Newton. To Kate Guiney for exceptional copyediting that came with thoughtful, insightful development notes, and for leading me to the self-publishing path. To my daughter, Selina, who read this well before she was Audrey's age and responded with her usual wisdom. Along with her brothers, Jake and Casey, all three of these wonderful people have made motherhood an experience of love and meaning beyond words. Finally, to Jeff Magid, for his encyclopedic knowledge of the music industry and its history; and for making a home with me be the place where I always want to live, without any remodeling.

About the Author

With the release of her debut novel, REMODELING EVE, Helen Kantor braids a narrative of mother around daughter as the events of a kitchen remodel transform both of their worlds. She has taught graduate and undergraduate writing courses, coached writers to develop their craft, and harnessed storytelling to develop social media and win philanthropic funding for nonprofits and institutions of higher education. She holds an MFA in Screenwriting from UCLA, a BA from UC Santa Cruz, and lives in the Los Angeles area.